XOXO, Valentina

JILL BRASHEAR

MOMENTUM PRESS

*For all the readers who have lost someone and learned to love again.
Hope you find your very own Joey.*

Book Review of "Love Trials" by Spencer Aaron

BY VALENTINA BLUERIDGEBOOKCLUB.COM

5 stars
5 hot peppers
5 book boyfriend hearts

DEAR READERS,

I'm back! Remember me, your friendly online reviewer? I know it's been a while, but I've been in a bit of a reading slump. Don't worry, I found the perfect book to fix it, and I'm sharing it with you, my dearest readers.

If you don't like male/male romance novels, this one will change your mind. It was the perfect escape from reality, full of romance, heat, and hope.

Plot Overview:

Kaiser Pierce is known for three things: winning more gold medals than any American athlete, his charity for funding swimming programs in underprivileged neighborhoods, and being openly gay.

In an effort to keep the public eye on his charity and swim career, Kaiser fiercely guards his privacy. The last thing he wants is to see his dating life splashed all over the tabloids.

After sixteen years of swimming and four times competing in the Olympics, Kaiser is nearing the end of his career. He has one last chance to qualify for the Olympics. At thirty-four years old, Kaiser knows it's a long shot to make the team.

As the pressure increases, Kaiser doesn't have the headspace to think about dating. He spends more time training than ever before.

Many of his coaches doubt he can compete with swimmers half his age, and even his closest friends don't believe he will earn a spot on the team.

The one man who believes in Kaiser more than anyone is his strength-and-conditioning coach, Trent Starsky. Trent has never been attracted to men before, but he finds himself falling for the fascinating Olympian. They are opposites in every way possible, but their souls are perfectly aligned. Kaiser awakens feelings Trent didn't know were possible. As the bond of their friendship grows, Trent falls in love with everything about Kaiser. For the first time in his life, he questions the labels put on love.

When they end up sharing a hotel room in Omaha, Trent finds the perfect opportunity to confess his feelings. As they begin a whirlwind affair, they think it's just a fling. But things turn serious pretty quickly, and they are forced to figure out what to do when love comes unexpectedly.

Pros:

- Trope: Just a fling turns into a helluva lot more
- Sexy main characters: A hot swimmer with superhero muscles and delicious tattoos plus a poetry-loving trainer with glasses equals double the charm in this male/male delight.
- Secondary Characters: Loads of interesting sidekicks in the athletes and coaches.

• Smoking hot sex: There are so many sex scenes in this book, and they are all on fire.

• LOVE is love.

Cons:

• I had to dig deep to find this one. But I am not a fan of the third-person point-of-view. I like first-person better. It's just more personal!

To sum it up, I loved this book! It was an intense read. I became emotionally invested in the characters and cheered for Kaiser to make his comeback. Trent and Kaiser's love scenes sizzled off the page. I also adored the sweetness of Trent falling in love with Kaiser for more than just his fame and physique. Their relationship went much deeper than just lust. It was a true inspiration.

Wouldn't it be nice if all of us were so lucky to find someone we were deeply attracted to on the inside as well as the outside?

I promise to be back again soon with more reviews!

Chapter 1

GABI

I wore my favorite outfit to fire Mr. Morales.

It was a Diane von Furstenberg knock off, which was still a splurge at half the cost of the real thing. But a good wrap dress never went out of style, so I'd justified the purchase. The dress was emerald green—my favorite color—with a frilly hemline perfect for salsa dancing.

I wasn't planning on salsa dancing my way down the halls of Pinewood Elementary School anytime soon.

In fact, I hardly ever wore dresses to work. They weren't practical for an elementary school principal. But I needed the extra boost of confidence my favorite dress gave me to fire Mr. Morales.

Not only was he the best Spanish teacher PES had ever had, he was also, quite possibly, the hottest man on the planet. My tongue tied in knots when I was around Mr. Morales. If I caught his eye during the weekly staff meeting, I would forget everything I'd planned to say.

Tall, dark, and always smiling, Mr. Morales had the same effect on women of all ages. He proved swooning was a real thing, and it happened outside of historical romance novels.

Since I'd hired him, there had been an uptick in parent-teacher conferences. I suspected the sudden spike in requests had more to do with Mr. Morales's sexy accent and dazzling good looks than underperforming students.

Firing him was going to be one of the most difficult things I'd had to do in my career. I hated firing people in general, but firing Mr. Morales was going to be extra hard because I'd have to give the reason. I'd have to tell him what I'd seen.

My cheeks burned when I passed his classroom, a.k.a the scene of the crime.

I hurried down the hall before visions of Mr. Morales half naked invaded my thoughts. Again.

Usually, this was my favorite time of day. In the quiet moments before children filled the halls, I felt a sense of pride and accomplishment. But all I felt was dread.

I passed the teachers' lounge and glimpsed Mr. Morales talking with some of the other teachers who were crowded around a box of pastries. The pastries were probably homemade, which was against policy.

He looked good enough to eat in a button-down shirt and fitted slacks. My pulse quickened when I imagined what he looked like underneath his clothes.

"Good morning, Mrs. Salinger."

The office door hit me in the back as I froze in the doorway. "Oh!" My heart leaped to my throat. "I didn't see you there, Mr. Collins."

My assistant popped up from behind the front desk, his face bright with a smile. "Here are this morning's messages. I marked them in order of importance."

Of course he had. Mr. Collins was ever the eager one. Always arriving before me. Always leaving after. But Mr. Collins didn't have a fourteen-year-old son who slept through his snooze alarm and needed a ride to tutoring after school like I did.

I took the messages and flipped through them, noting that Chelsea Taylor wanted to see me again regarding her daughter Kaylee. That message went to the bottom of the pile. I was 99 percent sure Kaylee Taylor wasn't being bullied. It was more likely *she* was the one doing the bullying. The little girl was cute as a button, but also a troublemaker. I would deal with Ms. Taylor later.

"Did you decide on the theme for spirit week yet?" Mr. Collins asked.

Spirit week wasn't until next month. Surely it wasn't top priority. "Not yet." I focused on my enthusiastic assistant. "Were those muffins I saw in the teacher's lounge again?"

Color stained Mr. Collins's round cheeks, and he dropped his gaze. "I'm not sure."

Last month, someone had brought in some banana walnut muffins, and they'd caused the technologies teacher to swell up like a science experiment gone wrong.

No one had owned up to being the baker, but I had my suspicions about Mr. Collins. With his plump tummy, he was likely the muffin man.

I upped the intensity of my glare until beads of sweat popped out on his prominent forehead. "We wouldn't want Mrs. Pfeiffer to have another reaction," I said.

His chin trembled. "Certainly not."

I let him quiver under my disapproving stare for another moment before I turned to hang my coat on the rack. "Include a reminder of the new lost-and-found policy in the morning announcement," I said.

Mr. Collins made a strangled sound from behind his desk, and I gathered he didn't approve of my new rule to enforce silent lunch after multiple lost sweatshirt violations.

I swiveled to face him. "Is there a problem?"

Mr. Collins's cheeks blazed brightly. "No, ma'am."

I raised my chin at him. "I don't need to explain the importance of keeping up with one's belongings to you, do I?"

"I understand," he said in a choked voice. "It's not that."

"Well, what is it?"

He sank into his chair. "It's nothing," he said.

I waited for a moment, but he remained silent and returned his attention to his monitor.

The teachers and administration at PES thought I was a strict boss. They called me Iron Lady behind my back, but I wasn't offended. I was proud to be compared to a tough-as-nails leader like Margaret Thatcher. As a single mom to a son who'd grown taller than me at eleven, I had to be tough.

My chest tightened when I thought about the next item on my agenda. "Tell Mr. Morales to come to my office during his planning period," I said.

Mr. Collins nodded, still not looking me in the eye. "I'll buzz him now."

I went into my office and closed the door with a firm click. Filled with comforts of home, my office was my sanctuary. School awards lined the bookshelves, and photographs of my son, Shane, topped my desk. Framed art projects hung on the walls, and a de-humidifier misted the air.

I settled in my ergonomically designed chair and tackled the important messages one by one. By the time I finished everything, my stomach alerted me it was time for lunch.

Tomorrow was shopping day, and our pantry looked like it had been raided by a swarm of hungry teens. Or at least one six-foot-tall teen.

I'd given Shane the last of the decent food I could scrounge up. Luckily, I had an emergency pack of crackers in my bag.

I grabbed my romance novel and tore into my crackers. I got little time to read, and I was behind on my to-be-read pile. Luckily, I fell straight into the narrative, and before I knew it, I was transported to the frozen forests of Alaska.

My busy schedule left little room for fun, so reading was my escape. I liked to read paperbacks, not ebooks, but I didn't like anyone to know what I was reading. If steam levels of books were like hot peppers, I preferred Carolina Reapers. Since my book preferences might be frowned upon by many of the parents in the carpool line, I hid the covers under a quilted book jacket and hardly ever read in public. No one would guess that underneath the fabric jacket was a smoking-hot lumberjack. And only my closest friends knew my secret identity as Valentina, a popular online book reviewer for the Blue Ridge Book Club who specialized in erotic romance.

My sex life was non-existent, but my book boyfriends were many.

My current boyfriend was a handsome, rugged outdoorsman with a penchant for flannel.

After a few pages of reading about the lumberjack's exploits in the frozen tundra, my mind drifted to Mr. Morales, who would be scrumptious in gray-and-green plaid.

A knock at my door startled me, and I dropped my book on the desk. I didn't have time to put it away before the door swung open and the object of my fantasies peeked around the corner.

"You wanted to see me?" Mr. Morales asked.

Adrenaline shot through my system. *Mother of Pearl!* He was gorgeous.

When I'd first interviewed Mr. Morales, it had been over the phone. He'd sounded young and full of life—exactly what we needed at PES. I'd had no idea the smile I'd heard over the phone would be so devastating in real life.

His hair was always perfectly tousled, as if he'd either been running his fingers through it, or just rolled out of bed. His eyes were caramel brown and tipped up in the corners, as if he had a secret he was willing to share with the right person. The perfect amount of stubble decorated his perfectly square jaw. I imagined what his scruff would feel like scraping along the sensitive skin of my neck... or against my inner thigh.

He smiled, and a bolt of desire shot straight to my core. I clasped my hands in my lap, trying desperately to block my inappropriate reaction to his extreme handsomeness. My mind reeled as I forced it out of the land of flannel-wearing heroes and back to the elementary school where it belonged.

"Come in, and close the door, please," I said.

Mr. Morales wasn't a hero in my novel. He was an employee who'd made a mistake and needed to be dealt with. It sickened me for PES to lose such a fabulous teacher, but it was my duty to fire him.

Chapter 2

Mr. Morales's dark eyebrows drew together. He closed the door behind him and stood just inside my office. "Is everything okay?"

"Sit down," I said.

He took the seat across from my desk, leaned back, and spread his large hands over the arms of the chair. While his gaze roamed around my office, I feasted my eyes on him. He wore a pale-blue dress shirt with a subtle check, which was rolled up at the sleeves to reveal tanned forearms. A leather bracelet adorned his left wrist, and rings decorated several of his fingers. The fourth finger on his left hand was noticeably bare.

I didn't care for jewelry on men, but the style suited Mr. Morales. The flash of silver on his hands and the aged leather at his wrists conjured up a whole slew of fantasies. My mind drifted to the bad boy of romance—the motorcycle club leaders, the pirates of the high seas, the unscrupulous rogues.

"I like your artwork," he said, turning in the chair to look at the framed drawings on the walls.

His words flowed in a uniquely Latin rhythm, conjuring up hot summer nights and flouncy-hemmed dresses. He leaned forward and looked at the framed photograph of Shane on my desk.

"Is that your son?"

Being alone with Mr. Morales made my blood heat and my tongue tie in knots. I gathered my composure and nodded at Shane's school picture, which showed off his metallic smile. Shane had begged me not to buy it, but I thought it was cute. And I'd paid a lot of money for those braces, so I might as well immortalize them.

"I can't believe you have a teenager," Mr. Morales said. "You look so young."

I was young for my position, but I'd earned it. My predecessor had held the job for over twenty years, and she was a tough act to follow. I'd spent the last two years proving my worth, so those words coming from anyone else's mouth would have set my teeth on edge. But everything Mr. Morales said sounded enchanting thanks to his sexy accent.

"I'm older than I look," I said, stacking his file on my desk.

His chin dipped toward my half-eaten pack of crackers. "I hope that's not your lunch."

I pushed the crackers aside. "Tomorrow is shopping day."

His eyebrows slanted in disapproval, and my mind shot straight into Fantasyland. Disapproving Mr. Morales was even sexier than smiling Mr. Morales. I imagined him hovering over me, promising to punish me for my irreverent lunch. Licking crumbs off the corner of my mouth and sliding his tongue along my lips, he would feast on me, devouring me inch by inch.

Good grief! I really must find a new genre. Too much erotica had warped my brain.

I flipped open his file. "Do you know why I called you into my office today, Mr. Morales?"

He sat back in his chair and clasped his hands in his lap. "You can call me Joey."

I'd heard some of the other teachers calling him Joey, but I'd always thought of him as Mr. Morales—or Fernando. According to his file, he was Fernando Morales, age twenty-seven, originally from Tamarindo, Costa Rica.

"Why Joey?" I asked. "It's nothing like Fernando."

"It's from *Friends*." He crossed his arms over his chest and gave me a chin nod. His entire demeanor changed as he flashed a flirty grin. "How you doin'?" he asked in a perfect New York accent.

My brain knew he was only doing an impersonation of the flirtatious Joey Tribbiani from *Friends,* but my belly still flipped. And other parts of me tingled in anticipation at the prospect of Mr. Morales flirting with me.

I halted my imagination before it could conjure any more embarrassing fantasies. I needed to get back on track. Time to stop letting him affect me. Time to end the small talk and get down to business.

My intercom buzzed, and Mr. Collins's voice crackled through the air. "Mrs. Salinger? Can you come to the main office?"

I pursed my lips and stabbed the call button. "I'm in the middle of something, Mr. Collins."

Flipping the pages in the file, I came to the recommendation letters from his former employers in Atlanta, Georgia, who'd hated to lose him. I would give him a good reference, of course. It would be too embarrassing not to.

"Did someone make that for you?"

His voice penetrated my concentration. "What?"

"The book cover," he said.

My hand shot out to cover the quilted jacket. Even though he couldn't see the half-naked lumberjack hidden under the book cover, I felt exposed. I should have tucked the book away before he came into my office.

"They sell them at Hyperbole's Bookshop," I said.

"My sister Ava would love it." He leaned forward to better examine the quilted pattern, which looked like it belonged in my grandmother's bedroom and perfectly disguised the sexy cover of the book. "She likes to read porno books," he said. "But she doesn't want my mom to find out."

My heart leaped into my throat. *Porno books.* What would Mr. Morales think if he knew what I liked to read?

Heat filled my cheeks, and I swept the book into my desk drawer. "Maybe you should buy her one."

He laughed, and the rich sound filled me like a beam of light. His gaze dropped from my face to the flush on my neck. "Maybe I will."

Could his accent be any sexier? And the lips forming the words were even better. Full and firm, they'd been made for kissing.

The intercom buzzed again. "Mrs. Salinger."

I straightened in my chair as if I'd been zapped and pressed the button on the intercom. "Yes?"

"Ms. Taylor is here. She wants to speak to you about Kaylee."

"Please tell her to make an appointment. I'm in the middle of something."

"Yes, ma'am."

I sat back in my seat and gave Mr. Morales a stern look, signaling it was back to business. No more leaning closer and imagining dragging Mr. Morales across my desk so I could devour his pillow-soft lips. My priorities were back in order. "As I was saying—"

The buzz sounded again. "Hi, Mrs. Salinger," said a female voice over the intercom. "This is Chelsea Taylor. Can you spare a moment of your time?"

Mr. Morales moved as if to stand. "Should we continue this later?"

"No." I rose and pushed back my chair. "I'll be right back."

Once in the main office, I approached Ms. Taylor with a tight smile. She cocked her head at me and straightened her shoulders. Ms. Taylor was an anomaly among elementary-school mothers. She never looked ruffled, her clothes were on trend, and her hair was perfectly styled in beautiful waves. I suspected the impressive smoothness of her face had something to do with injectables, but whatever she'd done had been well worth the money. Even though I knew she was older than me, she didn't look a day over thirty. If I ran into Ms. Taylor outside the office, I might be intimidated, but at school, I was empowered by my authority.

"Bullying is not tolerated at PES," I said, giving her the no-nonsense look I used on the children. "No matter who is doing the bullying."

When Ms. Taylor continued to question me, I told her I would be glad to have a conference with her and Kaylee's teacher, but she would need to make an appointment with Mr. Collins. Apologizing for my abruptness, I told her I needed to get back to my prior engagement and went back to my office without giving her a chance to respond.

I closed my door and paused for a moment, getting my priorities straight. Mr. Morales's back was to me, and to my chagrin, even the back of his head was handsome. My fingers itched to tangle themselves in the thick, dark waves of his hair.

He turned toward me in his chair and pinned me with his caramel-colored eyes. "I think I know why you asked to see me," he said.

Relief mingled with regret. The unavoidable moment had arrived. I squared my shoulders and crossed the room to stand behind my desk. "Good," I said.

"I know we aren't allowed to have homemade goods for school activities. But the food will make the Fun Festival come to life." He leaned forward in his chair and braced his hands on his knees.

A headache built behind my eyes. Because... firing him. When I finally got around to doing it, I would have to tell him why. I'd have to admit I'd seen him receiving sexual favors from a buxom blonde after hours in his classroom.

I'd have to say the words, and when I did, I was going to blush. And he was going to know I'd watched through the tiny glass partition of his door much longer than I should have.

The Iron Lady was only so strong. She didn't stand a chance against the image of Mr. Morales's strong thighs, his tight abs, his—

"Nina Valbuena is so excited to share her mother's tamales," he said. "And Summer Carleton is making a recipe from her favorite book. You could bring a dish of your own. Can't we bend the rules a little?"

What? Were we still talking about the Fun Festival? My mind had drifted to the scene I'd witnessed, the accidental hummer incident.

"I'm afraid not all rules were made to be bent, Mr. Morales," I said sternly.

"I understand." He clasped his hands in his lap. "It would just mean so much to the kids."

His mention of the students made me doubt my convictions. Mr. Morales was one of the most beloved teachers at our school. The kids would be devastated to lose him, and it was almost the end of the year. Maybe I could put him on probation?

Technically, I was the only one who knew about his inappropriate behavior. Well, I had told my book club friends, but they wouldn't say anything. And if I said nothing, no one would else would know.

It had been at night when no one was at school but me and the custodian. *Could I let him get away with it?*

It went against all my principles to let him break the rules and avoid punishment. Didn't he know his behavior wasn't to be tolerated? Even if no kids were around, sex on campus was a huge no-no. Maybe he'd thought he was safe since it was after hours. Maybe it wasn't his fault.

I flushed, my chest burning with heat. Of course it was his fault! How else could it have happened?

I was so torn; I felt like I was being split in two.

I stared at the folder. "I didn't bring you in here to talk about the Fun Festival."

"You didn't?"

Needing to put more distance between us than just the desk, I walked to the window and stared out at the kids in PE class skipping along the tarmac. What would they think about losing their favorite teacher? The teachers would hate me for getting rid of him, but I would never tell them the real reason.

I remembered the day I'd hired Mr. Morales. He'd said he'd run a race in the Blue Ridge Mountains and fallen in love with my hometown of Mossy Oak. The very next day, he'd started packing.

Tension filled the room as I stared out the window. The only sound was the distant noise of children's voices and the hum of the overhead lights. The longer the silence lasted, the more awkward the moment became.

I swallowed thickly. "You're in violation of dress code," I blurted.

His eyebrows rose. "I am?"

"Your hair is too long. Your clothing is too casual, and your jewelry is..." I waved my hand in the air, grasping at straws. "It's supposed to be kept to a minimum."

His hand lifted to touch his necklace, then drifted to rub absently over his heart. With a mysterious smile, he rose from his chair and crossed the room to stand next to me at the window. His nearness made every cell in my body sizzle, and when he dropped his gaze over me in a slow perusal, I felt ready to combust.

"I should point out you are violating this dress code as well," he said in a low voice. "I think you are having... How do you say it? A wardrobe misfunction?" He raised one eyebrow and pointed at my backside.

A sudden blast of heat filled my body as I reached around and felt the frilly hem of my dress tucked partially into the waistband of my panties.

Hello, mortification, my name is Gabi.

Chapter 3

Gabi

I needed my afternoon run through the park more than ever after surviving flashing the hottest guy on the planet my panties. The four miles at race pace cleared my head and cooled my blood. I worked up a sweat and pushed aside my embarrassment.

Life went on.

It could happen to anyone.

It wasn't the first time Mr. Morales had seen a woman's panties.

By the time I finished running, I had convinced myself I deserved a hot slice of greasy pizza for dinner. I stopped by Hawthorne's and ordered our family's favorite buffalo chicken pizza with an extra side of ranch dressing.

While at the counter, I spotted my friends Thatcher and Lacey in a corner booth. They were arguing over something, which was not an unusual sight. Lacey and Thatcher were more like brother and sister than boss and employee. They bickered over everything just for the fun of it.

I headed over to their booth to break up their squabble. When I planted my hands on their table, they stopped arguing and turned toward me.

"What's going on here?" I asked.

Lacey sat back in the booth and folded her arms across her chest. "I'm trying to talk Thatcher into sponsoring an indie author conference. He says he's too busy, but what he doesn't understand is how easy it will be. He won't have to lift a finger. I'll take care of everything."

Thatcher glared across the booth at Lacey. "And what Lacey doesn't understand is that I'm already in over my head." He rubbed his temples. "I'm so busy, I can't think straight."

I pointed at Lacey. "Put the papers away."

She opened her mouth to argue, then closed it and swept her papers back into a folder. My disappointed stare prompted her to look embarrassed.

"Sorry, Thatcher," she said. "I know those renovations are a real bitch."

He grimaced. "Don't get me started on the carpet in the upstairs bedroom."

Lacey arched a brow. "It can't be worse than the hideous tile in the kitchen."

Thatcher rubbed his forehead. "It's worse. Trust me."

"Scoot over." I bumped Thatcher with my hip. "You need a massage."

Thatcher slid over, and I slid in beside him. I rubbed his tense shoulders, working my knuckles into the knots.

"You're as hard as a brick," I said.

"Between the renovations gone wild, running the book club, the store, and Outside the Box..." He trailed off, and his shoulder stiffened again. "I really don't even have time to be here right now."

"It's one beer," Lacey said. "You can make time for one beer."

"Even I have time for a beer," I said, cheerfully. "Shane won't be home for another hour." I'd been planning to take a long shower, but I'd sacrifice the luxury for a drink with my friends.

"Hey, there's Mia," Lacey said, waving her hand in the air.

Lacey's sweater slipped down to reveal the colorful tattoos on her arm. I'd always wanted a tattoo, but I'd never been brave enough to ink myself permanently. If I got a tattoo, I wouldn't get something bold, like Lacey's bright designs. My ink would be private, my own little secret.

"Mia," Lacey called. "Over here."

"I bet Mia has time for a beer," I said as she approached the booth.

Mia checked her phone and slid into the empty booth beside Lacey. "A martini would be better," she said. "But I have to get back to work."

"It's after six," I said.

"There's fresh evidence against The Wolf," she said.

Mia was assistant district attorney in Azalea County. A few months earlier, she'd lost a case against a rapist on a technicality. Known as "The Wolf of Wolf Pit," the rapist had assaulted at least five women in the small town of Wolf Pit. Mia hadn't given up on putting him behind bars.

The server approached, and we ordered a round of drinks.

"I should have ordered a martini after the day I had," I said.

"What happened to you?" Thatcher asked.

I filled my friends in on my attempted firing, which had ended in a reprimand and a "wardrobe misfunction."

"My entire butt was out," I said, digging my fingers into Thatcher's shoulders.

"Ouch." He reached up and removed my hands. "Easy."

"Please tell me you weren't wearing mom panties," Lacey said.

I cringed. My underwear drawer was stuffed full of mom panties.

"Gabi's ass looks hot in mom panties," Thatcher said, reaching for his beer.

"How would you know?" Mia arched a brow at him.

"I'm a man," he said. "I can appreciate a fine ass on a woman even if she is just my friend." He raised his glass to me. "Gabi has one fine ass."

"Thanks. Right back at you."

Everyone in Mossy Oak knew what Thatcher looked like under his clothes because he'd posed in his underwear for a calendar to benefit the Canine Rescue Center last year. He'd been Mr. June, but I bet many women had kept him hanging up long after summer was over.

The server put our drinks and a basket of bread on the table. I grabbed the bread first, suddenly starving.

"Why the hell didn't anyone tell you your ass was out?" Lacey asked. "Mike Collins? Or Chelsea Taylor?"

I clapped my hand on my forehead. I'd forgotten about Chelsea Taylor. Son of a monkey! She'd seen my mom panties too, and she was always so gorgeously done up. How embarrassing.

"Mike Collins is one of those passive-aggressive types," I said. "I always knew he hated me."

"He doesn't hate you. He was probably too scared to tell you." Mia slathered butter on bread and pointed the knife at me. "Everyone is terrified of you."

"I'm five foot three!" I protested. "I'm hardly scary."

"Own it," Mia said. "You're tiny but mighty and scary as hell." She bit off a chunk of bread. "I say that with love."

"So, did you fire him or not?" Lacey asked.

I swirled my beer. "Not," I admitted. "I couldn't do it. He was so passionate about the Fun Festival."

Mia nodded knowingly. "He sounds very passionate."

I didn't pretend not to understand her meaning. My friends knew all about the accidental hummer incident and took every opportunity to tease me about my crush on Mr. Morales.

"Give the guy a break," Thatcher said. "Maybe he was attacked by the woman. You don't know the situation."

Mia laughed. "I can guarantee there isn't any evidence pointing to a BJ bandit on the loose."

"Maybe it was an accident," Lacey said. "Maybe he tripped, and his dick fell into her mouth."

My friends erupted in laughter.

I set my beer glass down with a *thunk*. "It's not funny. I can't even look at him without picturing the scene."

"I bet that's not the only time you've been picturing it," Lacey said, grinning.

My cheeks flushed, and I fanned my face. "I'm horrible, aren't I?"

Mia rolled her eyes. "I'm dealing with thieves, rapists, and murderers. In comparison, accidentally spying isn't so bad." She tore off another piece of bread. "And I don't think dating a teacher is criminal behavior. Unless it's against the rules?"

"Technically no, but it wouldn't be right." I buttered another piece of bread. "Plus, I'm too old for him. He's not even thirty."

Thatcher's eyebrows pulled together. "You're thirty-five. What's the big deal?"

"You should get laid. It will take the edge off," Lacey said before I could answer. "That's the advice you gave me, remember?"

"It was stupid of me to suggest. Having sex with Mr. Morales wouldn't solve anything."

"If not the Spanish teacher, then how about someone else? Look who's working tonight." Mia nodded at the bar. "He might be exactly what you need."

Aaron was behind the bar, shaking a cocktail tumbler with enthusiasm. The handsome bartender always flirted with me, but he probably flirted with all the single woman at the bar. He *did* work for tips.

"Aaron is such a hottie," Lacey said. "Check out those biceps."

He did have nice biceps. They bulged as he shook the tumbler.

"Go talk to him," Mia said.

I took a gulp of my drink. "Not tonight," I said. "It's Wednesday."

"What's that got to do with anything?" Mia asked.

"I don't hook up on Wednesdays."

Lacey burst into laughter. "Plus, she's wearing her mom panties."

Mia leveled me with her prosecutor's stare. "Do you really have a schedule for sex?"

"No. But Wednesdays are out. Shane is at basketball practice," I said. "I barely have time for a run and takeout."

"Shane isn't a baby," Lacey said. "He can stay home alone for a little while."

"I know, but I don't have a lot of time left with him." Sadness filled me at the thought of Shane's imminent departure. "I won't waste it on a Wednesday night hookup with a random man."

* * *

I got home before Shane and set the table for dinner. A few minutes later, he blew into the house like a six-foot-tall hurricane, scarfed down his food, and shoved back from the table.

"You forgot to chew," I said as he rinsed his plate and loaded it into the dishwasher.

He grabbed a chocolate muffin I'd swiped from the teachers' lounge and headed down the hall. "I told Jaden and Kendall I'd be online at seven forty-five."

"Wait a second," I said. "What about homework?"

He groaned. "I did it already."

"Are you sure?"

"Yes." He rolled his eyes. "I'm sure."

"How's your grade in Spanish?" I put down my fork and rose from the table. "You can't be on the team if you don't make good grades."

"I know, Mom. I'm working on it, I promise." He checked his phone, and his thumbs flew against the screen in the fastest text this side of the Mississippi. "By the way, Coach Marshall is making me try out for track," he said.

"Track sounds great," I said. "You know, I was the fastest miler—"

"I know. You were the fastest miler in the state of North

Carolina in, like, 1942." He grinned and shoved the muffin into his mouth.

I cocked an eyebrow at him. "Respect your mother."

He hurried down the hall, narrowly missing his head on the low-hanging light fixture. Had he grown in the last week? *Probably.* I added raising the light fixture to my ever-growing list of household maintenance items.

"I don't want to run track," he said around the mouthful of muffin. "I hate running. It's so boring."

I followed him down the hall. "Are you even my child?"

"Nope." He pulled his door open. "You're way too short to be my mom."

"Don't forget to brush your teeth," I said as he settled in front of his video game and pulled his headset on over his headful of springy curls. "And you need a haircut."

He gave me a thumbs-up sign and reached for his controller.

"You have until eight thirty," I said. "Then get to bed."

"Okay," he said. "No, I wasn't talking to you. It's my mom." He shifted his headset. "Jaden says hi."

"Hi, Jaden." I resisted the urge to wipe muffin crumbs from Shane's cheek and stepped into the hall. "Don't stay up too late. It's a school night."

Shane didn't hear the last bit of advice. He was already lost in the world of ultimate fighting or whatever game he was playing with his best friends. I knew I would have to go back to his room at eight thirty to make sure he was following the rules. It was the part of my job as a single mom I hated the most. I always had to be the bad guy. If his dad were around, I would get some relief. Montel had been in the military. He would have been a stern father with lots of rules and regulations.

Maybe Montel wouldn't have even let Shane play video games online with his friends. Maybe he would have insisted they were too violent or risky for predators. But it was some of the only time Shane had to spend with his friends. His life was busy with sports and school and his multitude of cousins, who always seemed to be having an event to attend. I didn't have the heart to tell Shane he couldn't have a little downtime with his video game and his buddies.

Deep down, I knew I was probably too soft on Shane, and I struggled to find balance. If Montel were here...

But he wasn't. He'd been gone for twelve years, and there wasn't a day that passed when I didn't think of him. Sometimes it hurt worse than usual, but it didn't rip my heart out like it once had. When Shane had been a toddler, I'd cried every single day.

It still wasn't easy, especially since Shane resembled his handsome father more and more every day.

As I took a quick shower and went through my nightly routine, I imagined how different it would be if Montel were alive. We would be living in one of the larger houses on base. Montel would be a sergeant or higher, and we would probably have a house full of kids. We'd wanted at least three.

I'd have a network of army wives, and I would plan charities and volunteer at fundraisers.

I would be a completely different person if Montel hadn't died in Afghanistan twelve years ago. I'd be a wife, and I wouldn't have to crawl into an empty bed every night for the rest of my life.

Despite my best intentions, my mind drifted to Mr. Morales. I imagined what it might be like to have his lips against mine.

I couldn't forget his expression when he'd pointed out my underwear mishap. How I wished I'd been wearing something other than sensible white cotton panties... Something silky and sexy enough to drive him crazy, the same as he did to me.

I slipped into bed, imagining what Mr. Morales was doing. Was he getting into bed too?

Longing coursed through me at the thought of Mr. Morales in bed. My heart quickened, and my skin tingled.

After twelve years of being single, I knew how to take the edge off desire without any help from a man. I slid my hand under the elastic waistband of my boring mom panties.

Guilt knotted my belly as I touched the aching bundle of nerves at my core. I knew it was unprofessional to think of kissing Mr. Morales while I touched myself, but I couldn't help it.

I bet his beard would feel soft against my skin, and he would taste as good as he smelled. Citrus and spice. His tongue would dip into my mouth and trace the seam of my lips until I opened for him.

A buzzing sound pierced the air, dragging me from my fantasies. I jerked upright, my heart hammering in my chest.

It was my phone, and it buzzed again. I went into mom-panic mode for a split second before remembering my only child was safe and sound, or as much as possible while playing video games.

Something else must be wrong. No one called this late unless it was an emergency. I grabbed my phone and saw it was my mother calling.

I swiped to answer. "What's wrong?"

"Hi, sweetheart," my mom said. "Is that how you answer the phone? You sound like you're out of breath. Did you just go running? You know I don't like you running at night."

Yanking the covers up to my chest, I sat back against the headboard. "I wasn't running. Why are you calling so late? What's the matter?"

My mom chuckled. "You have a few hours before you will turn into a pumpkin, honey."

"Is everything okay with Dad?" My father had recently retired and taken up adventure hiking. He was currently hiking the Grand Canyon with several buddies.

"Your father is fine. I was only calling to tell you *Forever Love* is on television right now. I thought you might like to watch it."

"Thanks, Mom."

"You're welcome. I've got to go; commercial break is over."

My mom had no idea about Netflix, and it wasn't the time to tell her. I hung up and put my phone back on the nightstand.

A moment later, there was a knock on my door, and then it opened.

"Can I go to a party at Zack's Friday?" Shane asked. "It's his birthday."

"Will his parents be there?"

"Yes, Mom."

"Will there be girls there too?"

Shane flashed his perfect smile, which had cost five thousand dollars at the orthodontist. "I hope so," he said. "I don't want to go to a lame party without any girls."

I swallowed hard, still uncomfortable with the idea of my son at a party with girls, even though he was in high school. He still seemed so young sometimes. "Okay. You can go."

"And is there anything else to eat? I'm still starving."

Chapter 4

JOEY

I wasn't built for cold weather.

Rain, I could handle. In Costa Rica, we have two seasons: the rainy season and the less rainy season. I'd take rain over cold any day.

The clouds hung so low in the air, they rested on my shoulders. A hazy fog clung to the treetops, and a smell I didn't recognize hung in the air. It might have been snow.

I pulled my knit cap tighter around my ears and set out on an easy jog toward Ginger Cake Acres. Normally, I avoided the trails winding through the busy park. I much preferred the challenging terrain of the Sapphire Hills to the dirt path, which wound around the pond and forked into town, but I wasn't training for anything. Without a marathon on my schedule, I ran to stay in shape, not to race. I didn't always have to pick the hardest routes. Sometimes I could go easy on myself.

With every step I took, my body warmed up a little. By the time I got to the path around the pond, I no longer thought my extremities were going to freeze off. I settled into an easy pace and let my mind drift. I imagined the perfect day on the beach with my toes in the sand and an ice-cold Imperial in my hand.

Another runner popped out from behind a grove of trees, pulling me out of my daydream.

Crazy woman—she had on shorts.

She kept up a fast pace, probably trying to outrun the cold. I watched her quick turnover, admiring her form. She was an excellent runner, with a high kick and minimal bouncing.

Despite the cold, her legs were hot. The nice view took my mind off my frozen nose. Wanting a closer look, I sped up to catch her. My legs burned as I pushed faster, sprinting through the trees to the other side of the pond. The effort was worth it when I caught her. She was even better up close.

Toned and tanned despite the winter, her legs went on for days. Her ass was cute, too. It was just plump enough to jiggle... Hold on. I'd seen that ass before.

All that shiny brown hair was familiar, too. Although I was used to seeing it secured in a tight bun, I recognized the rich shade of my boss's hair.

A grin tugged at my mouth when I recalled our meeting. When she'd left me alone in her office, I'd snuck a peek at the book she'd shoved in her desk drawer. I trusted my intuition, especially when it came to the opposite sex, and I knew by the way her eyes had widened when I mentioned my sister's porno books that Mrs. Salinger was reading one just like them.

Sure enough, the real book cover under the handmade jacket was a half-naked man with an axe slung over his ridiculously muscled shoulder. A quick scan inside the book confirmed it: she was reading a porno book. Just like Ava did.

When I saw the cover, I knew I'd misjudged Mrs. Salinger. She wasn't the Iron Lady everyone thought she was. Underneath those conservative outfits, Principal Salinger was as hot-blooded as a *Tica*.

I should have known she was a runner by her fabulous legs.

I sped up, letting my footfall thud harder than usual so she would hear me coming. There wasn't anything worse than scaring a woman running alone. I'd almost been maced a few times.

I cleared my throat as I ran up beside her. "Morning, Principal Salinger."

Her head whipped around at me. When she recognized me, her step faltered and her eyes went wide. She looked like she'd swallowed a box of fireworks.

"Mr. Morales?"

She was cute when she was startled. Her mouth formed a perfect circle, and a flush spread across her cheeks.

I grinned. "Call me Joey."

Her answer was a huff of frosty breath and a burst of speed. She left me in the dirt, her ponytail swinging behind her in a jaunty dance. I watched her for a moment, then I picked up the pace and caught her. She sped up again, and so did I.

If she wanted to race, I was game. I lived to race. We sped around the edge of the pond, startling several squirrels digging holes in the dirt.

As we neared the trailhead splitting off from the pond, I lost myself in the demanding pace. The thrill of racing brought back my competitive spirit. I didn't feel the cold anymore as my heart pounded and my legs burned. Cold air filled my lungs, and Mrs. Salinger's electric energy buzzed through my veins.

I glanced at my boss and saw she was pushing herself to the limit. Her cheeks were pink, and her gaze was fierce. She was adorably determined to beat me. I might just let her win.

"Race to the picnic shelter?" I asked, my breath puffing in a cloud between us.

Her chin lifted a notch, and without warning, she took off. After a moment, I followed her, catching up in three long strides. She glared at me when I passed her, and I threw her a wink. The path wound around a row of low bushes and then climbed a hill to our destination. I reached the bottom of the hill first and glanced back in time to see her vault over the bushes in a flying leap.

"Hey!" I yelled. "You're cheating!"

Her laugh was sweet music to my ears. She landed as light as a gazelle a few meters in front of me, shot me a smug grin, and sprinted up the sidewalk.

"Watch out!" I pointed at a dangerous tree root pushing up through the concrete.

But it was too late. Her toe hit the root, and she flew through the air, landing not-so-gracefully in the grass.

Chapter 5

GABI

My hands shot out in time to save me from planting my face on the sidewalk. I couldn't save my elbow or my knee, though. They both scraped the sidewalk as I crashed to the concrete.

Mr. Morales crouched over me and touched his gloved hand to my arm just above the torn sleeve. "Evil root," he said. "I've tripped over it myself."

I noted his twinkling eyes. "Go ahead and laugh. I'm sure it was pretty funny."

His smile was even gentler than his touch. "You fell very gracefully. Much better than I did." His gaze traveled over me, and his eyes narrowed on my elbow. "You're bleeding."

I sat up and inspected my elbow, where my favorite shirt was torn and my skin was scraped raw. "It's nothing."

He skimmed his hand along my arm, feeling for injuries. His touch made a tingle of awareness race down my spine. I felt as silly as a teenager with a crush, trembling because he touched me *through his glove.*

"You must be freezing," he said.

Since we weren't running anymore, the cold made me shiver. The temperature had dropped since I'd left home, and the sky had darkened. The forecast hadn't predicted snow, but I could sense it in the cold, wet air.

"I should get going." I was determined to get home before the snow came, and apparently I couldn't be around Mr. Morales without making a fool of myself.

He took my hand and helped me to my feet. "Can you walk okay? Your knee is scraped too."

I brushed aside his concern. I dealt with skinned knees on a regular basis. "I'm fine."

"Come with me," he said, wrapping my hand in his.

Even through his glove, I felt the warmth of his touch. My body didn't need skin on skin to react to him. Just being near him made my belly flutter and my heart race.

"Where?" I asked, forcing a laugh. "Is there a first-aid kit nearby?"

"My place is just over there." He pointed toward the park entrance.

I stiffened and pulled my hand from his. I couldn't possibly go home with Mr. Morales. What if someone saw us? It wouldn't look right. I had a reputation to uphold.

"Come on," he said, sensing my hesitation. "You can get cleaned up and warm. I don't know about you, but I could use a hot cup of coffee after freezing my ass off out here."

I shivered and wrapped my arms around myself. "I don't live far either," I said. "Just a few miles."

"I'm closer," he said. "Let me take care of you."

The protest died on my lips. How long had it been since a handsome man had offered to take care of me? Too long to remember. My rusty libido sputtered and kicked into gear, leaving me with an embarrassing flush on my cheeks. I fussed with my torn sleeve and avoided his eyes.

"I don't want to trouble you."

He took my uninjured arm and steered me toward the park exit. "It's no trouble."

I knew he didn't mean to flirt, but his sexy accent made my blood heat. It was obvious why they called him Joey. While he didn't much resemble the *Friends* character, they shared a similar vibe. They had the same serene confidence, nothing ruffled them, and flirting was second nature.

We crossed the pond over an arched footpath and came to the park exit. Even on a chilly morning, Ginger Cake Acres was busy. Dogs chased balls across the rolling lawn, kids whizzed by on bikes, and couples strolled along, holding hands.

Jealousy coiled in my belly as I watched the couples walk by. The last time I'd walked through the park holding hands with a man had been a lifetime ago.

Mr. Morales was just being nice to me. He was friendly and naturally outgoing. He didn't mean anything by offering to help. Sometimes my imagination got the best of me, and I had to remind myself this was real life, not an erotic romance novel where every scenario ended with a thorough ravaging.

Maybe it was time I branched out from lumberjacks and reverse harems. My love of erotica had gone to my brain. I loved reading erotica because the plots were so outlandish. The story lines were nothing like real life, which was stressful but often boring. Maybe reading so much erotica had warped my brain.

Reading was my escape. After Montel had died, reading had been my way to cope with raising a young boy on my own. More recently, reading had led me to a group of great friends with the Blue Ridge Book Club.

For the first time in my life, reading seemed dangerous. My books had planted seeds which could never bloom—deliciously naughty seeds involving Mr. Morales lifting me onto his kitchen counter and stepping between my thighs to bandage my scraped knee. He would kiss my wounds better, his mouth chasing away the pain. In the guise of checking for injuries, he would stroke my thighs, caress my hips—

"Careful," Mr. Morales said, steering me away from a low tree branch growing into the sidewalk. "The trees are out to get you today."

"Yeah," I muttered, telling myself to get a grip and pay attention. Maybe I should select an autobiography for my next book. I'd heard Gandhi's was excellent, and probably tame compared to the spicy stories I usually devoured.

We stopped in front of a white brick Colonial steeped in Southern charm. A North Carolina flag flapped from the upper porch, and the front and center door was painted royal blue to match the shutters.

Joey fished a lanyard with a key from the neck of his sweatshirt. "Here we are."

"This place is beautiful."

"I'm very lucky to live here," he said. "The neighbors are great, and there's a hot tub on the back patio."

The front door swung open, and a woman carrying a yoga mat walked out. One of the great neighbors? She was tall and curvaceous, with a headful of bouncy, red curls. Her face lit up when she saw Mr. Morales.

"Hi, Joey! How was your run?"

"Cold." He turned toward me. "Kaitlyn, this is my friend Gabriella."

Butterflies took flight in my stomach at the sound of Mr. Morales rolling his tongue over the *r* in my name. *Gabriella.* It sounded so sexy when he said it. I'd never been called by my full name before. Everyone, including my mother, called me Gabi. Mr. Morales made me want to be Gabriella. Gabriella would let her hair down, dance under the moon, and make love on the kitchen table any day of the week. Gabriella was a lot like Valentina, my secret identity, who loved erotic stories and was sexually adventurous.

"Nice to meet you." Kaitlyn's eyes drifted to my torn sleeve. "What happened to you?"

"A tree root tried to attack her," Mr. Morales said.

Her perky nose wrinkled. "Ouch."

I pressed my knees together. "It's not too bad."

"You're lucky I'm certified in first aid," Joey said.

"Are we still on for Thursday night?" Kaitlyn asked Mr. Morales.

"I wouldn't miss it," he said.

"Perfect," she chirped. She continued down the stairs, then stopped suddenly. "Hey, did I leave my bikini top at your place the other night?" she asked. "I can't find it anywhere."

He shrugged. "Maybe you left it down by the hot tub."

"I don't think so."

"I'll look for it," he said.

Kaitlyn waved goodbye and hurried down the stairs.

A bitter taste filled my mouth. If Kaitlyn was what Mr. Morales had meant by friendly neighbors, I wasn't eager to meet the rest of them.

Chapter 6

GABI

We entered the main door and stepped into a grand foyer with gleaming mahogany floors and paned windows. A crystal chandelier hung from the high ceiling, scattering light across the white walls. A traditional, wood-paneled staircase led to the second floor.

"I'm up top," he said, leading the way up the stairs.

I followed slowly, hobbling on my hurt leg. My knee smarted, and I shivered in my sweaty clothes.

"You okay?" he asked, slowing to wait for me.

Irritation coiled in my belly, and I gritted my teeth. I'd bet Kaitlyn never got attacked by a tree root. "I'm fine."

He unlocked his door and held it open for me. "Sorry about the mess," he said. "I wasn't expecting company."

I stepped into his sparsely furnished living room. There wasn't much of a mess because there wasn't much of anything. The only furniture was a low-slung sofa and a sleek coffee table. The walls were bare, and the mantle was empty.

"Did you just move in?" I knew he'd been in Mossy Oak since last summer, but maybe he'd switched apartments.

"No." He glanced around with a sheepish grin. "I just suck at decorating."

"Maybe you're a minimalist?"

"I guess."

A blur of orange raced across the floor and launched itself at Mr. Morales's shin.

"Is that a cat?"

He pulled off his gloves and bent to scratch the giant ball of fluff between its triangular ears. "This is Frodo. He doesn't know he's a cat."

"You have a cat?" I'd assumed Mr. Morales had an active social life that didn't leave room for a pet.

He tossed his cap onto the sofa and ran a hand through his hair. He'd had it trimmed, and it stood up at odd angles, sweaty and disheveled.

"Frodo's not really my cat," he said. "He came with the apartment. Frodo belongs to everyone in the building."

So the neighbors not only shared a hot tub, but also a pet.

"Everyone has a doggie door, and Frodo comes and goes as he pleases. I never know when he is going to grace me with his companionship."

He scooped Frodo into his arms and gave him a cuddle. Frodo went pliant in his arms, blissfully arching against Mr. Morales's hand. His loud purr echoed across the room.

If Mr. Morales rubbed his hand across my belly, I would purr too.

Mr. Morales set Frodo on the floor, and to my surprise, the cat ran toward me. He moved faster than a ball of fluff should and was at my leg before I could say *here kitty, kitty.* Frodo sniffed my leg, then flipped onto his back for a belly rub.

"He thinks he's a dog," Mr. Morales said.

I pulled off my gloves and stroked Frodo's belly. "Hello there, handsome."

Mr. Morales chuckled softly. "Don't flirt with him, I'll get jealous."

I raised my gaze from the cat and saw him looking at me with longing. A bolt of lust shot through me at the hunger in his expression.

Frodo meowed, demanding my attention. I rubbed my hand across his soft fur, distracting myself from Mr. Morales's intense gaze.

"Frodo," he said. "Leave the lady alone. I need to doctor her."

The phrase conjured up all sorts of delicious fantasies.

I followed him down the hall to the bathroom.

"Don't worry." He bent and rummaged under the sink. "I'm certified in first aid."

"It's only a scrape."

I tried not to stare as he reached into the back of the cabinet, but his sweatpants were doing wonders for his butt. A small swatch of bronzed skin showed between his sweatshirt and the waistband of his pants. The tiny glimpse of his bare skin sent a ripple of desire through me. Great Scott! I was turned on by looking at his lower back. What would I do if I saw his naked chest?

"What is it?" he asked, glancing over his shoulder at me.

"Nothing," I said. My cheeks felt like they'd caught fire. "You're just a little overdressed for the weather." It was the first thing I thought of, and it tumbled out before I could stop myself. He was wearing too many layers for a run in early spring in the Carolinas. Sweatpants, a shirt, and a sweatshirt were overkill. He'd already tossed his knit hat and gloves. "It's not that cold."

He went back to his search. "It's freezing outside. Aren't you underdressed?" He looked over his shoulder at my bare legs.

The heat of his gaze warmed me from the inside out. I had a serious case of the swoons for Mr. Morales, and the tight quarters of his bathroom weren't helping things. Luckily, the counter was right behind me. I leaned my hip against the cold marble as his eyes scorched over my legs. I would have thought he was flirting again, but then I remembered my bloody knee. He was probably looking at my injury, and I was standing there ogling a scant centimeter of skin above his waistband.

I reached over to turn on the faucet. What was wrong with me? Cleaning up a skinned knee was second nature to me. I'd had plenty of practice.

He stood and grabbed a washcloth before I could. His eyes danced with mischief as he moved closer, invading my personal space. I breathed in the musky scent of his sweat. Even his sweat was intoxicating.

"Let me," he said, pushing my hands out of the way under the faucet.

He was just being nice. He wasn't flirting with me. So why did my heart race when our hands touched? My heart definitely thought he was flirting. The most tender flesh between my legs thought he was flirting.

He pointed at the toilet. "Sit," he said.

My sprinting heart slowed. There was nothing less sexy than sitting on a toilet. Ordering my lady parts to calm down, I took a seat. This was a far cry from the romantic scene I'd crafted in my mind of Mr. Morales ravishing me.

He wrung out the washcloth and squatted. "What's so funny?" he asked, glancing up at my face.

"When I woke up this morning, I didn't picture this happening."

He bent over my knee, carefully bathing it with the warm, wet cloth. I hissed when the water stung my cut. It wasn't a deep cut, but it was strange to have someone doctoring me. I couldn't remember the last time anyone had taken care of me.

"Almost done," he said.

I leaned back and held my breath as he sprayed antiseptic on the cut. His fingers were strong but gentle. He leaned closer and blew on my cut the way my mom used to when I was little. My heart raced when I imagined him tracing a path up my thigh. A bolt of desire shot through me as the soft puff of his breath cooled the sting from the antiseptic.

As he peeled open a bandage and applied it to my knee, I held in a sigh.

"Take that off," he said.

"What?" My eyes snapped open, and I saw he was pointing at my ruined shirt. A bolt of lust zigzagged straight to my core.

Then, from the corner of my eye, I saw a scrap of brightly colored fabric hanging from the shower curtain rod. *Kaitlyn's missing bikini top.*

My racing libido slammed to a halt. This man was a player with multiple women in his life. He already had a blonde and a redhead. Now he wanted to add a brunette to the mix? No thanks.

I jumped to my feet. "I've got to go," I said, pushing past him.

"Wait." He came into the hall after me. "Your elbow. I wasn't finished."

I grabbed my gloves and hurried to the door. "Yes, you were," I said.

"Gabriella, what's wrong?"

I bolted out the door without answering and flew down the stairs as fast as my injured knee would allow. I wasn't Gabriella nor my sexy alter ego, Valentina. I was Gabi. I was safe, responsible, predictable Gabi, and I should have fired Fernando Morales a week ago.

Chapter 7

GABI

The bleachers trembled as we stomped our feet, cheering in one loud voice echoing all the way to Main Street three blocks away. Only two minutes remained in the championship basketball game, and Mossy Oak was down by six points. Our best player, a senior headed to UNC Chapel Hill, fouled out, and they brought Shane off the bench.

"Go, Shane!" my mom yelled so loudly in my ear I thought my eardrum would split.

"Drop the hammer, Shane!" my dad yelled in my other ear.

My parents were the two loudest people on Earth, and I was trapped between them.

"*Go!*" Mom screamed at the top of her lungs and clutched my arm.

I winced when her fingers dug into my injured elbow. "Ow! Mom, watch out."

My dad stomped the bleachers hard enough to make them shake. "Kill them, Shane! Bury the bastards!"

I elbowed my dad in the ribs. "Dad!"

He glanced down at me, his eyes shining with pride. "What?"

"It's a high school game, not a battlefield."

He pretended not to hear me and raised his fist in the air. "Drop the hammer, boy!"

"It's not just a game," my mom said. "It's THE CHAMPI-ONSHIP GAME!" Her voice boomed louder with each syllable until it could shatter glass.

The winner of this game went on to compete in the North Carolina state championship game in Charlotte next week. This was the biggest game of Shane's life. He'd barely touched the ball all season. As the youngest member of an all-conference team, Shane hadn't had many opportunities to play.

Now was his chance to shine.

Harding High had the ball and was trying to run as much time off the clock as possible. My focus was trained on Shane while he guarded the kid with the ball. Tension hung thick in the air as the boy stepped back to shoot a three-pointer. Shane jumped up as the boy shot the ball, slapping the shot wide. The crowd went wild as the Mossy Oak guard grabbed the ball and sprinted down the court. The center dashed under the goal and positioned himself perfectly to catch it and slam an easy dunk, which tightened the score to a four-point spread.

The bleachers shook again when my dad jumped up and down beside me. I was so nervous, I could hardly watch when Harding took possession again. I glanced around at the other spectators, feeling a sense of community. We were all in this together, holding our breath, biting our nails, cheering our hearts out for our teams.

Then I saw him. Mr. Morales was standing a few rows over, cupping his hands to his mouth as he yelled at the court. He wore jeans and a green-and-gold Mossy Oak T-shirt. The T-shirt hugged his broad shoulders and clung to his biceps, and the jeans did wonderful things for his butt.

"*Yes!*" Mom screamed in my ear.

"Air ball!" Dad yelled.

I tore my eyes from Mr. Morales's butt and looked at the court.

Mossy Oak had the ball again. They passed. They shot. They scored. We were two points away from tying the game, with only thirty seconds left on the clock.

Harding had the ball again, but I couldn't watch. It was too nerve-wracking. My eyes strayed to Mr. Morales again, and this time, he happened to be looking right at me. Our eyes met and held over the cheering crowd. He nodded his chin at me and smiled brightly. I remembered how he'd taken care of me after my fall, how gentle he'd been, and how easy things had been between us until I spotted Kaitlyn's swimsuit top.

Annoyed, I jerked my attention back to the court in time to see Mossy Oak get another steal.

With twenty seconds left, the team bounded down the court and set up for the final shot. Shane hustled down to the far edge of the court, and my heart beat kicked up speed. He'd spent hours shooting from his spot. It was exactly where he needed to be to make a three-pointer to win the game. But would his teammates trust he could do it? He was the youngest kid on the team. The only freshman.

The clock ticked and his teammates passed the ball back and forth, running out of options. Finally, one of them saw Shane was open and threw him the ball. He set his feet behind the three-point line, squared up to the net, and released it.

The ball soared in a perfect arc, hanging in the air for an ungodly long time before swishing through the net.

The final buzzer sounded as the ball hit the hardwood floor, and the sound of cheers was deafening. My mom and dad yelled so loudly, I thought my head was going to split open.

Fans swarmed the court, surrounding the players. Shane fought his way through the crowd.

My dad caught Shane in a bear hug. "Congratulations! You're going to states!"

Shane wrapped his arms around my dad, and they thumped each other's backs. In his high-top shoes, Shane stood taller than my dad, and his halo of curly hair gave him another few inches of height.

My throat clogged when our eyes met over my dad's shoulder. *Good job,* I mouthed over the noise. He nodded and smiled so big, I thought his face would crack.

"Can you believe my three-pointer?" he asked.

"Of course!" I hugged his neck, thinking of the endless practice shots he'd taken in our driveway. The sound of the basketball thumping on the concrete had driven me crazy. "It's your sweet spot."

"You looked so handsome!" my mom said, joining in the hug.

We laughed, but it was true. Shane was handsome. He was the spitting image of Montel. Same wide mouth and high cheekbones. Same stubborn chin. There was so little of me in him. People often asked if we were related. I thought maybe he had my eyes, but otherwise, he was all Montel.

"I'm so proud of you," I said, holding back tears. Montel would be proud. He'd been a huge basketball fan. I choked back my emotion and backed away from the family hug. "Pizza at Hawthorne's tonight?"

Pizza at Hawthorne's was our family tradition after basketball games. Hawthorne's had the best pizza in town, and usually half the team was there celebrating a win or commiserating over a loss.

"See if Kendall and Jaden want to come," I said. "My treat."

Someone yelled Shane's name, and he waved. "Zack is having everyone over tonight," he said. "Remember?"

My chest squeezed. I didn't remember, but I pretended. "Sure."

"We're getting out of here before the traffic," Mom said. "Don't be late for supper on Sunday."

I rolled my eyes. My mom was a stickler for two things: punctuality and avoiding traffic.

My dad hugged me again. "I'm proud of you, baby," he said.

The tears I'd kept at bay filled my eyes. "Why? I didn't do anything."

"You raised a great kid," he said.

I gulped air, trying to force the lump in my throat to disappear. My mom tugged my dad away before the dreaded traffic thickened. I watched them until they disappeared into the crowd.

"Hey, Coach Joey," Shane said.

I turned around and saw Mr. Morales coming up behind me. I read the lettering on his green-and-gold T-shirt: Mossy Oak Track and Field.

Mr. Morales was Shane's track coach?

They were only a few days into practice, and Shane was taking it easy until basketball season was over, but he'd come home every day more and more enthusiastic about running.

"With speed like yours," Mr. Morales told Shane, "I think you're better suited to sprint distances after all."

I agreed. My son had one speed: fast. Plus, he could jump. "Or maybe the hurdles," I said, raising my voice over the noise of the crowd.

Mr. Morales stepped closer, so we didn't have to yell. "One hundred meters or three hundred meters?"

"Three hundred."

He took another step toward me when a group of girls rushed past us. "I think you're right."

"Mom, I gotta go," Shane said, breaking in. "Is it okay if I go to Zack's?"

"Will his parents be home?"

"Yeah."

"Can you get a ride home, or do you need me to get you?"

"I can get a ride with Matt."

"Home by eleven thirty."

"Sorry about Hawthorne's," he said.

My heart squeezed. "It's okay. Have fun and be safe. Don't do anything stupid."

"I won't." Shane hurried off to catch his friends.

When he was gone, so was most of the crowd, but Mr. Morales was still standing close enough for me to smell his spicy scent.

Orange and cloves. I wondered what kind of cologne he used. Or was it his shampoo?

"You've been avoiding me," he said.

I stiffened. "I have not."

He crossed his arms over his chest and pinned me with his brown eyes. "I used to see you in the teachers' lounge almost every day, but I haven't seen you once this week."

My heart hammered, and my chest tightened under the intensity of his gaze. He'd noticed me in the teachers' lounge? "I've been eating lunch in my office."

He raised one dark brow. "More crackers?"

An ancient flirting mechanism in my brain, which hadn't seen the light of day in a decade, groaned to life. I tilted my head to the side and leaned in. "I switch it up sometimes and have a protein bar."

His eyes danced, and I noticed the gold flecks in his irises. "Have dinner with me tonight."

My pulse raced at the low vibration in his voice. A tremor shook my knees. I was out of my league with this man. I'd started this flirting train, but it was moving too fast. I wanted off.

Dating wasn't officially against the rules at PES. I knew several teachers who'd been in relationships, but this was different. I was his superior. It wasn't smart to get involved with Mr. Morales.

"I shouldn't." I forced air into my tight chest. "People might get the wrong idea. They might think we're on a date."

His eyes held mine. I thought he might protest it wouldn't be a date, that I'd gotten things wrong. He wasn't flirting, just being friendly, like he'd done with my scraped knee.

"What if we went somewhere no one knew us?" he asked.

Heat filled my chest and spread up to my cheeks. He hadn't denied he wanted it to be a date. I hadn't gotten it wrong. He was definitely flirting, definitely interested in taking this beyond the occasional run-in in the teachers' lounge. A lump formed in my throat. It had been too long since I'd sat across a table from a handsome man and shared a meal. Would it hurt to eat dinner with Mr.

Morales? To stare into his dark eyes across the table and have a dinner conversation which didn't revolve around tutoring, Snapchat, or video games?

It sounded like heaven, but my better senses prevailed. "This town is so small, we are sure to see someone we know."

Mr. Morales's mouth curved, and he leaned closer. "Have you tried Goodfella's? They have the best Italian food around."

I frowned. "Never heard of it."

"That's because it's in Hog Bottom. No one will know us."

I wrinkled my nose. Hog Bottom was a tiny town about twenty minutes outside Mossy Oak. It had a population of about four hundred and was known across North Carolina for its fly-fishing museum.

"Do they have any restaurants in Hog Bottom?"

His eyes sparkled under the florescent lights of the gym. "Is that a yes?"

I glanced around at the dwindling crowd and weighed my options. I hadn't been on a real date in ages, but this wasn't really a date. It was just a meal. And even if it was in Hog Bottom, it had to be better than the frozen pizza waiting for me at home.

"Fine," I said. "But you aren't paying for me." I stepped back in order to breathe easier. "And I'll meet you there."

Chapter 8

JOEY

I arrived at Goodfella's first and chose a booth in the corner with a high back for privacy.

When the server came to take my drink order, I gave him my credit card and told him to add a 25 percent tip. "Don't bring the bill," I said. "And make yourself scarce."

I didn't want distractions or any chance for Gabriella to pay. It didn't matter if she earned more money than I did. I'd asked her for this date; I was paying.

Gabriella didn't keep me waiting. She arrived a few minutes after the server dropped off two glasses and a pitcher of water.

I stood and helped her with her coat. She wore jeans and a Mossy Oak High T-shirt better than anyone. The jeans hugged her curvy ass, and the T-shirt was snug in all the right places.

Once she was settled in the booth, I slid in across from her and poured us each a glass of water. "Do you want wine?" I didn't know what she liked to drink. I knew almost nothing about her besides what I knew from work and that she read sexy books. I wanted to know it all.

She reached for the menu. "Maybe just one glass." Her eyes flashed around the restaurant first before settling on mine. "I shouldn't have come."

Ouch. That hurt. Luckily, my ego was bulletproof. "Why not?"

"Why not?" she asked in a strained voice. "Let's start with the fact that we work together."

I reached across the table and took her hand. "We aren't at work right now. And there aren't any rules about teachers dating."

"I'm not a teacher. I'm your boss."

Her palm was warm against mine. She wore a gold band on her ring finger that probably kept most men away, but not me. I'd asked around, and I knew she wasn't married. Her husband, Shane's father, had passed away a long time ago.

"You're right," I told her. "It's risky."

I loved my job at PES more than anything, except maybe coaching track, but I couldn't stop obsessing over my boss. I wanted to explore the chemistry sizzling between us. I smiled, trying to look effortlessly charming, even though my heart was beating out of my chest in anticipation.

Her fingers curled around mine, and she stared at our joined hands. "You're too young for me, Mr. Morales."

We'd both acknowledged the risk of starting something, yet we were still touching, still leaning toward each other across the table as if a magnet were pulling us together.

I squeezed her hand. "I'm almost thirty."

Her eyes flashed up from our intertwined fingers and narrowed on my face. "You're twenty-seven, eight years younger than me. I have a son who's half your age."

I lifted my shoulders in a shrug. "Americans are so uptight about age. It's just a number. And you should call me Joey. We're having dinner together." I waved my hand in the air. "No more of this Mr. Morales."

The server arrived, and Gabriella tugged her hand free from mine as if he were going to tattle on us. She ordered a glass of Pinot Noir, but I stuck with water. I needed to keep my wits about me while attempting to seduce the Iron Lady. Although, I didn't think the nickname suited her. Under her tough demeanor, I knew she was as soft as silk.

After the server left, she pretended to be absorbed in the menu. I knew she was pretending because the menu wasn't that interesting. It was pizza and spaghetti—well-executed pizza and spaghetti but not worth the attention Gabriella was giving it.

"Everything is good," I said. "The pizza is excellent. The lasagna is the second best I've ever had. And the company?" I waited until she lifted her gaze from the menu to look at me and flashed a smile. "Irresistible."

Her shoulders sagged as if she carried the weight of the world on them. "I really shouldn't be here."

I dialed down the wattage of my smile, going for smolder instead of scorch. "You really should."

She reached for her coat and purse. "I should have fired you last week," she said.

"What?" I snagged her wrist, stopping her. She couldn't drop a bomb like that and then run away. "You'd fire me for a dress code violation?"

Two spots of color appeared high on her cheeks. "It was never about the dress code."

Frustration made my chest tighten. I narrowed my eyes at her. "What then? Why would you fire me? I love PES, and the students adore me."

Her eyebrows knit together. "Not just the students," she said.

Was the chemistry zinging between us too much for her to handle? Was she so nervous about the attraction between us she'd get rid of me?

"Is it because we are attracted to each other?" It was so uptight of her. So American. Anger blazed through me.

"No," she snapped.

"Well, what then?" Some of my confidence returned. "Why would you fire me? I've never had one complaint, and the students are going to ace the end-of-grade tests."

Her eyes fired daggers at me. "You really don't know?"

The server approached with her wine, set the glass on the table, and made himself scarce, just as I'd requested.

"Sit down, please," I said once he was gone. "Tell me what this is about."

Gabriella eyed the wine, then looked back at me. For a long moment, I thought she was going to leave me in the dark, but she slid into the booth, picked up her glass, and took a long sip. She set the glass on the table and looked at me, a pained expression on her face.

"I saw you," she said.

I arched an eyebrow at her. *Go on,* my eyebrow said.

She took another swig of wine. "In your room." Her eyes flicked away from mine and then back. "At your desk?"

"I spend a lot of time at my desk, Gabriella." My voice was tense. I was a patient man, but this was ridiculous.

She leaned forward, her eyes clashing with mine. The color in her cheeks spread down her neck to the top of her chest visible above the V-neck of her T-shirt. "You were at your desk, and a blonde woman was on her knees sucking your—"

"Have you had a chance to look over the menu?" the server asked, coming out of nowhere.

We both turned and glared at him.

His eyes widened. "A few more minutes," he said, and quickly retreated.

I returned my gaze to Gabriella. The bomb had detonated. I closed my eyes in mortification, no longer able to meet her eyes. She'd seen Caroline giving me a blowjob. I deserved to be fired. The clanging sound of my heart filled my ears. No wonder she'd been keeping me at arm's length. I opened my eyes and saw her staring at me, waiting for me to say something.

"That wasn't my fault," I said lamely.

Her eyebrows rose dramatically. "So, I'm supposed to believe there's a BJ bandit running around Mossy Oak attacking innocent men?"

I winced. Caroline was a wine distributor, not a criminal. We'd met at a costume party on Halloween and had hit it off immediately. She traveled to Mossy Oak for work, and she called me when she was in town. We had an easy thing going. No strings, all benefits. We'd been on our way to dinner that fateful night when I'd stopped by the school to grab my laptop. The janitor had let me in, and Caroline had tagged along. Once we were in my office, she'd locked the door and confessed she had a teacher-student fantasy she was dying to act out.

I knew it was stupid and reckless, but as they say, one thing led to another, and the next thing I knew, she'd unzipped my pants and knelt in front of me. I wouldn't say Caroline was a "BJ bandit," but she had been very persuasive.

I knew nothing I said would make it right, but I had to try. "I didn't think anyone else was there."

Her eyebrows rose impossibly higher. "Neither did I."

"She locked the door."

"You forgot about the window."

I grabbed my water and took a long sip, wetting my dry throat. There was a slim window in my wooden door, but she'd had to have been at just the right angle to see in. She'd had to have been looking. I narrowed my eyes at Gabriella, and she glanced away.

"You should have fired me. Why didn't you?" I asked.

"I don't know."

Her brown eyes hadn't darted away quickly enough. I'd seen a gleam in them that screamed everything she wasn't saying.

She'd watched me getting a blowjob. And she'd been turned on. Gabriella Salinger definitely wasn't the buttoned-up prude her conservative appearance led everyone to believe. She read porno books, and she watched other people having sex. Beneath her iron exterior, she was soft as silk and hot as black sand in the sun.

I decided to take a risk. I eased out of the booth and slipped in beside Gabriella. Her eyes widened and her lips pursed. Electricity sizzled between us. She'd definitely watched. I could see it in her every movement.

I shifted closer, pressing my advantage shamelessly. "How much did you see?"

Her eyes fluttered closed, and the pink tip of her tongue peeked out to wet her lips. I slid my arm along the back of the booth and toyed with her long ponytail.

"Tell me."

She sucked in a sharp breath and looked away. She didn't have to say anything. I knew she'd watched. It was why she hadn't fired me, because she didn't want to admit that she'd watched an intimate moment and worse—she'd liked it.

I wrapped my hand around her silky hair and tugged until her eyes opened and met mine. "Tell me, Gabriella," I said, brushing my lips against her cheek. "Did you watch all of it? Did you watch me come?"

She gasped, and the sound went straight to my dick. The Iron Lady was making me as hard as steel. I pressed my thigh against hers and watched her nipples harden under her T-shirt.

So far, my risks had paid off. If I kissed her, would she push me away? I had to find out. Curling my hand around her neck, I moved in slowly, giving her plenty of time to slap me or tell me to go to hell with my bold intentions.

I brushed my lips against hers, and she went completely still. Her lips were cool, but her breath was warm, puffing against my lips in a sudden exhale. I backed away as slowly as I'd approached, watching the flutter of her long lashes against her cheeks. Before I could put more than an inch between us, her hand fisted my shirt, and she crushed her lips to mine.

Chapter 9

Oh, good grief. His lips were paradise.

His mouth was as perfect, as I'd always suspected. His lips were firm against mine with the right amount of pressure. He held me close, his fingers pressing against the nape of my neck to keep me from backing away. As if I would be so stupid. This might be my only chance to kiss him. We'd never get another opportunity like this. I wasn't stopping this kiss until I'd satisfied every craving I'd ever had for Joey Morales.

Easier said than done, considering I couldn't get enough of his mouth on mine. I clutched his shirt and pulled him closer. I threw my leg over his. I think I may have climbed him a little.

The vibration of his moan hummed against my mouth. The little noise made every cell in my body zing to life. A hot burst of desire swept through me, and I couldn't stop my hands from roaming his chest.

He groaned, and the sweet sound awakened a hunger deep inside me. Scorching heat blazed between us. I'd thought one kiss would satisfy me, but all it did was fill me with need. When I slid my tongue past his lips, he rewarded my boldness and touched his tongue to mine.

My heart sighed, and stars burst inside my chest. All those times I'd watched Joey from afar, wondering what his mouth would taste like, how his tongue would feel... It couldn't have prepared me for the real thing.

I climbed closer, pawing at his shirt, spreading my hands against his hard chest. The scruff of his beard rubbed my cheeks, softer than I'd imagined. Warm lips, full and pillow-soft, claimed mine in a sensual kiss. His spicy taste filled my mouth, making me hunger for more.

A soft mewling noise penetrated my ears. After a moment, I realized it came from me. I was whimpering like a kitten. Two more seconds of Joey's talented mouth on mine and the kitten inside would have turned into a lion.

I scrambled back in the booth, tearing my mouth from his. My hands got the message last and released their clutch on his shirt.

The server appeared at the end of the table. "Ready to order?" he asked, getting his pen and pad ready.

I grabbed my purse and climbed over Joey to get out of the booth. I slipped past the server and hurried to the exit. Outside, the cold air shocked my heated skin. I'd forgotten my coat, but there was no way I was going back in there. I couldn't seem to stop making a fool out of myself in front of Joey.

I heard footsteps behind me and hurried through the parking lot toward my car.

"Gabriella." Joey stepped in front of me, blocking the path. His eyes blazed with anger. "You can't kiss me like that and then run off."

A hot spear of embarrassment pierced my chest. I'd gone off like a firework with one brush of his lips.

He dropped my coat over my shoulders and pulled the sides closed around my chest. My arms were held straight against my sides, and I felt vulnerable yet protected at the same time. He used my coat to tug me forward against his chest. My head tipped back, and my belly flipped.

"Don't go," he said. "Come back inside and eat dinner with me."

"I can't."

He took a step back, unsettling me. I'd gotten used to his warmth, his solid presence.

"I promise not to touch you or violate any of your rules." Then, quirking an eyebrow, he added, "unless you want me to."

Desire tickled in my belly and then shot lower. I stared at his full mouth, framed by the dark stubble of his beard, and my mind veered straight back to Fantasyland.

I forced myself to think logically. There was no way Joey was interested in me. I was a widow, eight years older than him, and his boss. Hardly his type.

I took a step back. "I'll see you at work," I said.

He blinked a few times, and then his head bobbed in a nod. "Okay."

He walked me to my car and waited while I opened the door. "See you at work."

I started the engine and watched his long, loose-limbed amble through the parking lot until I couldn't see him anymore. My heart raced, and my vision blurred with tears of frustration. Joey Morales had awakened feelings I'd thought were long dead. His kiss was burned on my brain.

An icy finger of guilt pricked my skin, raising goose bumps. I hadn't felt these feelings since Montel. I choked back a sob. Life was so unfair. I was feeling lust for another man, and Montel was gone forever.

A numbness settled in my chest as I drove on autopilot, refusing to allow any thoughts of Joey to penetrate the steel trap of my mind.

When I was almost home, Shane's ringtone blared in the silence of my car. I pressed the button to answer, and the loud noise of a party rang out through the speakers.

"Hello?"

"Hey, Mom!" Shane shouted over the music.

"Hey, honey." I heard it in his voice that something was wrong. I gripped the steering wheel and tried to keep my voice calm. "What's up?"

He must have moved away from the party, because it got quieter. "I was just wondering if you could pick me up?" he asked.

"Sure." He didn't sound drunk or high. A mother knew these things. "Is everything okay?"

"It's fine. It's my friend Erin. She needs to leave. I'll explain when you get here."

My shoulders relaxed an inch. "I'll be there in fifteen minutes."

"Okay."

There was a long silence, and I thought maybe he'd hung up. "Shane?"

"Yeah?"

"I'll see you soon."

"Thanks, Mom," he said and disconnected.

I dropped my phone onto the console. It was a good thing I hadn't stayed for dinner. Being Shane's mother was my number one job, and I was always on duty. The hottest kiss in the world couldn't change that.

Book Review of "The Axe Man Cometh" by Ash Phoenix

BY VALENTINA BLUERIDGEBOOKCLUB.COM

4 Stars
5 Hot Peppers
3 Book Boyfriend Hearts

DEAR READERS, I'M BACK WITH ANOTHER OUTSTANDING book for your reading pleasure. If you are in the mood for a slow burn with high heat, this book will hit the spot.

Plot Overview:

A loner lumberjack spends all his days cutting wood and his nights alone in his cabin until a mysterious woman visits him. They begin a passionate affair, but she is always gone by morning. He thinks he might be imagining her, but he can still smell her on his sheets. He tries to stay awake so he can follow her and see where she goes, but what he doesn't realize is she is a wood nymph and has cast a spell on him.

. . .

Pros:
- Trope: supernatural beauties
- Meet cute: He wakes to find her in his bed.
- Ending: I won't give it away, but you guys are going to love it!
- Flannel: lots and lots of flannel

Cons:
- Suspension of disbelief is imperative

To sum it up, this took a while to get into, but once I got halfway through, I was hooked. You have to read this book to believe what happens. There are so many twists and turns I never saw coming.

xoxo,
Valentina

Chapter 10

Sally Ann Jenkins had thrown up again. I had done my best to clean it up, then after class, I went to the office for the keys to the supply closet so I could finish the job.

Gabriella's assistant gave me the keys. "You know Cliff can take care of it for you," he said.

"Thanks, Mike. I can handle it. Cliff is busy enough."

"You are a true team player, Joey." Mike pushed his glasses back up his nose and got back to typing.

Gabriella's door was closed. I hadn't seen her since our failed dinner at Goodfella's. Our last words had been, "see you at work," but it hadn't happened yet. She was avoiding me again.

Fine. I didn't need to chase women.

She'd made it clear she didn't want me complicating her life. She'd also kissed me like I was oxygen and she would die without me. My gaze swept back to her door again. "Is Principal Salinger in?" I asked.

Mike shook his head. "She's been scarce this morning since her conference call." He cracked a smile, chewing on the end of his pen. "Maybe she's chasing down the muffin man."

I shared a conspiratorial grin with Mike. We all knew who was bringing in the muffins. All of us except Gabriella.

Gabriella, who was so on top of everything, was a bit out of touch with her teachers' humanity. Yes, babe, we have sex. And guess what? We eat muffins at work. We are adults. We can choose to have a consensual relationship and eat an ingredient we might have a slight allergy to.

"Do you want to leave her a message?" Mike asked.

"No." I jingled the keys. "I'll check in later."

He grimaced. "I would steer clear of her if you can." He lowered his voice and darted a glance around. "She has been extra edgy all week. I was five minutes early this morning, and she told me to get my priorities in order." He glared at her door. "I was early!"

I shrugged in sympathy. Gabriella ran a tight ship, but she was great at her job. PES was ranked number one in the county for elementary schools, and top five in the state of North Carolina.

Evidence of the thriving school was everywhere.

In the east wing hall, a group of students sat on the floor, working on a timeline. At the end of the hall, several fifth graders painted their portraits on the wall. The students worked diligently, despite the constant distractions happening around them.

The hall smelled like twelve-year-old kids who hadn't started using deodorant yet and paint, but my classroom probably smelled worse. I really needed to convince Sally Ann's mom to quit with the tuna salad. Considering moving my fourth block class outside if the weather warmed up this afternoon, I fit the key in the lock and opened the door. Inside the supply closet, it smelled of pine and citrus. The windowless space was pitch black, except for a bright-orange light coming from the back corner.

I flipped on the overhead light and saw Gabriella sitting on a crate in the back of the closet. She jumped up when she saw me. Her phone clattered to the floor, and she yanked her earbuds from her ears.

"Close the door," she hissed.

I stepped inside and pulled the door closed behind me. "What are you doing in here?"

She tipped her chin upward to glare at me. "I'm trying to have a private moment."

I struggled to contain my grin. "What kind of private moment?"

She gave me a prim look. "Everything is sexual with you, isn't it?"

"Who said anything about sex?"

She rolled her eyes and retrieved her phone from the floor. "I'm watching the championship game," she said. "My mom is there, and she's sending me a live video."

"You're hiding in the supply closet, watching a basketball game?"

"Shh," she hissed. "What are you doing in here?"

I turned the lock on the door. "Watching the game with you." It was my planning period, which I had planned on using to clean up my classroom. This seemed like a better option.

Gabriella turned her attention back to her phone. "Get the light. Just in case."

I flipped the switch and joined her at the back of the closet. "What's the score?"

"It's tied, with eighty seconds remaining."

"Why aren't you in Charlotte?" I asked.

"I had a meeting this morning, and I had to be here. This is the best I could do."

My heart squeezed at the sound of guilt in her voice. My mom had struggled to work full time and raise four kids, but at least she had my dad to help. Gabriella did everything on her own. Shane was lucky to have such an amazing mom.

She scooted over to make room for me to sit on the carton. Despite the powerful scent of bleach in the supply closet, the smell of her shampoo tickled my nose. Gabriella handed me one of her earbuds, and the sounds of the game filled my ear as we huddled together, watching Shane dribble down the court for what should have been an easy layup. But nothing came easy in the championship game. The defensive player blocked Shane with an elbow to the ribs.

"Foul!" we cried in unison.

Shane hurried to the foul line and took his first shot. The ball swished through the net without hitting the rim. He missed the second, but Mossy Oak got the rebound and scored a quick two points.

We grinned at each other over the soft glow of light from her phone. Mossy Oak was up by three points. They had to hold on for one more minute, and they would be the state champs. The opposing team called a timeout, and everyone filed off the court.

"Have you been able to watch much of the game?" I asked.

"I missed almost all of it," she said. "But my mom will give me the play-by-play later. She never misses a game for any of her grandkids."

I shifted on the box, putting my arm around her shoulder to take up less space. "It must be tough not being there in person."

She stiffened under my arm. "No matter how much I'd like to, I can't do everything."

I rubbed my hand on her shoulder. "You're doing a great job. Shane is an awesome kid."

Her shoulder relaxed under my touch. "Thanks."

"How long have you been doing it alone?" It was the deepest we'd ever gone in conversation, and I wondered if maybe she wouldn't answer me.

"Forever," she said with a sigh. "My husband died when Shane was two."

It was hard to know what to say. "I'm sorry."

"It's okay."

We fell silent when the game started up again. The next few possessions were a battle as each team fought hard for the win. We held our breath while the other team missed a three-point shot.

Gabriella covered her eyes with her hand. "I can't watch," she said.

I took my arm from around her shoulder and pried her hand loose from her face. "Watch," I said, lacing our fingers together. "You'll regret it if you don't."

She clutched my hand. "I really can't watch."

But she did. Neither of us could tear our eyes away. The final ten seconds seemed to last forever. We hardly breathed as the clock ticked down to zero. The small closet heated with our rising temperature. When the final buzzer sounded, Gabriella's mom flipped the phone around to show her face. She was an older version of Gabriella with the same dark hair and eyes.

"We won!" she shouted.

She yelled so loud, Gabriella had to turn the phone off. Without the glow of light, we were back in the darkness. I heard the unmistakable sound of her choking back tears and shifted to put my arm back around her shoulder.

"It's okay." I squeezed her close, amazed at how perfectly she fit against me. "We won."

She sniffed. "I just wish I could have been there."

"I know." I hugged her tightly. "You can't do everything. You're doing the best you can."

"I just hope it's enough."

"It is, Gabriella. Trust me. It is." I stroked her arm. "You can relax now," I said. "The game's over."

She pulled away. "I need to get back to my office. Everyone will be wondering where I am."

And I needed to get back to the tuna salad. "Mr. Collins said you've been extra stressed," I said. "Maybe you can blow off some steam tonight since the game is over."

She laughed softly. "I don't have the time. It's shopping day, and Shane will be back in a few hours."

"Maybe you can indulge in one of those naughty paperbacks you love so much."

Her laugh ended on a choking sound. "What?"

"Maybe something with lumberjacks..."

Her shoulders stiffened. "I don't know what you're talking about."

I smiled in the darkness, turning my body toward hers. "You know exactly what I'm talking about. You read porno books."

I heard the sharp intake of her breath. "What?"

"I may have peeked at your book when you left me alone in your office. I saw the real cover." Even better, I'd gotten a glimpse of the private Gabriella. The one she kept hidden under those conservative clothes. "It's okay to have a sensual side," I said. "So what if you're a single mom and the leader of a school? No one expects you to stop living."

"Who says I've stopped living?" She scoffed, but her body softened against mine. "I live plenty."

"Oh, yeah?" I curled my hand around the nape of her neck, my blood warming at the memory of how she'd kissed me at Goodfella's. "When was the last time you did more than read about sex?"

"None of your business."

Her voice dropped an octave, soft and sultry—so sexy it made me want to pop the buttons on her blouse and press my lips to her throat. Tension pulsed between us, beating faster than my wild heart. "You could make it my business," I said.

Her palm rested on my chest. "That would be highly inappropriate."

My heart picked up the pace, and I felt like I was running the last lap of a race. "We're locked in this supply closet together," I said. "I'm pretty sure that's inappropriate."

Her fingers spread against my dress shirt, exploring. "We haven't done anything wrong."

I grinned, thinking how fun it was going to be to do all sorts of wrong things with Gabriella Salinger. "Not yet. But I want to do wrong things with you." I slid my fingers around her neck, seeking the top button of her blouse. "I'm dying to undo all these buttons."

She shifted closer, and my fingers worked open her button. The sound of our quick breath was the only noise in the room. The darkness cloaked us, and there was something erotic about touching her without seeing her clearly. It made every little noise ricochet off the walls, every breath echo in the silence.

Her other hand came to the front of my shirt and inched up to my shoulders. She pressed lightly, her fingers testing the flex of my muscles under the crisp cotton of my shirt.

I slid my thumb along the open collar of her blouse and bent my head toward her throat.

Her fingers dug into my shoulders before I could lower my mouth to her skin. "Stop."

Disappointment flooded my system. It wasn't the word I wanted to hear, but I stopped. Lifting my head, I wished I could see her face.

Gabriella pulled back a few inches, putting space between us. "Not here."

Hope sparked in my chest, reigniting the flame she'd just doused. "Where?"

She shifted away with a sigh. "I don't know."

"Let me take you to dinner this weekend."

She stiffened.

I backtracked. "Lunch?"

"Breakfast," she said. "On Sunday."

"My place, so no one will see us." I pulled her closer and pressed my lips to her cheek. "Nine o'clock?"

She lingered in my arms for a moment before moving away. "Fine." Her footsteps sounded on the floor, the door creaked open, and she was gone.

I stood in the darkness for a few minutes with a goofy grin and an uncomfortable erection, wondering how I'd gotten so hung up on a woman who not only had to have a head start, but the last word as well.

Chapter 11

GABI

Mossy Oak was a haven for outdoor enthusiasts. Although we had four distinct seasons throughout the year, they were all relatively mild and perfectly suited for outdoor activities.

Our town was full of hikers, runners, kayakers, and climbers. So I wasn't surprised to see people enjoying a stroll or a bike ride around Ginger Cake Acres, even though it was early on a Sunday morning.

I passed a young mother pushing a Baby Jogger, and I remembered the days of running behind Shane's stroller when he was a baby. Pushing a forty-pound stroller with a twenty-pound child inside wasn't easy. I remembered struggling to get up the hills and then flying to keep up on the downhills. Running had been my therapy, my escape from reality back when I'd been so lost without Montel, but lately I had been using the quiet time during my runs to clear my mind and work through my problems.

As my feet pounded the trail, my mind circled back to the problem of Joey. Agreeing to meet him for breakfast had been impulsive, but necessary. I couldn't go on ignoring Joey at school and pretending he didn't exist.

He'd gotten under my skin. He was an itch I needed to scratch.

But I was as nervous as a kindergartner on the first day of school. I'd slept poorly, awakened early, and laced on my running shoes. There was nothing better than a long run to sort my feelings. As soon as my feet hit the pavement, doubt filled my mind. I ran fast and hard but couldn't outpace my nerves.

Since Montel had died, I hadn't had a boyfriend. I'd had a few secret lovers, a couple of one-night stands, and the occasional friend with benefits, but I'd never brought a man around Shane. I didn't want him exposed to my dating life, so it was easier not to date.

I slowed my pace as I came upon two runners heading up to the pavilion water fountain, the scene of my humiliating fall. A man and a woman laughed and chatted as they ran at a fast clip, which would have most people gasping.

My attention gravitated toward the male runner, who had an easy, long-legged stride, and my heart raced. Joey Morales was easy to recognize. Even though the temperature was heating up, he was dressed for the tundra. His stupid cap covered his head, and he wore long sleeves and gray sweatpants. I was perfectly comfortable wearing a T-shirt and shorts, although my chest ached to see him laugh with another woman.

Doubts which hadn't left my mind all weekend grew stronger. Jealousy flared, hitting every nerve in my body like a pinball machine.

Joey never seemed to be lacking in female company. There was the BJ bandit—Caroline—Kaitlyn, and undoubtedly countless other women in his life.

I probably wasn't the only woman he'd had breakfast with this weekend.

Their laughter pierced the air again, and I ducked behind a row of tall bushes before they spotted me. From my vantage point between the holly bushes, I watched them take turns at the water fountain. I should have hightailed it out of there while they weren't looking, but I waited too long. The next thing I knew, the woman took off in one direction, and Joey headed down the hill, straight toward me.

I cringed and shrank back into the prickly bushes, hoping he would pass by without seeing me. My breathing slowed, and I held perfectly still as his footsteps neared. I listened to the even rhythm of his footfall, not daring to move as he zipped along the path.

He'd almost made it out of sight when my phone blasted to life in the pocket of my shorts. I scrambled to silence it, but I was too late. Shane's ringtone filled the air.

I was so busted. Joey's footsteps halted and his head turned. When he saw me crouching in the bushes, his eyes widened and then a slow smile curved his mouth.

I swiped to answer my phone. "Hello?" I whispered, even though the damage was done.

"Hey, Mom. I was just wondering... Can I go to the shooting range with Papa?"

Joey retraced his steps back to the row of bushes where I was only partially hidden.

My skin tingled as his eyes roamed over me. "You're supposed to be working on your English paper," I told Shane.

"You sound out of breath," Shane said. "Are you okay?"

"I'm running."

Joey heard me, and his grin burst to life. My cheeks burned with embarrassment, and I looked away.

"I'll do my essay tonight," Shane said. "Promise."

"Okay," I said. "You can go. But be careful and follow all Papa's rules. "

"I'm always careful around guns. Papa taught me."

"And don't forget your earmuffs. I'll see you at supper."

"Thanks! See ya!"

I swiped the phone to hang up and slowly lifted my gaze from Joey's running shoes to his face. He crossed his arms over his chest and nodded his chin at me.

"Lose something in the bushes?" he asked, barely holding in a laugh.

I plucked a holly leaf from my sleeve and tossed it to the ground. "I'm good. I found it."

He reached down and grabbed my hand, then hauled me to my feet. His arm wrapped around my waist, and he held me against him for a moment. The tall holly bushes gave us privacy, but not much. My heart raced both because Joey was holding me against the hard wall of his chest and because someone might come along the path and see us.

"Spying on me, again?" His voice was a soft whisper with a scorching hot edge.

My heart hammered as our eyes met and locked. "I didn't see anything good this time."

He let me go with a soft bark of laughter. "Have you met Coach Madison yet?"

"Who?"

"The woman I was running with," he said. "She's the other track coach at Mossy Oak High."

"Oh." My cheeks went up in flames.

He laughed again. "You're still coming to my place for breakfast, right?"

I hesitated, but only for a moment. I'd thought about nothing else since we'd made the date. "Yes. Nine o'clock."

He ran back toward the trail at an easy jog, and I joined him. We ran for a few moments before he glanced at me with a mischievous smile. "I'm hungry now," he said. "Are you?"

My footsteps faltered as his words sank in. "You want me to come over now?"

"Yes."

Even though I'd spent days thinking of this moment, I wasn't prepared for the rush of longing when it swept through me at the thought of being alone with Joey. I'd thought I'd have time to get through my run, sort my feelings, and shower before seeing him again, but life had taken a shortcut. And I was more than a little hungry.

"Okay," I said.

He lifted his chin in a challenge. "Race me?"

He couldn't possibly know it, but he'd said the perfect thing to make me forget my nerves. It wasn't in my nature to turn down a race. Plus, I needed to redeem myself for the epic fail of our last race.

I grinned up at him, feeling lighter than I had in years, and took off at full speed. The joyful sound of his laughter trailed behind me as I ran like the wind.

Chapter 12

J OEY

Gabriella jogged up the front steps of my house and slapped her hand on the door like the kids did when they were safe during tag. She whipped her head around at me and beamed triumphantly, her dark eyes sparkling. The expression of pure joy on her face went straight to my cock.

My gaze fell to her heaving chest. A ring of sweat spread around the neck of her T-shirt and dripped between her breasts. I imagined kissing the hollow of her throat like I'd wanted to in the closet, picking up right where we'd left off, but I couldn't kiss her on my front porch in case someone we knew happened by. I couldn't give her any reason to run away.

I pulled the key from around my neck and unlocked the main door, then tugged her inside. "Congratulations." I hustled her toward the stairs. "But you didn't win yet."

I started racing up the stairs, then fell back, letting her win. I would let her win every time if it made her shine like the midday sun. Gabriella got to my door first and stepped aside to let me open it.

I fit the key in the lock. "I can't wait to feed you something delicious," I said.

She laughed. "Why does everything you say sound sexual?"

I grinned. "It's my accent."

Her eyes roamed over my face. "Maybe." She dropped her gaze to my lips. "Are you trying to seduce me with pancakes?"

I smiled. "I was thinking French toast."

A laugh burst from her mouth, and something devilish flashed in her eyes. That earned a twitch from my eager dick, which hadn't gotten the message about being patient. Or at least that we needed to get to the bedroom before devouring her like a hungry wolf.

I pushed open the door and practically dragged her over the threshold into my apartment. Adrenaline coursed through my veins as I slammed the door and took her in my arms. Finally alone, we kissed. And it was as good as I remembered. Her mouth opened, and her tongue stroked mine in a curious exploration.

I'd often thought about kissing Gabriella like this and a whole lot more. I'd thought about unraveling her hair, untying her bows, and melting her iron exterior. But at that moment, she was the one melting me. She had me on the edge of reason with one hot kiss.

Our lips fused together, and every nerve in my body shot fireworks. Her tongue was in my mouth, her hands were on my chest, and her hips were glued to mine.

"Off." She tugged the hem of my sweatshirt. "Now."

Damn.

Who was I to argue? I stepped back and gripped both the hem of my sweatshirt and the shirt underneath it and stripped them off in one efficient move. Her eyes drifted down my chest, widening in appreciation. The energy between us surged, turning electric. Her gaze lingered briefly on the tattoo inked over my heart before snapping back to my face.

"And the cap." She smirked, humor sparking through the lust in her dark gaze. "Stupid cap," she muttered. "It's not even cold."

I scooped my hat from head and let it drop. "It's my thin *Tico* blood," I said.

She flattened her palm to my chest. "You feel pretty hot to me."

Hunger rose between us, so sharp and raw it hurt. I bent and touched my lips to hers. It was a soft kiss that turned hard in an instant. Our mouths were greedy, taking and giving, equally demanding. Our hands joined the party, grabbing with needy fingers.

When I pulled back to lift her shirt, she chased my mouth with hers. When she bent to shove my pants down, I kissed her neck and pressed her back against the door. I toed off my shoes. She did the same. When I peeled off her tight running shorts and cupped her hot pussy in my palm, her head shot back so fast she banged it on the door.

Her lips parted, and she let out a little moan that went straight to my cock. She was hot and ready. I'd barely touched her, but she was already on fire. We'd barely made it inside my apartment, and I wanted to take her right there against the door.

This wasn't the way it was supposed to happen. I was supposed to feed her, to seduce her, to get her into my bed where I could kiss every fucking inch of her.

I dipped my head to her shoulder, slowing things down a notch as I breathed in her heady scent. I kissed a path to her throat and flicked my tongue across the little bead of sweat on her skin. Salty and sweet. My Gabriella.

"Do you want to move this to the bedroom?"

Her eyes blazed open. "No."

The neediness in her voice made me lose my mind. I slid one finger inside her and felt her shudder. She leaned back against the door and moaned when I added another finger. I stroked her and then flicked my thumb against her clit. She cried out, something like my name. It was the first time I'd heard her say Joey, and I wished for a moment she'd said my real name in that guttural growl.

How sweet would it sound? *Fernando.* In her soft Southern accent, my name would sound like the hero of the story.

She slid her hand beneath the waistband of my briefs, and my thoughts froze. My name no longer mattered when she wrapped her hand around my throbbing erection and squeezed.

"I need this," she said.

It was a command. She was in charge. I didn't mind. I'd let her be in charge just as I'd let her win a race. Whatever turned Gabriella on, I was up for it.

She hooked her leg around my hip and arched her back, so we lined up perfectly. The sight took my breath away. Raw need burned through me. She stroked me. Once. Twice.

"Now," she whispered.

My cock throbbed at the sound of desperation in her voice. I liked sex, but I wasn't stupid. I got tested regularly, and I always covered up. I didn't take any chances.

"I'll be right back." I eased my hand from inside her. "Condom, baby."

I kissed her again, muffling her sounds of protests with my mouth, then left her long enough to grab my wallet from the coffee table and pull out the condom I kept there. I was back and opening the foil before she could blink. In one swift move, I rolled it on over my throbbing dick. Gabriella watched with a sexy little smile that made me stiffen even more.

I dipped my chin and took her mouth in a possessive kiss. "I want you so much," I said, and God help me, I didn't mean just her body. I meant her company in the break room, her feet pounding the trails next to mine, and her ear on the other end of the headphone wires.

Her lips curved. "I want you, too." She arched her back so that the head of my cock lined up at her entrance. "Now, screw me senseless."

Chapter 13

Joey

A roar of need filled my ears. I couldn't say no to Gabriella's request. I would fuck her brains out against the door if it was what she wanted. Even though standing up wasn't the easiest way to get the job done, I would oblige her. She probably read about it in one of her porno books and wanted to try it out.

I was game. We would do it against the wall, or at least we would start there.

I filled my hands with the sweetest ass in town and lifted her. She was light, with a runner's athletic build. I hoisted her up and pressed her back against the wall. Freeing one hand, I fisted my erection and guided it inside. With one thrust, I buried myself deep.

She gasped when I was fully inside her.

I drank in the sight of her bliss. Her eyes were half closed, and her lips were parted. A blush of color blossomed along her neck and up to her cheeks. She was still wearing her bra, but it was too late to do anything about it now.

I shifted my hands to the backs of her thighs and lifted her higher as I plunged deep. I fucked her fast and hard, the way I knew she wanted it. She may have read about getting fucked against a door, but she'd never experienced it with me before. Not like this.

And I'd never had it like this before, either. She felt so tight and hot. We were a perfect fit. Her legs locked around my hips, and her hands gripped my shoulders. She rocked against me, writhing on my cock like she couldn't get enough of me.

The musk of our sweat filled the room. Slick with heat, our bodies slid together.

I lowered my head and kissed her. She kissed me back, her eager tongue filling my mouth just as I filled her. She was velvety warmth surrounding me, and it was easy to get lost in the blistering heat of her kiss. Her sweet pussy clenched tighter on my cock, and the first twinge of a powerful orgasm tightened my balls. I held myself back, but she felt so good. So right. So perfect in every way. I fucked her faster and harder, determined to make her come at least once before I let her off the door and carried her into my bedroom.

Blown away by how good we were together, even in this ridiculous position against the door, I kissed her harder. Judging by the sounds she made, she was close. So was I.

I shifted my hand to her back and gripped her thigh, changing the angle. "Put your leg down, Gabriella," I said, guiding her.

The new position was perfect for freeing up my hands. Regret reared its ugly head when I skimmed a hand along her sports bra. I should have gotten rid of that earlier. All in due time.

I slid my hand down her belly and paused at the horizontal scar just above where we were joined. The scar made me want her even more. She was so beautiful, and she had been through so much. I wanted to be tender with her, but that was not what she'd asked for. She'd asked for this, and I was thorough.

I hooked her leg higher and changed the angle, so our bodies rubbed together. We were slick with sweat from the run and the frantic heat between us. I put a hand on her thigh and held her down, basically pinning her to the wall as I stroked into her.

Her gasps of pleasure filled my ears, urging me on. I pounded into her, grinding against her clit with every stroke. We kissed with open mouths and greedy tongues. I couldn't get enough of the taste of her tongue.

Sweet.

Salty.

Spicy.

Gabriella.

I hadn't realized I'd said her name aloud until her eyes sharpened on mine. Sudden heat exploded inside me when our eyes locked and held. Neither one of us looked away as I thrust into her. The door rattled and shook as we slammed against it. She had nowhere to go as I drove faster and harder, desperate to give her what she'd asked for.

I saw in her smoky eyes the moment she couldn't hold back any longer. Her sheath tightened on my cock, and the orgasm I'd been holding off roared for release. Her eyes drifted shut, and a flush swept across her cheeks.

I closed my eyes and focused on driving into her as she convulsed and contracted around me. Fire raced through me, but I held strong. My plan was to make her come and then take her to my bedroom and make her come a few more times before I found my own release, but then I made the mistake of opening my eyes.

One look at her gorgeous face, and my whole body tightened. The orgasm I'd kept at bay thundered through me. I lost control.

I groaned and kissed her hard, locking our mouths together as I came so hard, my whole body trembled. I managed not to fall down or crush her by bracing my hands against the door. All I could think about was how disappointed I was that I'd shot off earlier than I'd planned. I just needed a little time to recuperate and then I'd make up for my transgressions.

Round two, coming right up after some breakfast and maybe a shower. Or maybe round two in the shower? That sounded intriguing. I imagined soaping Gabriella up and rinsing her off, touching every inch of her body.

I disengaged from her body and steered her into the bathroom, where I got rid of the condom and grabbed a washcloth.

"Lift your arms, baby." I don't know why I called her baby. The word just fell out. I felt possessive of Gabriella, and I liked the way the word felt on my lips.

Our gazes met in the mirror. Her eyes were wide, and her cheeks were sex-flushed. She lifted her arms, and I stripped off her sports bra. Her body swayed back into me, and our gazes locked as her naked breasts spilled free. My dick responded with a hard jerk. Maybe I didn't need recovery time after all.

I wet the washcloth and cleaned both of us up, paying extra attention to the center of paradise between her legs because I had big plans for spreading her out on my bed shortly. When I finished, I wrapped her tightly in a towel.

"French toast in bed, coming right up. I hope you're still hungry."

She made a funny noise and reached for my hand when I ducked into the hall. "That's never happened to me before." Her eyes darted away from mine. "I mean..."

I took her chin and tilted her face upward. "That wasn't what I had planned."

"Oh, really? So you had no intention of having sex with me when you invited me up here?"

"Well, yeah, but I thought we'd make it until after breakfast. I was perfectly content to whip up something to satisfy your hunger, but then you were all like, 'Screw me, Joey! Screw me brainless!'" My impression of her husky voice was good enough to earn a smack from Gabriella. I raised my shoulders in a shrug. "What was I supposed to do? I couldn't say no."

She smacked me again. "Shut up."

I gathered her close, wishing I hadn't bothered with the towel so we could be skin-to-skin. "Are you brainless?" I asked, stopping myself just in time from calling her baby again. I needed to pull in the reins on all the sweet stuff. It was overkill, considering the frantic way we had just fucked against the door. She'd made it clear she didn't want me for anything more than a hookup. She wouldn't even risk being seen with me.

She rolled her eyes. "Senseless. Not brainless."

Chapter 14

GABI

Joey in person was infinitely better than any fantasy I had conjured.

He was all sleek skin poured over tight muscles. Sculpted and roughened by a smattering of dark, masculine hair, his chest belonged on the cover of a romance novel. My eyes couldn't get enough of him. My hands were greedy too.

When he started to leave, I reached for him. He grinned and pushed me back onto the bed, his mouth finding mine for a smoldering kiss. His body was heavy, pinning me to the bed with a solid, heavy, all-male weight.

GodblessAmerica!

How long had it been since I'd been crushed between a gorgeous man and a soft mattress? I couldn't begin to count the years. I melted against the cool cotton of Joey's bedspread, and my hands spread against the smooth skin of his back.

His tongue parted my lips, and after a long, slow perusal of my mouth, he traced a hot path to my neck, pressing feather-soft kisses along my arched throat. I was surprised I felt like this so soon after sex, but I did.

"I'm going to make breakfast." His voice was a soft, silky promise in my ear.

"Now?" I came up onto my elbows as he rolled off me.

He pressed me gently back to the bed. "Don't go anywhere." With an easy grin, he left the bedroom.

When I could no longer see him walking down the hall, I lay back on his bed and turned my face into his pillow. It smelled like him. I'd truly lost my mind against the door. I couldn't believe I had been so bold to demand he screw me against the door. I didn't even insist he use protection. I knew better than to be so irresponsible. I was the same woman who gave my son lectures on safe sex and preventing pregnancy. And Joey was obviously not a one-woman man.

Thankfully, he'd been sensible, while I'd been a fool. It felt strange to be the one making bad decisions. It felt even stranger to let someone take care of me.

I wondered what Joey's version of breakfast would be. As a bachelor, he probably lived off frozen waffles and cereal. I heard him moving around in the kitchen, banging pots and muttering something unintelligible. From the one-sided conversation that drifted down the hall, I surmised that Frodo was back, and apparently, the cat understood Spanish.

It was silly of me to hang around. I'd gotten more than I'd come for already. Much more.

For a long time, I'd thought I was broken. My body didn't respond like those women in the books I'd read about. I could get close to an orgasm with a man, but I'd never gotten all the way there. Sex had always been fun, even without the big O. I enjoyed the intimacy, the connection, the sensuality. All of it was great. But I'd never had an orgasm like they did in the books and movies. Not even close.

Until today.

Joey was the sexiest man I'd ever been with. He was handsome, charming, funny, and one of the best teachers I knew. He was also a player who had a woman's bikini top hanging over his shower rod and a condom within an arm's reach.

He could have a different woman in his bed every night of the week. He probably did.

The rich aroma of coffee filled the air. It didn't smell like instant.

"How do you like your coffee?" Joey called from the kitchen.

The question startled me. No one besides a barista had asked me how I wanted my coffee in years.

I figured a bachelor living alone wouldn't have milk, let alone fancy creamers. "Black is fine."

A few minutes later, Joey came down the hall carrying two cups of coffee. I propped myself up on the headboard and tried to appear casual, but the closer he got, the harder it was to keep my cool, because he was only wearing a towel, and I knew exactly what was under it.

"Here." He handed me a cup of coffee.

When the rich aroma of roasted beans reached my nose, something other than sex filtered through my foggy brain. I took a sip and savored the rich flavor. "Delicious." The coffee was so good, I didn't even miss the cream.

"Mm-hmm." Joey watched me with a sexy half smile and sipped from his own steaming mug. "My mom sends me a care package from Costa Rica every month."

I took another sip and sent a silent thank-you to Joey's mom. "I forgot Costa Rica produces some of the best coffee."

His white teeth flashed in a smile, and his eyes danced. "And the best men."

My gaze drifted over his towel-clad body. "Are you saying all men in Costa Rica look like they belong on book covers?" *One ticket to San José, please.*

"You think I could pull off an axe and a flannel shirt?"

I blushed at the mention of my naughty romance reads. No one except my closest book club friends knew about my guilty pleasure or my secret identity as Valentina. Mossy Oak was small enough that I knew I couldn't stay hidden forever, but denial was my best friend. I would never admit my identity, even if someone figured it out. Valentina was my little secret.

And now I had another one. A six-foot-tall secret with a sexy accent. I squinted at Joey, pretending to consider the idea of him on the cover of a romance novel, as if I hadn't pictured his face the entire time I'd been reading *The Axe Man Cometh*.

"You're more of the beach type," I said, letting my imagination run away with the idea of Joey shirtless on a sunny beach.

He leaned down and pressed a soft kiss to my lips, reminding me I didn't need to use my imagination. I had the real thing right there in front of me. In. A. Towel.

Joey's kisses reminded me how much I missed the intimacy of kissing. The feeling of being so close with someone else, breathing their air, tasting the exotic flavor of their tongue. Kissing Joey was like stealing a moment in time. I didn't want it to end.

It helped that Joey was the king of kissing.

Joey went back to the kitchen and came back a few minutes later carrying a tray. The smell of cinnamon and fried bread wafted into the room.

"I hope you like it, even if it's not pancakes."

Pancakes were the furthest thing from my mind as Joey sat on the bed. The towel stretched across his hips, leaving nothing to my imagination. I tore my gaze from his body and glanced at the tray, expecting cinnamon bagels or frozen waffles. To my surprise, the plate was piled high with thick slices of browned French toast topped with powdered sugar.

He picked up a fork and loaded it with a bite. "Eat it while it's hot." He held my eyes as he lifted the fork to my lips.

Longing rocketed through me as I leaned forward and opened my mouth. Joey's eyes dropped to my lips as they closed over the fork. He paused for a second as I chewed and swallowed, then loaded up a bite for himself.

"Mmm," he said around his mouthful. "I'm good in the kitchen as well as against the front door."

I pictured my earlier fantasy involving the kitchen counter and Joey's hands on my thighs. He forked up another bite, still smiling.

"You're very cocky," I told him.

"Cocky?" He asked, glancing down at the obvious outline of his male appendage beneath the towel.

"Not that kind of cocky," I said. "You know, like..." I searched my Spanish vocabulary. "*Un pollo!*"

One dark eyebrow rose, and the hint of a smile curved his mouth. "*Un gallo,*" he corrected, offering me another bite.

I took the food off the fork, but what I really wanted was another kiss from him. My eyes must have given away my thoughts because he put the fork down and leaned forward to give me what I wanted. He kissed me long and slow, his tongue licking the sensitive skin on the inside of my bottom lip. There seemed to be a magnet connecting our mouths. I needed to catch my breath, but when I did, I couldn't let it go. Breathing meant not kissing him again.

He tasted of earthy coffee and cinnamon. He smelled like sex.

His mouth left mine, and I shamelessly chased it.

"Are you still hungry, baby?"

I wasn't sure if he meant food or sex, but the answer was yes. I nodded. He fed me a bite of toast with his fingers. As I chewed, he tugged down my towel, exposing my peaked nipple. He dipped his head, took my nipple in his mouth, and sucked.

I moaned and slid down the bed, suddenly feeling boneless. Joey pushed my towel aside and sucked my other nipple into his mouth.

I gasped. "Oh!"

He lifted his head and nodded at the nightstand. "Hand me the syrup," he said.

I obeyed. A moment later, I felt the thick, warm liquid spread up and over the curve of my breast. Joey's tongue lapped at the syrup, licking my nipple clean.

His eyes darted up to meet mine. "I'm starving," he said.

He poured a thin line of syrup across my chest to my other nipple. His tongue chased the thick syrup and darted over my nipple. I shuddered and clutched the quilt. I wanted him again, but was it too soon? My experience with the men in the last dozen years had been a series of one-night stands and awkward hookups in the dark.

He pulled hard on my nipple, and a trail of fire shot straight from my nipple to the V between my legs. I moaned and arched against him. His lips continued to the underside of my breast, tasting every inch of me.

He drizzled the smooth, thick syrup lower, kissing a path down my belly. For once, I wasn't ashamed of my imperfections. The possessive spread of Joey's hand on my belly made me feel so sexy, I forgot about my annoying pooch and the thick, horizontal scar that had granted Shane's entry into the world.

Joey pressed his lips to my scar, then trailed lower.

I froze. "You don't have to do that," I said.

He peered up at me. "Why not?"

"It's not necessary."

"I disagree." He squinted with determination. "It is very necessary."

I put my hands on his shoulders, urging him upward. "I'm just not that into it."

He raised an eyebrow. "Why?"

"It doesn't work for me," I admitted, my face flushing.

His eyes twinkled mischievously. "You don't like it?"

I shrugged. This was embarrassing. I was pretty sure oral sex wasn't for me. I'd never had an orgasm from it before, and most of the time, I suffered through the entire act, trying not to laugh or squirm. I was always too worried about what the man was thinking to relax. And then I got bored.

"Not really," I admitted. His breath was warm on my thigh as he hovered over me. Okay, that felt kind of good. And seeing his dark head poised over my center was doing all kinds of things to my raging libido, but I felt like I should let him off the hook. "We just had sex," I said, as if it was in any possible to forget what we'd just done against the door. "You don't have to do it."

"Let me try." His cocky smile said he was ready for the challenge. "I want to taste you."

Joey's voice reading an email turned me on, but him talking dirty in his sexy accent sent a bolt of lust zigzagging through my body. He kissed lower on my belly. The soft scrape of his morning scruff against my heated skin made me think this wouldn't be so bad. I lay back on the mattress and closed my eyes. If Joey was determined to do this, I would let him. I just hoped he'd give up before we hit awkward territory. I really hated faking orgasms, but I would do it to soothe his wounded pride.

"Tell me if you want me to stop," he said.

I forced myself to relax and lay back on the bed. *This isn't a big deal.* This was just me receiving oral from a man I'd been fantasizing about for months—moments after I'd begged him to fuck my brains out. *Not embarrassing.* Not at all.

Joey bent to his task. My hips jerked, and he planted his hand firmly on my belly to hold me down. And then his tongue was on me. He sucked the tight bundle of nerves at my entrance, and a spark that rivaled the Fourth of July burst inside me.

His tongue swirled against my clit, and my hips bucked. I was eager for more. This wasn't so bad. Unsurprisingly, Joey was good at this, too. He dragged me to the edge of the mattress and hooked my thighs over his shoulders.

Then his mouth was on me again and I was suddenly very into it—so into it, my next breath depended on his tongue, licking me into oblivion. He alternated some magic formula of flicking and sucking that made me throb all over. Little quakes of pleasure spread through my body until I felt like I was a mass of sensations. Just when I thought it was too much, that I would explode from the friction inside me begging to be let out, Joey pulled back.

"Want me to stop?" His teasing tone told me he knew the answer.

"Don't stop," I begged. "Please don't stop."

He slipped a finger inside me, and I gasped. He eased another finger inside and went back to work, sucking and licking my swollen clit. I dug my fingers into his hair, and my thighs locked around his head. I was probably killing him and would end up in cunnilingus jail, but I no longer cared as shockwaves of pleasure rolled over me, and I came against his mouth.

GABI

I blacked out for a minute in a state of pure bliss. When I came to my senses, I was staring at the ceiling, not quite sure what had happened. Then I realized I'd had an earth-shattering orgasm, and I finally got it. That was what all the fuss was about.

I floated back to reality, feeling carefree and weightless.

All I could think was wow. Just wow.

The fuss had been worth the wait.

I blinked at Joey as he rose from between my legs and reached for the nightstand. A moment later, he was back, nudging my thighs apart to stand between them. A foil packet dangled between his teeth. He scooped both hands under me and scooted me farther back on the bed. The hunger in his hooded, brown eyes made me shiver.

My gaze drifted down his rock-hard torso to the heavy erection in his grip. Staring openly at his beautiful body, I watched him roll the condom over his length. Did the man have condoms ready in every room of his house? At least he was thinking responsibly.

He gripped my thighs and spread them apart, then teased my

opening with his cock. Aftershocks of my recent orgasm rippled through me, and suddenly I wanted another one. I was greedy, needy, and probably whimpering as I arched off the bed, desperate to get closer.

He entered me slowly, one inch at a time. My body seized around him, pulsing and twitching. I was so tight I must have been strangling him, and each inch he slid into me sparked a riot of sensations that scorched every nerve in my body. He sank all the way into me with a hiss of pleasure. Hearing that noise rip from his clenched teeth drove me over the edge. I felt another orgasm building inside me. I tried to hold off, eager not to chase it away.

My brain couldn't compete with what was happening to my body, and before I knew it, I was lost. I was wild. I was flying and floating and never wanted to come down.

And then Joey moved.

Oh, sweet mother of pearl, did he ever move.

Long, deliberate strokes. Slow and sensual. He slid back and forth, teasing every nerve in my body into a frenzy. Our bodies pressed together, sticky with syrup and slick with a fine sheen of sweat. His dark eyes searched mine, deciphering exactly what I needed without either of us saying a word. He slid his hands under me and boosted us higher on the bed.

My heart pounded in my ears, drowning out every thought as his mouth met mine. We kissed, our tongues teasing and tasting. He tasted sweet and tangy—like me and maple syrup.

I locked my legs around his hips, cinching him against me. He said something in Spanish in a husky voice, and I responded with something that made sense in my brain but came out as rubbish. I don't even know what I said, but it obviously turned him on because his eyes went wide, and he drove into me harder.

Another powerful orgasm came over me, and Joey moved right through it, thrusting into me as I came apart around him. I finally felt him let go and give in to his own pleasure. My eyes flew open when he groaned and shuddered, and I watched shamelessly while he climaxed. He was mesmerizing, so sexy and sensual, with his dark hair falling into his face, his eyes closed in fierce concentration.

I'd spied on him before, but it was nothing like witnessing it up close and knowing that I was the one giving him the pleasure.

When it was over, he gently pried himself from my arms and rolled off the bed. I collapsed back on the bed, unable to move. A moment later, Joey returned, sprawling next to me on the enormous bed.

"I knew you'd be sexy under all those buttons." His brown eyes twinkled. "You're even better than I imagined."

My heart pounded at his confession. I'd certainly thought about him, and he'd far exceeded expectations. "You imagined me?" Coherent sentences were a struggle. After all the orgasms, my brain was scrambled. "I mean this? You imagined this?"

"Maybe not the door."

He slid his arm under me and pulled me on top of him. I braced my elbows on either side of his head and blinked at him. I probably wore the goofiest grin in the world, but I couldn't help it. I felt happier than I'd been in a long time.

Joey cupped my jaw in his hands and smiled. I don't know which one of our grins was goofier.

"Que linda."

My smile widened impossibly. I searched for words, but there weren't any. This was all too much. I hadn't felt like this in years. Not since I had met Montel.

A lump formed in my throat. This was definitely not the same as Montel. Ours had been a whirlwind romance. We'd met at a bar while he was on leave. I'd been out with my roommates for a much-needed celebration after exams. By the time Montel had reported back for duty, we'd decided to get married. It had been silly and stupid and awesome. It had been love.

Guilt knotted in my belly. This wasn't love. This was sex. And multiple orgasms. Who knew orgasms triggered such powerful emotions? Not me, that was for sure.

The doorbell rang, and I jumped at the sound.

"Ignore it," Joey said, nuzzling my neck.

I realized I'd left my phone in the pocket of my shorts, which were by the front door. What if someone needed me? What if there had been an accident at the shooting range? I knew I shouldn't have let Shane go shooting with my dad today. I never liked the idea of guns.

"It could be important," I said. "It could be Shane."

Joey lifted onto his elbow. "Does he know you're here?"

I realized Joey was right. Shane didn't know I was here. No one did. The tension in my body eased, and then the doorbell rang again and I stiffened all over. "You should get it." I nudged Joey. "It could be important."

Joey groaned and rolled off the bed. He bent and tugged on a pair of shorts. He tried to wipe his chest with a towel, but it was hopeless. We were both a sticky mess.

"I'll get rid of them and be right back," he said.

A horrible thought occurred to me. My clothes were by the front door. What if someone saw them? My gaze darted to the door, fear paralyzing me.

"Don't move," he said, bending to kiss me.

I scrambled into a sitting position. "No one can know I'm here."

His brows pulled together, and his dark eyes narrowed. "Just hide back here," he said sharply. "No one will know."

I knew he was angry by the set of his shoulders and the tension in his jaw. He marched out of the room and disappeared into the hall. I heard the door open and then a woman's voice.

The sound of her voice cleared the haze in my brain. My logical thoughts came rushing back.

Having sex with Joey had been a terrible idea. Now I was naked and trapped and possibly caught. Guilty feelings about Montel were the least of my worries.

Chapter 16

JOEY

When I opened my door, I saw one of my students, Kaylee Taylor, accompanied by her mother, who was one of those hovering types of mothers who demanded monthly conferences even though their child was making As. Ms. Taylor was dressed in a tight dress and boots with a thin high heel.

"Hello," I said warily.

"You have a cat?" Kaylee squealed, dropping to Frodo's level.

Frodo wound his way around my ankles and made his presence known with a loud meow. Frodo technically *was* a cat, even if he didn't act like one.

"Do you remember how to say cat in Spanish, Kaylee?" Ms. Taylor asked.

Kaylee beamed up at me. *"Gato!"*

"Good job, kiddo," I said.

"We brought you brownies!" Kaylee thrust a covered dish at me, her blonde curls bouncing.

"That's very nice of you," I said. "Why don't you take them into the kitchen and give Frodo a treat? His bag is on the counter."

At the mention of treats, Frodo's tail twitched, and he strutted toward the kitchen. He pranced out of the room, turning his head to make sure Kaylee followed.

"He only gets five," I said. "*Cinco*. And he must do a trick each time."

Kaylee's eyes went wide. "He does tricks?"

"Of course. Doesn't your cat?"

"We don't have a cat," Kaylee said, frowning. "Mommy's allergic."

When Kaylee was gone, Ms. Taylor wrinkled her nose. "I'm not really allergic. I just don't like all the hair." She swept past me into my apartment and glanced around curiously.

I followed Ms. Taylor into my living room. I hated being the bad guy, but I didn't want parents or students showing up on my doorstep.

"Ms. Taylor," I said. "I don't know how you found out my address, but you absolutely cannot come to my apartment. It's wrong."

Her face fell. "Kaylee was the one who found it. And she made these brownies for you. She was so excited! She couldn't to wait to give them to you."

"I appreciate it," I said, trying not to come off like a jerk. "But this is my home. My students need to respect that. I wouldn't come to your home."

Her eyes widened. "I would never disrespect you," she said, batting her eyelashes as if blinking back tears. "You're a wonderful teacher. The best. I just wanted you to have the brownies Kaylee made. She's been so sad since the divorce."

I stood in silence, giving her a moment to pull herself together. When she was finished, I cleared my throat and said as gently as possible, "I need to keep my outside life and my inside life separate. You understand?"

She sniffed back tears. "Your personal life?"

I nodded. "You understand."

She dabbed her eyes. Ms. Taylor's theatrics didn't work on me. I had two sisters. Rosa and Ava weren't above using waterworks to win a fight. I'd seen enough fake tears to form an immunity. I stepped into the hall, blocking the view of the rest of the apartment from Ms. Taylor's prying eyes.

Gabriella was just down the hall, and she was terrified of being discovered. I could still feel her on my skin and taste her on my tongue.

I rubbed my tattoo out of habit. The thin material of my shirt stuck to my chest with syrup, which made me think of Gabriella. Usually, my tattoo reminded me why I kept my affairs casual and didn't get into relationships. At this moment, my tattoo wasn't working, because I wanted more with Gabriella. One morning of sex wasn't enough.

"I haven't done much baking since my divorce," Ms. Taylor said.

I nodded absently and steered her toward the door.

Ms. Taylor spun around so quickly I hadn't seen it coming and put her hand on my arm. "Do you like baking?" She blinked up at me, batting her spidery-long lashes so rapidly they stuck together, forcing her to blink even faster.

I waited until she got her lashes under control before nodding. "Sure. Everyone likes baking." Stepping away from her, I looked toward the kitchen. "¡Es suficiente! ¡Frodo! ¡Vamos!"

Frodo came trotting down the hall, reluctantly obedient. He'd definitely had more than his share of treats. I knew the feeling. I'd been greedy with Gabriella, and I wasn't ready to stop, either.

"¡Muy bien!" I bent and scratched Frodo's head.

"Your cat thinks he's a dog," Kaylee squealed. "Does he walk on a leash?"

I imagined walking Frodo at Ginger Cake Acres among the dog owners. I had a strange feeling Frodo might be into it.

"I haven't tried that yet," I said. "He's not really my cat. He just came with the apartment."

"But he speaks Spanish," Kaylee said, rubbing behind Frodo's small ears. "He must be yours."

If I had a pet, he would be one like Frodo: a big muscular beast with a showy tail and a confident attitude. Frodo was a pretty cool cat who didn't know he was a cat, and he was popular with the ladies.

I stepped around the pile of clothes on the floor and opened the door. "Thanks again for the brownies," I said.

Kaylee went into the hall. "Bye, Frodo!"

Ms. Taylor stopped with one foot in the hall. "Go on down to the car, Kaylee. I'll be right there." Her gaze dropped to the women's shoes and shorts on the floor just, naked curiosity on her face. "You have company?"

I narrowed my eyes at her. "I'm enjoying my day off." I put my hand on the door. "I hope you will as well."

"You're allowed to have a life, Mr. Morales. I'm not judging you." Her eyes roamed over me. "After my divorce, it took me a while to want a man in my life again."

It was all I could do to keep my eyes from rolling. In my mind, I was already back in my bedroom with Gabriella. "Uh-huh." I eased the door closed, trying to shut her out. "Good luck with that."

"It's not about luck." She tossed her hair over her shoulder. "It's about opportunity."

I nodded. Anything to get her out of here. "Right. Of course."

"Don't miss out on life's opportunities," she said.

"Couldn't agree more." The opportunity in my bedroom was waiting. "See you later." I shut the door before something rude slipped out of my mouth. I wanted to tell her to fuck herself and her brownies, but she wasn't worth it.

When I got back to my bedroom, Gabriella was standing at the door, wrapped in the towel. Her eyes were wild, and her hair looked like a tornado had whipped through it. She was gorgeous.

"Was that Chelsea Taylor?" Gabriella was ready to bolt. Lucky for me, her clothes were in the living room, so she would have to pass me to grab them. "What was she doing here?"

I blocked Gabriella's exit by leaning against the doorframe. "I got rid of her. Don't worry about it."

Her chin came up, and her jaw flexed. "Why was she here, Joey? Do you have something going with her too?"

My body tensed. Gabriella assumed I couldn't keep my dick in my pants. It was true I was no saint, but I wasn't a lowlife. "I don't have anything going with Chelsea Taylor." I placed my hands on her shoulders and lowered my chin so our eyes met. "Believe it or not, I don't have anything going on with anyone—besides you."

Her breath hitched, and her eyes softened. I could tell the idea of having something going with me intrigued Gabriella. She couldn't argue that we had a good thing going, but we just had to figure out how to keep it.

"What about the BJ bandit?"

The question baffled me. "What?"

"The woman on her knees behind your desk." Gabriella crossed her arms over her towel-clad chest. "It was only a few weeks ago, Joey. What about her?"

My stomach clenched. There had never been anything of substance between me and Caroline. When she was in town, we met up. It had been fun, but nothing more. Nothing like Gabriella. I wanted more than an occasional meet-up with Gabriella if we could somehow make it work. I'd settle for keeping it a secret if that was how it had to be.

"She doesn't matter," I said, shifting my hand from her shoulder to curl around her neck.

She leaned into my touch for a second, then stiffened. "What about Kaitlyn's bikini top? Did you give it back to her yet?"

Frustration mounted inside me when she pulled away. "Gabriella." I tightened my hold on her. "Kaitlyn was changing in my bathroom. Everyone from the building was over here watching Manchester City play Club América."

Gabriella rolled her eyes. "You have an answer for everything."

I shrugged. "It's true."

She stared up at me, a war going on behind her eyes as she decided whether to trust me. I stood patiently under her thorough inspection. When a reluctant smile tugged at her lips, I knew she'd made her decision. "Stop looking so cute," she said. "You make it impossible to concentrate."

I swept my thumb across her collarbone, smearing syrup. Bringing my thumb to my mouth, I sucked off the syrup.

Gabriella moaned and melted against my chest. "I really need to go," she said, her hands snaking around to my back.

"You're covered in syrup. Why not stay and take a shower?"

Her hands spread over my back, and she leaned against my chest. "I have to be somewhere."

A fist tightened around my heart. "Somewhere like a date?"

"Supper at my parents' house." She dropped her hands from my back and pulled away. "I don't date."

That was a relief and a tragedy. "Why not?"

"I need to go." She eased out of my arms. "Have you seen my phone?"

I jerked my head toward the door. "Probably still in your shorts."

She brushed by me, heading toward the living room.

"Wait." I snagged her wrist. "Why don't you date?"

A frustrated huff escaped her mouth. "I don't have the time or energy for dating."

I wrapped my fingers around her wrist and tugged her closer. "Maybe you should make time." Dipping my head, I kissed the corner of her mouth. "Start with a shower. With me." I trailed my lips across her jaw. "My friend in Costa Rica owns a hotel with outdoor showers. Mine doesn't compare, but it isn't so bad."

She turned her head, and we kissed again. Freeing her wrist from my hold, she hooked her arm around my waist and pulled me closer. Our tongues slid together, and my body filled with heat. Kissing her was like a drug, and I was already addicted.

A song burst into the air, and it took me a moment to register the noise as Gabriella's phone. She jerked away from me and scrambled to grab her phone.

"Hello?"

I watched her face change as she listened. Her alarmed expression softened, and she laughed.

"That's great, buddy! Tell Papa better luck next time."

She listened for a moment, her fingers twisting at the knot in her towel. Our eyes met and held, and her expression closed up. She looked away.

"Okay. See ya." Gabriella hung up and gathered her clothes.

"Everything okay?" I asked.

"It's fine." She straightened and hugged her clothes to her chest. "I really have to go."

I didn't try to argue. The moment was over. For now.

"I have Shane to think about," Gabriella said. "He doesn't need a parade of strange men in his life."

I managed an easy-going smile despite my stinging pride. "What about one not-so-strange man?"

She shook her head and went down the hall toward the bathroom. When she came out a moment later, she was dressed in her running clothes with her hair pulled back in a ponytail. She had her boss-lady face on, but her nipples were showing through her sports bra.

"This can't go anywhere." She gestured between us. "This is just a one-time thing, an itch we needed to scratch."

Ouch. Usually I was the one saying those lines. It didn't feel so great being on the other end. "If that's what you want."

"I'll never love anyone again," she said, almost apologetically.

Tension knotted in my gut. "I get that."

Her eyes fell to my chest, and I knew she was thinking about the tattoo under my shirt. I braced myself for her to ask, but she didn't. A moment ticked by, then another.

"I should go."

"Okay."

Neither of us moved. We were standing close enough to touch, but we didn't.

"I'm sorry, Joey."

My heart ached at the finality in her voice. Gabriella's world was black and white, with no room for anything in between. "Relax, baby."

She scoffed. "Relax? How can I relax? I'm the principal of the school. You're a teacher. And one of my students was just here."

I used some of Chelsea Taylor's wise words on Gabriella. "You are allowed to have a life."

"Not with you."

I winced at the disgust in her voice. Frustration mounted inside me, and my patience snapped. I strode to the door and closed my hand over the knob.

"That came out wrong, Joey. I didn't mean it as an insult. I just meant we can't be together. It would never work."

I shrugged and pulled the door open, ushering her out. "It's cool." I nodded at her, flashing my grin despite the pain in my chest. "Thanks for a good time."

She stormed out, but not before getting in the final word. She tossed her ponytail over her shoulder and glared at me. "It was my pleasure."

Chapter 17

Gabi

Gabi [3:30 p.m.] : Emergency book club meeting tonight?

Sloane [3:32 p.m.] : Can't. I've got an anniversary party. R u ok?

Lacey [3:32 p.m.] : What's wrong

Gabi [3:33 p.m.] : I'm good r u in

Lacey [3:35 p.m.] : In

Mia [3:35 p.m.] : In

Kennedy [3:45 p.m.] : I have to teach tonight, but I can come late. What's wrong????

Gabi [3:45 p.m.] : I'm fine don't worry

Mia [3:45 p.m.] : Then don't say emergency bitch!!!

Kennedy [3:46 p.m.] : Someone is sassy

Thatcher [4:45 p.m.] : Can we do my place?

Gabi [4:47 p.m.] : Does that mean we have to help with the cabinets?

Thatcher [4:47 p.m.] : duh

Sloane [4:48 p.m.] : keep me posted

I barely made it through supper with my family. My mother's meatloaf was dry as a bone, my brother moaned about not getting the promotion he'd wanted, and there wasn't any wine. I choked down the meatloaf because I was starving. All I'd eaten the entire day were a few bites of French toast and half a bacon sandwich. Thinking about the delicious food I'd eaten for breakfast made me think about Joey, which made the meatloaf even harder to swallow.

After dinner, I dropped Shane off at home and told him I would be back by nine.

"Thatcher needs my help with his renovation," I said.

"Cool!" Shane's face lit up. "Can I come?"

I pushed the button on the remote to open the garage door. "English essay."

He rolled his eyes and pushed the car door open. "Okay. But I want to come next time. I told him I would help lay the tile."

"As long as it doesn't involve you operating a saw," I said.

Shane scoffed. "I'm almost fifteen, Mom." He slammed the door and stomped up the driveway.

I drove back through town, toward Thatcher's house. A few years ago, Thatcher had moved to Mossy Oak because he'd inherited his uncle's bookstore and old family house. Thatcher had revamped the bookshop into a thriving business, but he hadn't touched the house until recently. He was in the middle of a messy renovation, which he was determined to do by himself.

When he didn't answer my knock, I let myself in. His fluffy companion, Daisy, bounded down the hall, her long golden tail swishing behind her. "Hey, pretty girl. Where's your dad?" I bent and petted Daisy's soft coat, letting go of some of my frustration over Joey go as I stroked her. "Men aren't worth the trouble, are they, Daisy?"

She wagged her tail in agreement, and I buried my head in her furry neck. A muffled thump came from upstairs, and I lifted my head.

"Thatcher?" I called. "Where the heck are you?"

"Up here!" His voice came from the rooms above.

I went up the stairs and found him on his hands and knees in one of the bedrooms, battling a piece of carpet. I clapped my hand over my mouth to keep from laughing when he tugged with too much force and landed on his ass. He wore a pair of carpenter overalls, rubber rain boots, and swim goggles.

"Perfect timing," he said, pushing to his feet. He slapped his hands on his denim-covered thighs, and a cloud of dust rose in the air. "Grab it over there." He pointed at a piece of the carpet he'd just torn up.

"Oh my God!" I stared at the grass-green carpet. "What have you done? You've ruined the fairway!"

He glared at me, his eyes magnified behind the goggles. "Shut up and help me."

I picked my way over the debris-covered floor and joined Thatcher in his battle with the hideous green carpet. "Is this turf?" I asked.

He shrugged. "I think so. On the count of three?"

It was hard to take him seriously in the swim goggles. "Don't I need my own eye protection?"

"I'm allergic to something," he said. "My eyes are killing me."

He counted to three, and we both pulled hard. Finally, the turf budged. An inch. Thatcher grunted and sank to the floor.

"I give up," he said. "Maybe I'll turn this room into a putting green."

I joined him on the floor and glanced around, taking in the high ceilings, ornate crown molding, and glass-tiered chandelier. Except for the garish wallpaper and the emerald-green carpet, this place had potential. After seeing what Thatcher had done with Hyperbole's Bookshop, I knew he could find the inner beauty of his old family house.

Back in the day, everyone had thought Hyperbole's Bookshop was haunted. Thatcher had transformed the musty relic of a shop into a thriving attraction in the heart of Mossy Oak's Main Street. His methods were unorthodox, but the finished product was worth it. He would do the same with this place, even if it took years.

Thatcher pushed the goggles up on his head, revealing his swollen, bloodshot eyes. Daisy nudged his chest, and he put an arm around her.

"You need an antihistamine," I said. "You're having a reaction."

He sneezed. "Probably all this dust."

"Bless you."

He shot me another dirty look. "Why are you so chipper?"

"I'm not chipper."

Thatcher cocked his head, his blue eyes studying me intently. His close inspection made me twitch.

"Did you get laid?" His lips twitched. "You did, didn't you?"

My cheeks burned brighter. Was it so obvious? Was I wearing a sign around my neck that read Sex Deprived Spinster? Oh, beans! Had my parents noticed?

"Hello?" Lacey's voice sounded from downstairs.

Daisy scrambled to her feet and raced out of the room to greet Lacey. Dogs loved Lacey. She was some kind of dog whisperer.

"Who's the guy?" Thatcher asked, grinning.

"You look like an idiot in those overalls," I said. "And I won't even ask why you're wearing rain boots."

He glanced at his boots. "Daisy has a thing for shoes. She keeps hiding them from me, and these were the only ones I could find. Now spill your guts," he said, poking my leg.

"Wait!" Lacey burst into the room. "No one is spilling anything until Mia and Kennedy get here."

Thatcher got up and took the bag Lacey carried. "Gabi had sex."

He peered into the bag and pulled out a beer. "Oh, you brought my favorite."

Lacey planted her hands on her hips and looked Thatcher up and down. "Don't ever say anything about my wardrobe choices again."

He tugged his goggles off and tossed them to the floor. "Let's go down to the kitchen, it's less..." He glanced around. "Green."

The kitchen was less green, but it was no less dusty, and no less a mess. The cabinets were halfway hung, the hardwood floors were torn up, and wallpaper sagged off the walls. The only appliance was a pea-green refrigerator.

"Are you sure you shouldn't hire a contractor?" I asked.

"I'm sure." Thatcher put the beer in the fridge and pulled out a bottle of wine.

My eyebrows rose at the sight of my favorite white wine dangling from his fingertips. One of the cheaper wines from the local winery, it still cost thirty dollars a bottle. I never bought it unless it was a special occasion.

I eyed Thatcher skeptically. "Why do you have fancy wine?"

"Your emergency book club alert made me think you needed a treat."

I didn't need treats. The opposite. I'd had too many treats, and I didn't know what to do.

"I brought chocolate," Lacey said, slinging her arm around me.

My favorite wine. Chocolates. Multiple orgasms in one day. It was too much. I choked back a sob. Wow, orgasms made a person weepy.

"Hey, don't cry." Thatcher popped the cork. "It's just wine."

"I'm not crying." I sniffed and pulled myself together. "It's been a day."

Thatcher held back a smirk and handed me a cup of wine. "I don't have any glasses," he said. "They're all boxed up."

Lacey raised her eyebrows at Thatcher. "Yet you found rain boots?"

"Daisy keeps stealing my shoes."

"Daisy-Do," Lacey said in a conversational voice, dropping into a squat so she was eye level with the golden retriever. "You wouldn't want someone coming into your space and taking your toys, would you?"

Thatcher and I exchanged a look over Lacey's head. Lacey was like a sister to us, an odd younger sister who we adored despite—or maybe because of—her strange habits.

"I wish Mia and Kennedy would hurry," he said. "I want to know who made the Iron Lady all mushy."

"Don't call me that."

He brushed by me and took the chips out of the bag. "It was a compliment."

"You know I don't care for it."

Thatcher tugged on my ponytail. "But it suits you so perfectly."

"Bite me, Sarge."

He smiled mischievously. "I'll leave that to the mystery man."

Lacey finished whispering to Daisy and got to her feet. "Did you finally follow your own advice?"

"What advice?"

"Yeah, Gabi is full of advice." He tugged my ponytail again.

"You told me to jump Beckett's bones, if I recall."

I shrugged and sipped my wine. "It worked, didn't it?"

A goofy grin stretched her mouth. "Perfectly."

"How is Beckett?" Thatcher asked.

"He's in London, but he told me to tell you he's still on for the batting cage next week." Lacey turned her attention to me. "So, did you jump his bones?"

I cleared my throat, staring at my feet. "It was just a one-time thing."

Mia swept into the room. "Whose bones did you jump?" she asked.

Kennedy followed on her heels. "I got here as quickly as I could. What did I miss? Gabi jumped somebody's bones?" She rubbed her hands together in excitement. "Tell us everything."

"Let's take this upstairs," Thatcher said. "I need to get back to my carpet war."

Mia and Kennedy helped themselves to cups of wine and we went back to Thatcher's hideous bedroom.

"Holy garden of shamrocks," Mia said, glancing around the room.

"It's not so bad." Kennedy planted her hands on her hips and surveyed the room. She'd come straight from teaching yoga class and was positively radiating good vibes. "The chandelier is cool."

"The wallpaper makes me want to puke," Mia said.

"It's coming down. Don't worry." Thatcher bent over the upturned piece of carpet. "Everybody grab hold."

"Yeah!" Kennedy shouted, exuding a little too much energy.

"Was it Aaron?" Lacey asked, grabbing some turf.

"Who's Aaron?" Thatcher and Kennedy asked in unison.

"The bartender at Hawthorne's," Mia said. "The hot one with the biceps."

Thatcher scoffed. "Everyone has biceps."

Mia pursed her lips. "Not like Aaron's."

We tugged together, pulling up most of the carpet and a lot of dust. Underneath the carpet was a thick layer of glue and stained particle board. Thatcher sneezed. Mia coughed. Daisy growled at the dust balls floating in the air.

"It wasn't Aaron," I said.

"Oh no, not Mr. Morales?" Lacey asked. "You were supposed to be staying away from him."

"The teacher?" asked Mia. "Gross."

My pulse quickened. "It wasn't gross." I bit the inside of my cheek. "It was... magical." I sank to the ground, feeling light-headed. "It was incredible."

"How incredible?" Lacey passed around the bag of chips. "Tell us everything."

"I thought I would just have a bite to eat with him and maybe kiss him again."

"Again?" Kennedy asked.

"We may have kissed once before."

Mia's brows rose. "May have?"

I flushed, remembering the hot lip-lock in the booth at Goodfella's. "We definitely kissed."

Mia crunched a chip. "Then what happened?"

"We didn't make it to breakfast." My pulse raced again as I remembered Joey pinning me against the hard wood of the door. "We barely made it inside the door."

"Whoa." Kennedy grabbed a chip. "Hardcore."

A smile fought its way across my lips. "We eventually made it to the bedroom."

"You did it twice?" Thatcher's eyebrows shot up toward his hairline.

Even Lacey was impressed, which was saying a lot, considering she and Beckett were doing it like bunnies every chance they got.

I bit the inside of my cheek and squeezed my eyes shut. "It was like nothing I've ever felt before."

When I opened my eyes, everyone was staring at me, even Daisy.

"So what's the problem?" Kennedy asked.

I stared at the wallpaper, wishing the garish pattern would reveal the solution.

"It's just sex," Mia said. "It's not like you're marrying the guy."

"You're allowed to have a life," Lacey said.

"That's what Joey said too."

"This Joey sounds like a smart guy," Thatcher said.

"He *is* a teacher," I said.

"Gross," Mia said softly.

"Teachers are not gross," Kennedy said. "I'm a teacher. Am I supposed to abstain from sex?"

"Good point."

"It sounds like you need more yoga in your life," Kennedy said. "It will make you feel so much better."

"Yoga is your solution for everything," Thatcher said.

Kennedy pointed at him with a corn chip. "I remember

someone having a very good time on the yoga retreat to Aruba a few months ago."

Thatcher grinned. "That's because I was the only guy. The women couldn't get enough of me."

I rolled my eyes. "I've had enough of you."

"You need more wine," he said.

"And I need a cigarette," Mia said. "All this talk about sex is making me feel deprived."

Kennedy tapped her lip in thought. "His name is Joey?"

"Yeah, why?"

"He's a little taller than average, dark hair, athletic build?"

I pictured Joey wearing nothing but boxer briefs, and my blood heated. "Yeah, why?"

"He has a tattoo right here?" She pointed to her heart, where Joey had a woman's name inked on his pectoral muscle. *Maria.*

Lucky Maria. It was hard to keep the bitterness from my voice. "Yeah."

"I know him from class. His name isn't Joey in the computer system, but that's what everyone calls him."

"Fernando Morales." His exotic, sexy-as-sin name rolled off my tongue.

Kennedy nodded. "He comes to my Thursday at six p.m. regularly." Her eyes widened. "He's hot."

I scoffed. "I know."

"He's good at yoga, too." It was high praise coming from Kennedy, who took her yoga as seriously as I took my lost-and-found policy. "He comes with his neighbor and her girlfriend a lot. Gorgeous redhead with long curls." Kennedy snapped her fingers until she remembered her name. "Kaitlyn!"

My jaw dropped. "Kaitlyn is a lesbian?"

Kennedy scowled. "Labels, Gabi," she warned. "People don't have to fit into boxes."

Of course I knew that, but I really hoped Kaitlyn was a lesbian with a capital L, because it would make me feel better about the whole swimsuit-top-in-the-bathroom thing.

"I haven't told you the best part yet," I said.

"There's more?" Lacey asked.

I nodded and drank a long sip of wine to fortify myself. "I think I had my first orgasm today."

Everyone stared at me, jaws slack.

Thatcher recovered first. "You mean multiple orgasms, right?"

"No."

"You mean with just the D, right?" asked Lacey.

I shook my head. "I mean a real orgasm. Toe-curling, earth-shattering, mind-blowing orgasm." I took another gulp of wine. "A lot of them."

That shocked my friends into silence. I stared at them, waiting for someone to say something, but I'd rendered them speechless with my truth-bomb.

Finally, Mia broke the silence with a click of her lighter. She fired up a cigarette and took a long drag.

Thatcher didn't even tell her to put it out.

Chapter 18

JOEY

Gabriella and I avoided each other for a week. Instead of spending my planning period in the teachers' lounge, I sat outside on a bench in the school's garden. I stood in the back of the room during the staff meeting, and I changed my weekly long run from Sunday morning to Sunday afternoon, when I knew Gabriella would be at dinner with her family.

If she didn't think we were a match, who was I to argue? I had plenty of other options. The manager at Hyperbole's Café had been flirting with me for months. And every time I took my shirt off at yoga, at least three women tried to strike up a conversation after class.

A month ago, I'd have flirted back. These days, I could barely muster a nod and a smile.

Gabriella's voice over the intercom for morning announcements stirred my blood. Catching her eye in the staff meeting made my dick swell. Seeing her at the track meet with her family made my heart ache.

I envied Gabriella's interaction with her parents and the man who resembled her enough to be her brother. Watching them made me miss my family, even my pain-in-the-butt baby sister, Ava, the attention hog of the family.

I tried to focus on the meet, but it was hard to ignore Gabriella's family shouting cheers for Mossy Oak from the bleachers. It was an away meet at Windy Rush High, but Mossy Oak supporters were there in record numbers, making it difficult for our rival school to have much of a home field advantage.

Mossy Oak won the four-hundred-meter relay, and the energy surged in our favor. But Windy Rush had a talented hurdler who'd crushed everyone in the one-hundred-meter race, and the outcome of the meet would probably come down to the final event.

I usually stayed calm during a meet, but watching Shane line up at the blocks for the last heat of the three-hundred-meter hurdle race made my heart jump into my throat. The favorite from Windy Rush was in lane five, the most desirable lane where the turns weren't too wide and the main competition was in view during the entire race. In lanes three and six were two runners who'd already qualified for the state championship race with smoking-fast times.

This was going to be one of the tightest races of the meet, and tension filled the stadium.

If Shane raced the way I knew he could, he would beat most of them, and earn a state qualifying time for himself. Shane had drawn lane one. Some people considered the inside lane to be undesirable, but it wasn't any longer than the other lanes. Everyone ran the same distance and jumped over the same number of hurdles.

At practice, I'd reminded the kids about Olympians who had won gold from the outside lanes. "Run your own race in your own lane," I'd said.

I hoped Shane remembered my advice as he lined up on his block. As a former hurdler, I knew the race was mental as well as physical. Winning from lane one took focus and confidence. It was easy to get discouraged on the tight curves of lane one when the rest of the field seemed so far ahead. But it was all about perspective, and by the time the track straightened out, everything would look different.

The gun went off, and the runners exploded off their blocks to a loud cheer.

Shane had a good start and cleared the first hurdle with minimal effort. I smiled, remembering the way Gabriella had hurdled those bushes on the first day we'd run together. He'd obviously inherited his talent from his incredible mother.

I glanced away from the race for a split second to watch Gabriella. Her hands were clasped under her chin and her gaze was glued to Shane. My heart squeezed when her brother threw his arm around her shoulder and pulled her to his side.

I turned my attention back to the race where the runners in the outside lanes were slowly losing their leads. From lane one, it was hard for Shane to see where he was in relation to the others until the end of the second curve, but according to the timing of his touch down, he was right where he needed to be.

My muscles twitched with memory while I watched Shane's flawless execution. The kid was something special, and I had the feeling I was watching history in the making. I checked the clock and realized Shane was on pace for a school record. Even if he didn't win, he could possibly go down in the books tonight.

Gabriella's family shouted from the bleachers as the race tightened. Shane moved up to third place after clearing his sixth hurdle. The stands went wild, and both teams crowded the edges of the field, shouting at the tops of their lungs.

Lanes one, four, and six battled it out to the final hurdle. The favorite from Windy Rush touched down first, then lane six, followed by Shane in lane one. The runner from Windy Rush was closing in to win, but two steps before the finish line, he stumbled. The crowd let out a collective "ooh" as his feet tangled up and he hit the ground hard.

The kid in lane six crossed first with a time of 39.6 seconds. I clocked Shane at 39.9. I whooped and pumped my fist in the air. If my time was accurate, he'd beaten the school record from twelve years ago and qualified for the state meet.

The sidelines were celebrating, but on the track, the mood was somber as Shane and the other competitors crowded around the Windy Rush athlete who'd fallen over the last hurdle. Together, they helped him to his feet and wrapped him in a group hug.

Cheers from the crowd reached an all-time high as the athletes led the fallen runner off the track.

I tore my gaze from the incredible display of sportsmanship and found Gabriella in the crowd. She was smiling from ear to ear and swiping at her cheeks. Her father threw his arm around her shoulder, and she grinned up at him through her tears. My ribs squeezed tightly, and I wished it were my arm around Gabriella's shoulders.

Her head lifted, and she caught my gaze from across the field. Our eyes locked, and over the roar of the crowd, I felt connected to her on a level more intimate than sex. My stomach felt queasy, and my heart raced as if I'd been the one sprinting to the finish. Her mouth curved in a bright smile, and my world tilted. I didn't just want to kiss the smile off her lips. I wanted to be the one responsible for it.

The gun went off for the eight-hundred-meter race, shattering the spell between us. I snapped my attention back to my team and hurried to the officials to confirm Shane's time. He'd smashed the former record by 0.3 seconds, and he was going to the state meet.

The rest of the meet passed in a blur as I focused on coaching and securing a win against our biggest rival. Back at the bus, the other coaches and I split it into thirds. Madison took the front, Tommy had the middle, and I settled into the second-to-last row. Although it was a happy occasion and the bus shook with cheers and laughter, my mood was somber.

I stared out the window, letting most of the conversation drift around me. Memories of my racing days flashed through my mind. I remembered what it was like to shoot off the blocks and sail over the hurdles, my heart pumping full blast. My days in college had been lonely as hell. My teammates had become my substitute family, but it hadn't been the same as being home.

Spring break couldn't come soon enough. I was going home for ten days. I would get my fill of suffocating hugs from my mother, late nights drinking Imperials and watching football with my dad and brother, and catching up on the local gossip with my sisters.

"Dude, your mom's a MILF."

"You're sick, bro," Shane said. "She's my mom."

My head snapped up, and I focused my attention on Shane and the pimply faced kid sitting two rows ahead of me.

"I'm just saying... She's hot. She doesn't look too old. I bet she likes—"

Shane cut him off. "If you don't shut up about my mom, I'm gonna kick your ass."

"She's got a great ass for an old lady," the kid said. "I wouldn't say no if she threw it at me."

Shane started to get out of his seat, but I was up first. I shot down the aisle quicker than the racers had gotten off the blocks and loomed over the little asshole.

"Watch your mouth," I said. "You think you're a big man talking about a woman like that?" I itched to grab him by his skinny neck and yank him out of his seat, but he wasn't worth the trouble. I lowered my voice to a growl. "She's Shane's mom. She's a person with feelings, not just some object for you to fantasize over." I refrained from smacking him on the back of his head like I wanted to and glared at him. "You understand me?"

A sneer twisted his lips, but he nodded. "I was just messing around, Coach."

"Have some respect," I said.

"Yes, Coach. Sorry."

The noisy celebration on the bus continued as I made my way back to my seat. Anger coiled in my belly. I cracked my knuckles and flexed my fists.

"Thanks for having my back."

I glanced up and saw Shane leaning into the aisle. I relaxed my fists and spread my hands out over my knees. "No problem," I said. "But I kinda wish you would have kicked his butt."

Shane grimaced. "I still might."

I nodded in understanding. If anyone talked about my mom like that, they would regret it. "Maybe not on the bus," I said. "Or school property either."

Shane laughed, and I saw Gabriella in him for the first time. They had the same expressive eyes framed by long, dark lashes. Otherwise, he didn't favor her very much. He was tall and lanky, with big hands and feet, a sure sign he wasn't done growing. Once he added in lifting weights, he was going to be unstoppable in any sport he chose.

"Nice racing tonight," I said, leaning into the aisle for a fist bump.

His smile faded, but he reached out to tap my fist with his. "Thanks."

Obviously, he wasn't satisfied with his performance. "You broke a record as a freshman," I said to remind him.

"Yeah." He shrugged.

My jaw tightened. I hated to think Shane was the kind of kid who wasn't happy unless he won. I leaned farther into the aisle. "Are you upset about not winning?"

His shoulders lifted again. "Nah. I don't care about getting first. I just thought I was gonna do a lot better." His mouth twisted, and he hung his head. "I know I can go so much faster." He lifted his eyes to mine. "I'm running in the low forties at practice, so I should be much faster on race day."

My shoulders relaxed when I recognized the tone of impatience in a gifted athlete. "You'll get there."

"You think it was because I had lane one?"

I shook my head. "Lane one can be an advantage." I'd run some of my best races from lanes one and six. "No one's expecting the outside smoke. They can't see you coming, and they aren't prepared for you."

Shane leaned forward, hanging on my words.

"If you train for lane one, think how good you can be in lanes three and four. We'll focus on your start next week, get rid of your initial stutter step, and I bet you can go under thirty-nine at the next meet."

Shane's eyes widened. "You think so?"

"I know it."

"That's dope." His smile returned. "I saw your race at Great Southern Conference Championships. You crushed everyone. What did you go? Thirty-seven fifty?"

"That's right." I thought fondly of my fastest race. The best part was my family had been there to see it. Mom and Dad had taken a rare vacation from the restaurant and brought the entire family to Dallas.

"Where'd you see my race?" I asked.

"YouTube."

I nodded. "That's pretty dope."

Shane gave me a funny look, and I realized he thought I was far too old to use teenager slang.

I was dying to pull out my phone and watch my race on YouTube, but I couldn't afford to lose any more cool points.

Shane got up from his seat, came closer to the back of the bus, and sat in the empty seat across the aisle from me. He leaned forward, suddenly serious, as he studied me. "You like my mom, don't you?"

His question was like a cold splash of water on my face. "What?"

His brown eyes crinkled with laughter, and he snorted. "It's so obvious. You're always making heart eyes at each other when she picks me up from practice. And I caught her listening to *Spanish for Dummies* on audiobook."

Gabriella was learning Spanish? Warmth spread through my chest.

"You like her, don't you?" Shane asked again.

"Your mom is pretty amazing, but she's my boss."

Shane's eyebrows pinched together. "So?"

Frustration coiled in my gut. "Between you and me?"

He leaned into the aisle. "Yeah."

I saw in Shane the man he would be in a few years—a man raised by an extraordinary mom. I felt a camaraderie with him, and I didn't want to lie to him.

"I like your mom a lot, but she doesn't like me. And she doesn't date."

Shane frowned. "All my mom does is work and read books. She has no life. None." His voice cracked. "I wish she had some fun once in a while. I wish she had somebody cool to hang out with."

"Your mom is smart," I said. "She'll be okay. Don't worry."

"Okay."

One of the other kids called to Shane, and he went back to his former seat. I was glad to hear Shane wanted his mom to have a someone special. I just wished it were me.

My chest felt hollow, and I scrubbed a hand over my heart, reminding myself what happened the last time I had fallen for a woman. I'd ended up with a broken heart and a permanent tattoo.

Chapter 19

J OEY

My long run stretched from its usual ten kilometers to fifteen as I circled the pond at Ginger Cake Acres on Sunday morning. I wasn't sure if Gabriella would even show up to run, but it was my only chance to see her outside of school or a meet. She was the kind of person who lived on a tight schedule. If I didn't see her running, I would try the supermarket on Thursday. Stalking the supermarket wouldn't be easy, so I was glad when I finally spotted her on the other side of the pond.

She was running at a fast pace, and I had to push to catch up to her. If she told me to fuck off, at least we would be talking, which was better than the strange dance of avoidance we'd been doing since we had sex.

"Gabriella," I called.

When she saw me, the pained longing on her face gave me all the confirmation I needed. She was as hung up on me as I was on her.

I was breathless from sprinting to catch up to her brutal pace. "Can you slow down?"

She brought her pace back a notch and studied the trail in front of her as if she hadn't run it a thousand times before.

I fell into stride beside her, and we headed into a grove of flowering trees. "I think we should talk."

Her chin lifted, but she stared straight ahead. "What's there to talk about?"

I grabbed her hand and tugged her to a stop, then pulled her into the cover of trees. "This." I grabbed her face and pressed my mouth to hers. I kissed her with all the pent-up energy I'd been holding onto for weeks. I poured every moment I'd thought about her into the kiss, and she kissed me back just as hard.

She wound her arms around my neck and clung to me, her mouth fighting mine for control. We stumbled farther into the cover of woods, and I pressed her back against a tree. Her hands slid under my shirt, and I hissed when her warm fingers grazed my nipple.

"This." I groaned, grinding my erection against her hip. "We need to talk about this."

She reached between us and flattened her hand against the bulge in my running shorts. "Talking is not what we need."

I groaned again when her hand slid over me. "Stop." I grabbed her hand. "Not here. Anyone could walk up and see us."

She blinked a few times, coming to her senses as she glanced around. "Your place?"

My eyes widened. I'd expected it to be a lot harder to convince her. She must have missed me as much as I had missed her. I didn't hesitate. I led the way out of the trees back to the path and we ran to my apartment in silence. I opened the main door for her, and we hurried up the stairs.

This time we made it farther than the front door. We got to the kitchen before I had her clothes off and her hoisted on the counter. By the time I had my cock sheathed in a condom, I was almost ready to come just from looking at her. She was so sexy, sitting on my counter with her legs spread. I almost dropped to the tile floor so I could taste her, but she grabbed my hips and pulled me between her legs.

"I had a fantasy about this." She locked her legs around my hips. "The day I fell, and you played doctor?"

I lined my cock up at the gates of heaven. "Yeah?"

"I pictured you giving me this instead of a bandage." She wrapped her slim hand around my aching flesh and guided me inside. "I wanted this."

Our mutual groan filled the air as I sank home. She pressed her hands into the counter and ground into me. I buried my face against her neck, breathing in the erotic scent of sex and sweat.

"I wanted this too." I licked a path up her neck to her jaw, then found her lips again.

Our tongues tangled frantically. I thought my heart was going to explode as I pumped into her. We burned to get closer to each other. Her hands clawed at my shirt, then yanked it up and over my head. My fingers dug into her hips, pinning her to the counter as I pounded into her.

I knew by the change in her breathing, she was close. She cried out, and I covered her mouth with mine, swallowing ripples of pleasure as they rocked through us. Her pussy clenched my cock so tightly I couldn't hold on much longer. She raked her nails down my back with enough pressure to mark me as hers, and I lost control. I came so hard my knees went weak and I had to lean against the counter until my toes uncurled.

We clung together while the last spasms swept through us. When we'd both caught our breath, I slowly eased back and cleaned myself up. The thought of making muffins on this counter struck me as funny, and I grinned.

Gabriella's eyebrows rose, and her flushed cheeks burned brighter. "Why are you smiling?"

I dragged her off the counter and set her on her feet. "I was just thinking about making some breakfast."

She bent down to get her shorts and wiggled them over her

shoes. After plucking her phone out of her pocket, she scrolled through her messages. "I need to go."

"Everything okay?"

"Fine."

"Where's Shane?"

She cocked an eyebrow at me. "He spent the night at my brother's. My nephew is a year younger than Shane."

I pointed at her phone. "Was that him?"

She shook her head. "He probably isn't up yet."

"Then you have time for breakfast." Sex in the kitchen was proving to be convenient.

Gabriella eyed me as I filled the kettle with water and set it on the stove. "You don't have to cook for me."

I wiped down the counter before grabbing everything I needed from the fridge. "I want to."

She yanked the elastic band out of her hair and fixed her ponytail. "I don't think this is a good idea."

"If you keep saying that, you're going to hurt my feelings." I smiled and grabbed a pan for the eggs. "I just ran about fifteen kilometers waiting for you to show up at the park, so this food is more for me than you."

"Fifteen kilometers? That's like nine miles."

I set the pan down and placed my hands on either side of her, trapping her against the counter. "It was worth it."

She spread her hands across my chest, her throat working as she swallowed. Her long lashes fluttered as she blinked at me. "I rarely eat breakfast."

I rarely cooked for people, or ran circles in the park waiting for them. And I didn't beg women to come back to my apartment to "talk," or spend nights lying awake in bed missing them.

A loud *meow* split the silence. Frodo stared up at me. I scowled at him. *"No seas metiche."*

Frodo ignored me and leaped onto the counter, nosing his way between us.

"Frodo understands Spanish?" She rubbed him behind the ears. "*Hola*, Frodo."

Frodo purred and leaned into Gabriella's touch. I didn't blame the orange beast one bit.

"What did you say to him?"

"I told him to mind his own business." I gave Frodo a stern look and pointed. "Down."

After whipping his tail against the counter a few times, Frodo jumped to the floor and padded around my feet.

"He's very obedient for a cat."

"Only when he wants to do what he's asked." I tucked a loose strand of her hair into her ponytail and smiled at her. "I heard you were learning Spanish."

Color stained her cheeks. "Who told you that?"

The kettle screeched. "Is it true?" I asked, taking the kettle off the stove.

She shrugged. "I've always wanted to speak another language."

"Why Spanish?"

She huffed out a breath and moved to the sink to wash her hands. "If I'm staying, put me to work. What can I do?"

I pointed at the bread box and didn't comment on how neatly she'd avoided my question. "Slice some bread for toast."

I spooned ground beans into the coffee press and tried not to smile while I watched Gabriella fumble around in my kitchen.

"What?" She glanced over her shoulder at me after finally choosing a butcher knife from the knife block.

"Use this one." I pulled the proper knife out of the block and handed it to her. "It will slice better."

She nodded and pulled the bread out of the box. "Don't tell me you made this bread."

"Okay." I winked. "I won't."

"Seriously? You made this bread?"

"I made it in the bread machine. Does that count?"

"You have a cat and a bread machine?"

I laughed and reached above her to pull a bowl from the cabi-net. "He's not my cat."

On my way back to my side of the kitchen, I dropped a kiss on her cheek. The bowl in my hands clattered to the counter as I wrapped my arms around her waist. At this rate, breakfast might not be served until lunch.

Her phone buzzed in her pocket, vibrating against my hip. Gabriella dug it out and glanced at the screen.

I eased back to give her privacy and cracked eggs into the bowl while she responded to the message.

"My mom wants me to bring rolls to dinner tonight."

I added a splash of milk and a dash of hot sauce to the eggs. "What kind of rolls?"

She shrugged and picked up the knife. "Is there more than one kind of dinner roll?"

I tried not to cringe when she hacked into the loaf of bread. "Yes. There is more than one kind. My mom makes the best garlic rolls." My stomach growled at the thought of tasting my mom's cooking again.

Gabriella smiled. "You must be starving after running nine miles."

I shrugged. "At least it wasn't a marathon."

Her brow wrinkled. "You wouldn't have run that far."

Running was the last thing I wanted to talk about. I pushed the plunger on the coffee press as if it required all my attention. "You've been avoiding me at work again."

The tension in the air thickened.

"You've been avoiding me."

"Maybe." I reached for two mugs and filled them with steaming coffee. I handed her one. "Black, right?"

She took the mug and stared into it with a frown. "This isn't going to work between us."

"Because of work?"

She nodded at her coffee.

"You wouldn't want to be with me even if we didn't work

together," I said. Before I could shut my stupid mouth, I went on, "You don't date, especially not men like me."

Her eyes flashed up to mine. "I didn't mean that."

I poured the eggs into the skillet, wishing I wouldn't have brought it up. "Let's just forget it."

Her phone buzzed again, and she wrenched it out of her pocket. She fired off a rapid text as I scrambled the eggs and popped the bread in the toaster.

"Shane's going on a church group retreat for spring break," she said, shoving her phone in her pocket. "The list of supplies he has to bring keeps growing."

"A lot of the kids from the team are going. He will have a blast."

"He won't have his phone for the entire week." She laughed. "He may not survive."

I scooped eggs onto two plates. "You'd be surprised."

"This looks delicious," Gabriella said. "I'm impressed."

The scrambled eggs and toast weren't fancy. "At home, we eat rice and beans with our eggs. We call it *gallo pinto*."

"Spotted Rooster!"

I winked at her. "Very good."

We sat at my breakfast table as if it were the most normal thing in the world for us to share a meal. Gabriella fired off a few more texts in between bites of food.

She glanced up and saw me watching her while I ate. "Sorry." She slapped her phone face down on the table and picked up her fork. "I broke my own no-technology-at-the-table rule."

"More for the list?" I asked.

She nodded. "I don't know why he has to have two sets of sheets. They're camping."

I laughed, picturing the camping I'd done growing up on the quiet beaches of Playa Langosta. It didn't involve sheets.

"What do you call it?" I took a bite of toast, trying to remember the right words. It was a funny American expression of two words mashed together. "Expensive camping?"

Gabriella took a sip of coffee. "Glamping." She took another sip and groaned. "This coffee is so good. I don't even miss the cream."

"You said you liked it black."

She scrunched her nose. "I just said that because I thought you wouldn't have any."

"*Hablar papaya,*" I muttered under my breath as I slid my chair back from the table. I went into the kitchen and grabbed a carton of half-and-half and some flavored creamer from the fridge. "Which one do you want?"

Gabriella's fork paused in the air, and her eyes widened. "It's fine without," she said, reaching for the flavored creamer. "But I'll take a dash of this."

I watched her splash creamer into her coffee. "Why wouldn't I have cream?"

She reached for her fork again. "I misjudged you in many ways," she said. "Take these eggs, for example. I've never had scrambled eggs so perfect. How did you get them to be so fluffy?"

"You thought about me making eggs?" I asked. "Why?"

She forked up the last of her eggs. "I can't explain it. I'm just surprised you're so domesticated."

"Because I don't eat cardboard crackers for lunch and have cream in my kitchen, I'm boring? Is that what you mean?"

She put her fork on her empty plate. Her eyes raised to mine, and a bolt of desire zigzagged between us. "You're definitely not boring."

A slow smile spread across my mouth. I pushed away my plate and reached for her hand. Her phone buzzed, but she ignored it and placed her hand in mine.

"It's probably more for the list," she said, running her thumb along the rings on my middle finger and fourth fingers.

I stroked her hand and touched the gold band on her ring finger, wondering if she ever took it off.

"Spring break can't come quickly enough," she said. "The teachers have done such a great job, but everyone is ready for a week off."

"Ten days," I said.

"That's right. Shane will be gone from Saturday to Saturday, and we won't be able to talk the whole time. It's going to be the longest we've gone without contact." She shook her head. "I'm sure he'll be fine, and if there's an emergency, one of the counselors will call me."

"A glamping emergency?"

She laughed. "Not likely, right?"

I shrugged. "Anything can happen, but there's no sense in worrying."

"I know, but worrying comes with being a mom. I try to live in the now as much as possible, but it isn't always easy." Her phone buzzed again, and we both glanced at it. "I should get going," she said.

We stood and cleared the plates. "What will you be doing with an entire week to yourself?"

"Stuff around the house and catching up on my reading." She rolled her eyes. "Sounds exciting, right?"

I smirked. "Depends on the books."

She put her plate in the sink and slapped my shoulder. "Stop it." Her hand lingered on my sleeve.

I nudged her away from the sink. "Leave those. I'll get them later."

"What about you?" She traced the seam of my shirt on my shoulder. "What are you doing for spring break?"

For the first time, I regretted my travel plans. Gabriella would be responsibility-free for a week. It would be the perfect time to see more of each other.

I took her into my arms. "I'm going to Costa Rica," I said. "Sun, sand, and delicious meals cooked by someone other than me."

Her hand stilled on my shoulder. "Sounds fantastic."

I stared into Gabriella's pretty brown eyes, and an outrageous idea sparked to life. What if I could visit home and spend more time with Gabriella? It might be tricky getting some alone time with her and seeing my family, but with a little planning, I could make it work.

"What is it?" Gabriella asked, narrowing her eyes at me.

"You're going to think I'm crazy."

"Why?"

I tightened my arms around her waist, lifting her off her toes. "Do you want to come with me?"

Her eyes went wide. "I can't," she said.

"Why not?" The idea took root and bloomed. I pictured Gabriella joining me for leisurely breakfasts and long walks on the beach. I thought about everything I wanted to show her. "Shane is gone all week, and you said you don't have any plans. I'll be there for ten days. You don't have to come the whole time." I worked out a plan as I spoke. "We can stay at my friend Santiago's hotel, the one with the outdoor showers."

I stopped talking when I saw the look on her face. She had completely shut down.

"I can't do that, Joey. You know I can't." She reached up and brushed her lips against my cheek, then stepped out of my arms. "I should really go."

I nodded, realizing it had been dumb of me to ask. She wouldn't even meet my gaze during a staff meeting. Why would she want to come home with me?

Book Review of "The Night Shift" by Mackenzie Austin

BY VALENTINA BLUERIDGEBOOKCLUB.COM

5 stars
5 hot peppers
5 book boyfriend hearts

DEAR READERS,

This book was an unexpected delight. I'm a Mackenzie Austin virgin, but I'm on my way to being a SuperFan. This book was full of action, adventure, witty banter, and steamy sex. If anyone knows how I can step into The Shimmer, please let me know.

Plot Overview:

Jade Ringley has never been an ordinary girl. Her skills with a sword or a bow are unsurpassed. It isn't until she is hired as a guard at a graveyard that she understands her destiny. One night when she is patrolling the ancient section of the graveyard where a thief had recently stolen priceless relics from a tomb, Jade comes face-to-face with one of her ancestors who should have been long dead.

Jade takes the biggest risk of her life by "stepping into The Shimmer," a secret world of danger and desire. She meets two men on opposing sides of a war and falls in love with both of them. Tristan and Vox couldn't be more different, but Jade is drawn to them with a depth of passion that will shake you to your core. She finds herself in a love triangle destined for disaster. She must choose sides in the war, but she can't untangle the savior from the villain. Her decision is clear: choose one man or return home and lose both loves forever.

Pros:
- Trope: shifters, witches, alternate worlds
- Heroine: Snarky, funny, and smart, Jade Ringley is a must for fans of Charley Davidson or Stephanie Plum.
- Smut: If you like it hot, you will not be disappointed. There's a scene in a cave where Jade accidentally takes a serum that causes her to hallucinate. The threesome she imagines between her and her two lovers is enough to make you melt.

Cons:
- Cliffhanger: You guys know how much I abhor a cliffhanger. Austin delivers a story with enough intrigue to make me forgive her.
- The length: It was so short, I finished it in about three hours. I would have liked more, but I guess I will have to wait for book two.

To sum it up, I'm counting down the days to the release of the second book, and you will be too!

xoxo, Valentina

Chapter 20

GABI

"Some of us are going to yoga tonight," Shane said when I picked him up from track practice. "Wanna come? They say it's good for stress."

"I'm not stressed," I said, slapping my turn signal with more force than necessary.

Shane raised both eyebrows. "Whatever."

"I'd love to come, but I'm not stressed. I'm fine."

"Cool. Can we give Erin a ride?"

"Sure."

Erin was one of Shane's best friends, but I suspected he wished they were more. Erin was the reason I'd picked Shane up early from the party at Zack's house after the championship game. She had drunk too much, and she had been scared to call her parents, so Shane had called me.

"Erin's great at yoga," he said. "She was showing us some stuff before practice yesterday. She can do a handstand and everything."

"Nice." I prepared myself to get schooled at yoga by a fifteen-year-old.

When we got home, I texted Kennedy to let her know I was taking her up on her advice and going to a yoga class. She was thrilled but warned me to get there early because Mallary's class was popular.

We arrived ten minutes early, but there were only a few spots left in the room. I couldn't believe so many people had nothing better to do on a Friday night than sweat their butts off in a hot yoga class.

"It's packed," I said, glancing around with no small amount of pride for my friend. Kennedy had made Namaste Yoga a welcoming place, and the studio was like a slice of life cut straight from Mossy Oak. The variety of shapes, sizes, and ages of my fellow yogis was impressive.

"This is nothing," Erin said. "By the time class starts, we'll be like sardines."

My stomach clenched at the thought of being so close to my sweaty neighbor. "You say that as if it's a good thing."

Erin gave me a look that every teenager seemed to have perfected: disbelief at my utter uncool-ness. "It's about the energy," she said, with a sympathetic shake of her head. "You'll see."

"Erin! Shane!" A petite blonde dressed like yoga Barbie in a hot-pink matching set waved at them. "Over here."

Shane took my mat and told me he would find us spots while I put my bag in the locker room and filled my water bottle.

I found one of the few empty lockers and was making my way through the crowded hall when I saw the back of Joey's head above the crowd.

Holy guacamole! His hair was all tumbling waves and chestnut highlights. It had grown out since his last haircut, and only a small swatch of tanned skin was exposed above the neck of his shirt. Had I kissed that spot before? I didn't think I had, but I was suddenly overcome with the need to do it.

A woman in her fifties with a body fitter than most twenty-year-olds' was chatting him up, and he leaned against the wall with his customary casualness, listening raptly.

My heart slammed in my chest as I watched him. I'd successfully avoided him at school all week, but I hadn't forgotten him. His invitation to Costa Rica had echoed in my head. I'd never been to Central America, and the thought of going with Joey was enticing.

I dreamed about spending long lazy days on the beach and even longer nights in the bungalow he'd described. My mind fixated on the outdoor shower, and I imagined how good it would feel to stand naked under the hot spray with Joey. To drink rich coffee and eat *gallo pinto* for breakfast. To touch him whenever and wherever I felt like it without hiding.

Joey was so engrossed in his conversation I thought he wouldn't notice me, but as I squeezed by him down the hall, his hand snagged mine.

"Gabriella." He cleared his throat. "Mrs. Salinger. It's nice to see you."

I raised my chin at him. "Mr. Morales."

"I didn't know you practiced yoga."

"Guess I'm full of surprises." I slipped my hand from his and squeezed through the crowded hall into the studio.

I hoped my dizziness would fade once I was in the studio, a safe distance away from Joey.

Good grief, was I wrong. The room was so hot it hit me like a punch to the gut. Outside it was early spring. Inside it was tropical rainforest. Erin had been right about the energy. I felt the buzz in the air rising above the cloud of humidity.

Yoga mats, placed scant inches apart, lined the room from front to back. Mirrors covered the front wall, and the side wall was made of windows looking out over the tree-lined Main Street.

Shane pointed at my mat, near the front row on the other side of the room from his. "There weren't many spots left," he said.

I made my way through the yoga mats to mine. The woman next to me was dressed in shorts and a sports bra that covered little more than a bikini. I tugged at my tank top, feeling overdressed.

The instructor came in as everyone was settling into their spots. A few latecomers breezed in from the hall as class started right on time.

"Find child's pose," Mallary said, turning on the music.

A wave of silence swept through the room as everyone knelt on their mats and pressed their foreheads to the ground.

"Welcome, everyone. My name is Mallary, and I am going to lead you through your practice tonight." Her voice was calm and confident, inspiring us to do our best.

"It's called a practice because it isn't perfect," she said, walking to the front of the room. "Don't try to be perfect. Just do what you can do."

I smiled to myself. For some reason, this reminded me of Joey. He was always effortlessly perfect. The way he mastered the English language with ease. His wonderful cooking. The flawless way he ran at a fast pace, which would have most people panting. How he made everyone feel as if they were his closest friend.

"I'm going to call out poses," Mallary said. "But they are all optional. Everything I say is optional. The only thing you *have* to do here in this space is breathe."

Relief flooded through me. The pressures of the stressful week lightened. For one hour, all I had to do was breathe. I could handle it.

"Take a deep breath in and fill your body with light," she said. "Now let it go. Share that light with everyone in the class. Take another deep breath and inhale a fresh start. It's never too late to start again. As long as you're breathing, you can start over."

Upbeat music filled the room, and Mallary's gentle voice led us through another round of breaths.

"I'm going to challenge you to stay grounded on your mat," Mallary said. "Ignore the distractions of what might be going on around you. Everyone come up to all fours and take a look around the room. Go ahead, you know you want to."

There were a few chuckles as everyone shifted.

"Check out your neighbor. Say hello. Get it out of your system because I'm going to ask you to forget them for the rest of class and focus inward."

I smiled at the woman next to me and then turned to my right. A familiar pair of warm brown eyes met mine.

"How you doin'?" Joey nodded his chin at me and winked.

My muscles clenched, and I nearly fell over in my tabletop pose. Joey couldn't be my neighbor! There was no way I would get through class beside him.

My gaze fell from his face to his naked torso, and I felt dizzy.

I'd spent the entire week avoiding Joey, and Lord take me now, I was inches away from his half-naked body.

"Now it's time to focus inward," Mallary said in her encouraging tone. "Keep your eyes on your own mat. Ignore the person beside you and their energy. Stay in your own lane."

Fat chance.

My entire body sizzled from Joey's nearness. My nipples could put an eye out, and my thoughts were deserted on Naughty Island.

"Close your eyes and concentrate on your inner drishti," Mallary said, but it wasn't helpful. Not even her soothing voice could take the edge off my fractured thoughts.

My inner drishti was preoccupied with Joey's lean torso glistening with sweat.

"Keep your eyes closed," Mallary said. "And on your next inhale, come into downward facing dog."

I snuck a peek at Joey and regretted it instantly. His eyes weren't closed. He was shamelessly checking me out, his eyes roaming over my body with undisguised appreciation.

My skin tingled, warming under his inspection. His gaze crashed into mine, and he winked.

"Follow your drishti," I hissed.

His smile turned wicked, and I didn't have to guess where his drishti led him.

"Turn to face the window wall," Mallary instructed.

The students rotated to face the wall of second-story windows overlooking Main Street below, but I was a distracted by the view of Joey's naked back.

His broad shoulders tapered to a narrow waist. Carolina Blue shorts hugged his hips and contrasted with his golden skin. The view of blooming cherry trees and glowing streetlights on Main Street couldn't compete with Joey's muscular back.

When we turned to the other wall, I had a moment's relief. It was much easier to focus on my drishti when Joey wasn't blocking my view.

I darted a glance at the clock on the wall by the door. Only fifty-five more minutes until the torture was over. I didn't think I could make it.

Joey seemed to be handling it like a champ. He flowed from one pose to the next with impressive grace. He radiated strength and vitality, somehow making the hardest poses look easy. It was the way he did everything, never frazzled. He flowed through life with a calm focus, as if nothing could derail him.

I tried watching my own hand like Mallary advised, but my eyes drifted to the eye candy next to me. His upper back rippled and bunched as he reached his arms in opposite directions. His damp hair clung to his neck.

It was time for another haircut. I might have to give him another reprimand. Dirty thoughts invaded my mind, and I imagined the ways I might punish him. The supply closet popped into my mind. A tingle of excitement rushed through me.

Then I remembered my son was in the room, and my worlds collided with a crash that sent me reeling.

Suddenly the heat, humidity, and Joey were too much to handle. I needed to escape. Tears clogged my throat. Breathing felt like trying to suck through a straw. Everything was crashing down on me, and I had to get out. Now.

Chapter 21

J OEY

It was impossible not to feel every move Gabriella made. In the tight space, I felt her as if she were under my skin.

When she left abruptly, I watched her pick her way toward the door in the mirror. She seemed upset, but maybe she just needed air. It was hot as hell in the studio. I tried to listen to the instructor and focus on the poses. I stared at my hand and watched it reach for the ceiling. Up and back. Up and back.

Fuck it.

I broke my pose and hurried out of the room, threading through a dozen yogis to get to the door. In the hall, I found Gabriella sitting on a long wooden bench with her head in her hands. Her back heaved as she sucked in air.

I slid onto the bench beside her. "You okay?"

She didn't lift her head, but her shoulders shook. I realized she was holding back tears. I moved quickly, wrapping my arms around her. I knew she was really far gone when she didn't resist but sank into me instead.

After a week of not touching her, I thought I would explode at the feel of her silky skin against mine.

The door to the locker room opened, and two women walked out. They hardly noticed us, but I knew I had to get Gabriella out of there, away from prying eyes.

I hustled her up from the bench and led her down the hall. There was a door I'd never noticed before. I grabbed the handle, and when it opened, I tugged her in with me.

The room was dimly lit by the faint blue light of a computer screen. It was someone's office—empty, thank God.

I locked the door just in case and pulled her into my arms. Her body shook as she sobbed silently. I held her and brushed her hair away from her face.

"What's the matter, baby?" I brushed away the tears on her cheeks.

"It's too much. I can't do it."

"It's just breathing."

She choked on a sob. "I can't. I'm falling apart."

I pulled her against my chest and rested my chin on top of her head. Her arms laced around my waist, and she leaned into me. Eventually, her breathing slowed, and her body relaxed. I stroked my hands along her back, fitting my palms against her slender waist.

She lifted her head, and our mouths met as if they had their own agenda. We kissed softly.

"Better?" I asked, rubbing my cheek against hers.

She melted into me a little more. Our lips found each other's again, and our tongues touched tentatively. Her hands laced around my neck, fingers tangling in my hair.

I'd missed this more than I thought possible. I pulled back, breaking the kiss that threatened to put a hole in my heart.

"It's okay," I said, trying to lighten the mood. "It's hot in there."

She shook her head. "I feel crazy."

"I know. Me too." I'd done nothing but obsess over her for a week. She hadn't been at recess. She never came to the break room anymore. I had been dying to see her, but our paths had stopped crossing. "I'm leaving tomorrow," I said. "I won't see you for ten days."

Her eyes found mine and held. "I want to come. I want to be with you."

I hooked my arm around her waist and backed her up against the desk. I forced myself not to pounce on her like a hungry lion. "You do?"

"Yes, Joey."

She said my name as if she wanted to devour me. A stray lock of hair fell from her ponytail, and it was all I could to do to keep from brushing it off her cheek.

I wanted to rip her clothes off and fuck her right on top of the desk, but it wouldn't be enough. I needed more than a quickie with Gabriella. I needed more than a stolen afternoon or a forbidden breakfast.

I dipped my head and kissed her, taking more than I should. She met my kiss with her own demands. I broke away, content to know I had her to myself for at least a few days.

"You missed me, didn't you?" I teased.

"Don't be *un gallo*." She grinned up at me, and her hand snuck to my package and stroked me through my shorts.

I grabbed her wrist with a growl. My swelling dick didn't need encouragement. "Don't start."

She stretched up on her tiptoes and kissed my cheek in an innocent gesture that felt sexy as hell. "Sorry."

"When will you come?" I asked, already eager to lie beside her on a deserted beach where no one would know us.

"Wednesday?"

I nodded. That would give me four days to visit with my family before I made everything about Gabriella. I grabbed her ponytail and tugged. "Let's get back to class before anyone notices we're gone."

She glanced at the front of my shorts, eying my hard-on as if it were a dangerous weapon. "You can do yoga like that?"

I grimaced. "I might have to skip eagle pose." I cracked open the door and peeked into the hall. The coast was clear. I nudged Gabriella out, then followed a moment later.

Chapter 22

GABI

I had a list of things to do before Wednesday, including underwear shopping. I jotted down the items I needed to take care of before flying out of the country. My passport was current from a missionary trip to Haiti with our church group, but my swimsuit collection was from five years ago. I was debating on whether to drive to Charlotte to do some shopping when Kennedy called.

"How was yoga?" she asked.

I pulled a brush through my tangled hair. "Hot."

She smothered a cough. "The studio wasn't the only thing that was hot," she said. "How's Joey?"

I dropped my brush. "How did you know Joey was there?"

She laughed. "You know what? My office has a security camera."

"What?" My cheeks flamed, and I paced into my bathroom.

She choked with laughter. "Yep. I get a notification if the motion detector goes off. Usually I lock my door, but I guess I didn't tonight. You're welcome."

My hand flew to my mouth. "I'm so sorry, Kennedy."

"Don't be. He looks like an excellent kisser. Please tell me he's a good kisser."

I grinned and sank to my bed. Joey was an amazing kisser. "He's the best."

"Knees weak?"

"Check."

"Panties wet?"

"I wasn't wearing any."

"God, I miss having a boyfriend. Maybe I should call Dustin back."

"Don't you dare," I said. Dustin was Kennedy's ex who'd cheated on her and then tried to make it seem like it was her fault.

"I might have to take my mom up on her bridge partner's nephew, but he's only five foot ten. It would never work."

"Five ten isn't short," I said. Kennedy was just under six feet tall, and some of the men she'd dated had a problem being shorter than her. "Maybe he has enough confidence not to be intimidated."

"He'll need it if he wants to go out with me."

Kennedy frequently wore outlandish outfits and dyed colorful streaks in her hair. Any man who dated her needed more than height. He needed a sense of humor and a hunger for adventure.

"What's next for you and Joey? Are you going to tell Shane you're seeing someone?"

"We aren't even seeing each other."

"That's not what the security cam footage showed." She laughed. "*He* is hot."

"I know." I was getting all hot and bothered just thinking about the way Joey kissed me, as if he had a secret map to my erogenous zones. "I'm going to Costa Rica with him," I said.

"What? When?"

"For spring break. He's going home for a week, and he asked me to come."

"When do you leave?"

"Wednesday." Tension coiled in my belly. "Maybe I shouldn't go."

"Of course you're going. Why wouldn't you go?"

"The garden needs planting, the shutters need painting, the light fixture in the hall needs to be raised, and my to-be-read stack is a mile long." I scowled at the stack of books on my nightstand. I hadn't been in the mood to read lately. Every hero between the pages made me think of Joey. "And what about our spa day? I shouldn't cancel on you guys."

Kennedy made a choking sound. "You can't be serious."

"And then there's Shane..."

"The excuses are stacking up, Gabi."

My temper flared. "Shane isn't an excuse. He's my son. What if he..."

Kennedy cut me off. "You've got about three more years to use your son as an excuse to avoid your intimacy issues."

"I'm not—"

"Do you want to borrow my leopard-print swimsuit?"

"Absolutely not."

"I'm bringing it over tomorrow, and I'm helping you pack. This is a thong-only trip. No mom panties allowed."

I cringed. "You heard about that, huh?"

"Everyone knows about your mom panties," she said.

Kennedy continued talking, listing reasons I should go to Costa Rica. I tuned her out while she blabbed on about a yoga retreat, surfing, and acai bowls. My mind drifted to Joey as she prattled on.

* * *

Four days later, I stepped onto the dirt airstrip in Nosara, Costa Rica, carrying a suitcase stuffed with sensible vacation outfits, a few outrageous swimsuits courtesy of Kennedy, and two paperbacks I hoped I wouldn't have time to read.

I should have been exhausted. My long day of travel had begun at the crack of dawn with a two-hour drive to Charlotte, followed by a six-hour flight to San José and a forty-minute flight on an eight-passenger plane to Nosara.

A colorful sign announced I had arrived at the surf-and-yoga capital of the Nicoya Peninsula, but there was nothing but dirt and weeds for eternity. The sun blazed overhead, baking everything in sight to a brown husk.

After the plane took off and the family of four who'd traveled with me from San José boarded a shuttle bus, I was alone on the abandoned strip of concrete.

Joey had warned me the Nosara Airport was hardly more than a drop zone, but I hadn't expected to be in the middle of nowhere. Other than a shed and a few bicycles propped against a chain-link fence, there was nothing to see but dirt, grass, and blue sky.

I dragged my suitcase to the only shady spot around and stopped when I heard a rumbling sound in the distance. A cloud of dust rose along the dirt road in front of a black truck. I almost squealed when I recognized Joey behind the wheel.

The truck stopped, and Joey hopped out, looking even more handsome than I remembered. How could that be when he'd been drop-dead gorgeous in Mossy Oak a few days ago? His smile was radiant as he strode across the field to greet me. Scooping me off my feet, he buried his face in my neck and kissed the sensitive spot below my ear.

I knocked the baseball cap off his head and threaded my fingers through his hair, holding him closer than I would have dared to at home.

"I hope you weren't waiting too long," he said. "The roads are bad from a big rain yesterday."

I silenced him with a kiss. The spicy-sweet taste of him filled my senses. I locked my legs around his hips and clung to him. The sun beat down on us, and a breeze lifted my skirt. I hadn't felt this free in years, and I wanted to drink in every moment.

Joey shifted his hands to carry more of my weight and walked me back to the truck. He pulled open the door and set me inside, then scooped me close again, settling himself between my legs.

"Did you miss me?" His hands slid under my dress to cup my hips.

"Yes." I braced my hands on his shoulders, feeling the flex of his muscles beneath the soft fabric of his shirt.

"What did you miss most?" He nibbled my bottom lip. "My mouth?" His tongue skimmed over my top lip. "My tongue?" He yanked me closer, and I felt the hot steel of his erection. "My cooking?"

A laugh burst from my tight chest. His accent was thicker since he'd been home a few days, and I loved it. He seemed even more exotic in Costa Rica than he had in Mossy Oak. I curled my fingers in his hair, which was definitely in need of a trim, and tugged his head back to look at him. It was his eyes. I'd missed his eyes the most. Those dazzling, smiling, enchanting eyes. So dark brown they reminded me of a warm cup of melted chocolate.

"I missed everything," I said.

The grin I'd missed so much beamed. "I have so much to show you, Gabriella," he said. "I have a full night planned for us." He dipped his head and kissed me firmly on the lips. "We should get going."

Chapter 23

JOEY

The rocky, dust-covered roads curved dangerously and were riddled with hidden potholes. I drove at a snail's pace, giving Gabriella plenty of time to comment on the scenery as we crawled by.

"Monkeys!" she cried, craning her neck to look out the window.

Monkeys were everywhere, filling the air with their chatter. The locals barely noticed them. They were as plentiful as squirrels in Mossy Oak.

I had to slow even more when we came upon the main part of town, where the roads had been carved from the overgrown vegetation.

Unlike many other beach towns, Nosara didn't have a main strip along the shore. A thick buffer of jungle separated the shops and restaurants from the beach.

At first glance, Nosara seemed wild and remote, but it was a true paradise. The town had been built into the thick jungle, and the roads were a tangled mess, barely wide enough for a single car.

The town had a laid-back vibe with funky shops, boutique

hotels, and cafés catering to vegans. Bikes and quads were more numerous than automobiles, and every other person carried a surfboard under their arm.

Visitors seeking a rustic beach town with surfing, fishing, and yoga found Nosara and didn't want to leave.

"Everyone looks so happy," Gabriella said.

"Life is much simpler here. It's slower paced, but you get used to it." I pointed out the window at a sloth lounging on a tree limb. "That guy isn't going anywhere for a while."

Gabriella dug out her phone and snapped a photo. "My niece Becca loves sloths."

Her brow furrowed as she swiped her finger across her phone and realized she didn't have cell service.

"Like I said, it takes getting used to." I laughed when she dropped her phone in her lap. "You can send it from the hotel. They will have Wi-Fi."

We turned onto the bumpy, pitted lane that led to Santiago's surf and yoga retreat.

"I feel bad for taking you away from your family," Gabriella said.

I grabbed her hand and squeezed. "Don't worry about it. I will be here all summer. My family will be sick of me."

When I'd told my family my plans to stay at Santiago's for a few days, they'd given me a pretty hard time. Rosa had piled on the guilt and Ava had given me the cold shoulder, but my parents seemed to understand. My mother was more curious than upset. She had made me promise to bring Gabriella to dinner.

We arrived at the hotel, which was barely visible from the road behind a canopy of trees. I parked the truck and hopped out to grab Gabriella's suitcase.

She climbed out of the truck and turned in a circle, taking in the views of the mountains and the ocean.

I gave her a minute to take more pictures, then led the way up the wide stairs to the lobby of the retreat. The hotel was rustic, with wooden-beamed ceilings, handcrafted furniture, and open terraces overlooking nature.

"Fernando! My brother. I thought you were going to be here an hour ago." Santiago came out from behind the front desk, grabbing two cocktails from a tray. "I was going to send out a search party. Thought you forgot how to get here."

"Santiago, this is Gabriella Salinger."

"*Pura vida*," he said, handing her a drink.

"Pure life?" Gabriella asked.

"Yes," I said, pleased she'd been keeping up her Spanish studies. "But it means a lot more than that in Costa Rica. It's the Tico way of life. No worries. No stress. No fuss."

Gabriella laughed. "In a nutshell: you."

I winked. "That's right."

Santiago's eyebrows raised, but he said nothing. The boy he'd known growing up had been just the opposite of laid-back and easy-going. I'd been driven and determined. I'd refused to settle for anything less than perfection. I wasn't that kid anymore after living in America for nearly a decade.

Ignoring Santiago, I took a sip of the ice-cold drink. "You must be starved," I said to Gabriella. "We can grab a snack at the bar or get changed and go into town for dinner."

Gabriella slid her arm around my waist and stretched up to whisper in my ear. "I'm starving."

The husky tone of her voice told me she wasn't talking about food. I brushed her lips with mine. Electricity sizzled between us. Our connection seemed to have grown since we'd been apart.

Her scent overwhelmed me. I hadn't even realized I'd missed it, but breathing her in made me want to scoop her up and carry her off to our bungalow for the rest of her stay.

I tightened my arm around her waist and kissed her again, tasting the mint and lime on her lips.

"Get a room," Santiago said and laughed at his own joke.

I lifted my head and looked at my friend. Santiago was laughing, but his brown eyes were full of bewilderment. He was my oldest friend, and he'd never seen me like this with a woman. I'd never brought anyone home before, and he hadn't known me to have a girlfriend since Maria. I was sure he was dying to know our story. He would be peppering me with questions at the first opportunity.

I grabbed her luggage and led the way out of the lobby. "Come see the pool first, then I'll show you the room. Bye, Santiago."

"Bye, Fernando," he said, then added in Spanish, "She's too classy for you, you know?"

"I know," I said in Spanish.

"What do you know?" Gabriella asked.

I winked at her. "He said you were too good for me."

She took a sip of her drink. "He doesn't know you very well then."

I laughed softly, pleased that she would pretend it wasn't true. "Maybe not so much as he used to," I said.

We stopped at the pool, but Gabriella wasn't interested in the fantastic view. She put her drink down on a table. "Does everyone call you Fernando here?"

I nodded. "Joey is my American name."

Her eyes searched mine. "Why?"

"Joey is easier. And everyone knows *Friends.*"

"Don't you want people to call you your real name?"

I finished my drink and placed my glass next to hers. "It doesn't matter," I said with an easy shrug. "I'm the same person either way."

She reached for my hand. "You're the only one who calls me Gabriella. Did you know that?"

I shook my head. Everyone at work called her Mrs. Salinger to her face and the Iron Lady behind her back.

"Even my parents call me Gabi. But when you call me Gabriella, it..." She trailed off and stared out at the view without finishing.

"It what?" I pulled her closer.

She dragged her gaze away from the ocean and met my eyes. "It makes me feel like a woman."

A spark of desire surged between us. I cupped her cheek and pulled her close for a kiss.

Knowing I was the only one who used her given name made me feel like I had a key to her that no one else knew existed. I felt suddenly possessive of her. It wasn't enough to make her feel like a woman. I needed to make her feel like she was mine.

Chapter 24

G ABI

Joey slid his arm around my waist and pulled me snug against his chest. His hard body braced mine, and the heat... the unbearable heat. I leaned into him, letting my head fall back against his chest. It felt so good to touch him out in the open in broad daylight. I didn't have to worry about being seen with him. Everyone I knew was a thousand miles away.

"Do you want to swim?" His voice rippled over my skin like moonlight. In his delicious accent, every word he said sounded like a naughty promise.

"Yes." I wanted to swim in this refreshing pool while looking out over the canopy of trees and dazzling blue ocean. I kissed his jaw, running my lips along the soft scruff of his beard. "Later," I said, unable to contain a tiny grin.

Joey grinned back, and his arm tightened around my waist. His lips grazed mine, soft and teasing. "A lot later," he said against my lips. "You ready to see our place?"

I didn't think I'd ever wanted a man more than I wanted Joey. A stab of guilt pierced my heart, and I silently apologized to Montel, the man who'd been on a pedestal in my mind longer than he'd been my partner in marriage. Had I wanted Montel like this? It suddenly seemed like a million years ago when I'd given my heart to my husband. Joey was present, and he was right where I wanted him. Well, not quite. I wanted him in the privacy of our room, where his magic tongue would make me come again and again.

We left the pool, and Joey led me to the bungalow we'd be sharing for the next few days. We followed a path of stones through a secluded garden away from the rest of the hotel until we reached a private bungalow tucked into a canopy of trees.

Joey stopped in front of its tall wooden door. "Santiago always gives me the best room." He pushed open the door, revealing a rustic room with red clay tile and wooden-beamed ceilings. Four sets of double doors opened to a private terrace overlooking the tropical plants and a white sand beach. The jungle outside vibrated into the room, filling the space with the chatter of birds, the rustle of palm fronds, and the smells of rich earth and salty sea.

A brightly colored quilt covered the enormous bed, and paintings in jewel-toned hues adorned the walls. A leaf-blade fan pushed a sea breeze through the room that stirred the hem of my skirt.

I crossed the room and stepped onto the terrace. A beam of golden sun cast shadows over a swaying hammock big enough for two. Hidden behind a stone wall was an outdoor shower with wrought iron fixtures.

I swept my gaze across the view of waves lapping the shoreline, taking in the peaceful view. I'd heard Costa Rica was one of the happiest countries in the world, and it seemed true. The laid-back atmosphere, beautiful scenery, and perfect weather fostered a serenity that could not be replicated.

The bungalow was gorgeous, but the man was the reason I was smiling. He'd been worth every minute of the hard, long day of travel.

He was so handsome. His skin shone like bronze, and the tousled waves of his mahogany hair gleamed with honey highlights. The top three buttons of his linen shirt were undone, revealing the strong, tanned column of his throat and a leather necklace. Several days' worth of dark stubble defined his square jaw, and his brown eyes tilted upward in the corners because he was smiling.

Joey was always smiling. Tiny smirks, full-blown grins, sultry half-smiles. I was smitten by all his smiles.

I stepped toward him even as he was stepping toward me. We met at the edge of the bed.

"Did you see the shower?" he asked, reaching for me.

Goosebumps pebbled along my skin at his touch. "I did."

He worked the top button of my dress free and spread the fabric open, then dipped his head to kiss my collarbone. His lips were cool against my skin. I shivered despite the heavy humidity.

He took his time undoing each button on the bodice of my sundress. When he reached for the tie around my waist, he paused and spread his hand over my ribs.

"Have I told you look beautiful?" he asked.

My chest ached when he looked at me with such tenderness. "No," I answered finally. "Not today."

His lips curved. "That's embarrassing." He slid his thumb into the knot at my waist. "You are the most beautiful woman I've ever seen. These dresses you wear drive me crazy." His fingers worried at the knot, tugging it loose to hang at my sides. "You walk down the halls at school in your buttoned-up dresses, looking so perfect all the time."

I laughed, remembering my embarrassing panty reveal. "Not so perfect all the time."

Joey winked. "That was one of the best days of the year."

I looped my hands around his neck and gave in to the temptation to touch his hair. I loved touching his hair, and I wouldn't have to stop myself from sliding my fingers through it, not once, for the next three days. "Not for me, it wasn't."

He pushed my dress off my shoulders and cupped my breast over the lace of my bra. My nipple responded immediately, puckering against the thin fabric. He squeezed, and I inhaled sharply. My head fell back when he pinched my nipple.

"I loved seeing your gorgeous body under that dress so much I almost didn't say anything."

"Joey!"

He laughed and rubbed the pad of his thumb across my aching nipple. "But I didn't want Mike Collins seeing your cute little ass in those hot panties again, so I told you."

"Mr. Collins doesn't look at me like that." I sucked in another breath as he pushed my dress down over my hips. It pooled around my bare feet.

"Every man looks at you like that, baby. Especially me." He took a step back and let his gaze drop over me in a slow, appreciative sweep.

Kennedy had insisted I refresh my underwear collection, so I was wearing a new set in blush pink. I felt exposed in the skimpy bra and panties. My hand fluttered to my stomach, automatically covering the scar that wasn't even visible under the pink lace.

"No." Joey pushed my hand away, trapping my wrist with his long fingers. "Don't cover yourself." He let his eyes drop over me, his fiery eyes searing every inch of my flesh. "Beautiful."

I reached for his shirt. "Why are you still dressed?"

His lips curved. "You want me naked?" He pushed my hand away, then pulled his shirt off in one swift move. Buttons be damned. His shorts were next. He kicked them off, and, *oh snap*, he wasn't wearing any underwear. His cock sprang at full attention, already glistening at the tip.

He closed his fist around the base and pumped slowly. "This what you want?" he asked, licking his full lower lip.

I nodded again because words were beyond my grasp. My breasts felt full and achy. I rubbed my thighs together, trying to ease the throb between my legs.

He curled his hand around my braid and tugged it back, so my eyes came up toward his.

"Next time, I want you to ask for what you want." He winked at me. "'Screw me senseless,'" he said with a little chuckle.

Frustration coiled in my belly. He would never let that one go. "Why aren't you kissing me?" I demanded.

"My baby wants to be kissed?"

I flattened a hand to his chest, feeling the flex of his supple muscles under my fingers. He gave my braid another solid tug, and I looked into his eyes. Son of a mother ducker! There was so much to admire about Joey. His chest, his abs, his mouth, his eyes... those smoky eyes that never shied away from anything.

"Kiss me, Joey."

As soon as the words were out of my mouth, his lips sealed onto mine.

Chapter 25

JOEY

Her mouth was hot and wet, open for my assault. We were kissing with an urgency that was completely unnecessary. We had three days of nothing ahead of us. We didn't even have to leave this room if we didn't want to. We could kiss languidly through the heat of midday, straight into the cool evenings if we chose. But we weren't. We were devouring each other. Drowning in each other.

I loved every minute.

Gabriella was a greedy kisser. She kissed with her lips and teeth and tongue. Her fingers tangled in my hair, her hips ground against me, and her legs locked around my thighs. I kissed her harder, pressing, groping, tugging, and she practically climbed me.

"We can slow down," I said between hard, open-mouthed kisses.

"Yes," she said, gasping when I bent my head to claim her breast, shoving aside the pretty lace bra.

"We don't have to rush." I unclasped her bra, so her breasts spilled out.

"Yes." She arched into my hand. Her breathing was so ragged she could hardly get the word out.

I cupped her glorious breasts, filling my hands with their soft weight. She was perfect. Her breasts were just the right size, exactly what I wanted. I sucked her nipples until they were slick little buds against my tongue, then I got to my knees and kissed a path along her soft belly to the cleft between her legs. I kept my touch light, a teasing coax, reveling in the fact that this wasn't our first time and I knew what she liked. Although, I still didn't know all her secrets. An eager student, I wanted her to teach me everything.

"Que linda," I said, directing my words to the pink petals of her pussy hidden beneath the nest of her soft curls.

Her thigh quivered against my cheek as I nestled closer to the heaven between her legs. I pressed soft kisses to her inner thigh, and she relaxed inch by inch as I licked, nipped, and nudged my mouth closer to what I wanted. What we both needed.

"That's it, baby," I murmured, dragging my tongue through her slick, wet heat.

She trembled and cried out. I pushed my tongue past her succulent folds, tasting the honey cream of her arousal. I sucked her clit between my teeth. The tight bud swelled against my tongue, and I sucked harder, until she writhed against me, her fingers fisting painfully in my hair. I flicked my tongue over her just the way she liked it, and she cried out, coming for me almost immediately. She spasmed against my mouth as I continued licking and sucking every drop from her orgasm. I hadn't wanted her to come so fast. I wished to make every moment of these next few days last forever, but I reminded myself not to worry.

I could make her come again, and I would.

When I let go of my hold on her hips, she sank onto the mattress. I pushed her down and crawled up her body, lavishing her satin skin with kisses. My cock was a hot, hard brand between us. She slid her hand down my stomach and wrapped her cool fingers around my dick.

I hissed, holding back the urge to ram myself into her fist like a horny teenager. One careful breath later, and I had myself under control. I reminded myself we could stay like this all night, touching and kissing, making love without a care in the world.

She pumped me harder, stroking me with her tight little fist, squeezing me at the tip and then sliding down my shaft in a quick motion that made my balls tighten.

"I want you in my mouth."

I grinned, not too far gone with lust even as my dick swelled to tease my sweet girl. "You want my *what* in your mouth?" I asked, cocking my head at her.

She licked her lips, and my dick pulsed in her hand. A knowing look came into her eyes. It turned me on more than anything to see her realize her power. She was too sexy not to know it.

"I want this in my mouth." She slid her hand down my shaft, using a bead of pre-cum as lubrication.

"Better," I said, holding back a groan when her hand moved in long, lazy strokes, sliding up and down. "But not good enough."

I kissed her collarbone, scraping my beard against her soft skin. When I thought about her lush lips wrapped around my impossibly hard cock, fire streaked through me. But I needed to hear her words. Needed to know exactly what she wanted. Why? I had no idea. Maybe it was a sick fantasy of hearing my boss tell me to do dirty things. I was a motherfucker for thinking that way, but I couldn't help it. My mind got caught up in my own teacher fantasy. I remembered Caroline sucking me off that night at school, and I wished it had been Gabriella on her knees under my desk.

"Say it," I said, my words like sandpaper against my raw throat. "Say you want my cock in your mouth, and I'll give it to you." I nipped her throat, just a little bite that wasn't quite hard enough to leave a mark. She smelled good enough to eat, and she tasted even better. I rocked my hips, pushing into her hand. "Say it? Please?"

She blinked up at me, her eyes so dark with lust they were nearly black. "Joey, please."

Although her tight, little hand on my cock was making it hard to think straight, I formed words. "Please what, baby?"

"Your. Cock. In. My. Mouth." She tugged on me wickedly. "Now."

I couldn't deny her when she asked like that. I grabbed her under the arms and positioned her higher on the bed, so her shoulders were propped up by the pillows. I straddled her hips, trapping her body under mine. She was small and delicate against the colorful quilt, her hair mussed from its tidy braid and falling over her shoulder. A quick flash of something fierce struck me, tightening my chest and clenching my throat without warning. Her sweet vulnerability made me want to do dirty things to her, but it also made me want to fold her in my arms and keep her safe from everything evil in the world. I vowed to protect her from the hurt and anger and disappointment that inevitably came with love. If only I could. Love. Was that what this was?

Her eyes met mine and held. Something nameless passed between us. It felt familiar and impossibly new at the same time—scary, but also exhilarating, like standing on the edge of a cliff ready to take a leap. My heart pounded so hard in my chest, I felt like I was sprinting against Olympians.

A dewy flush stole over her cheeks and spread to her chest. She was breathing hard, her chest rising and falling. She gripped my hips and slid down the bed, and then she was kissing me the way I'd kissed her. Soft lips against my thighs. The flick of her tongue along the underside of my cock. Her lips parted, and even though she'd been eager to do this, practically begging, she hesitated before taking me into her mouth.

I stroked her cheek, so soft in the tropical heat, and pressed my thumb against her bottom lip. Sparks of gold glinted in her brown eyes, and her lip trembled against my thumb.

I fought the need to shove into her tender mouth and feel the tight, wet heat against my aching cock. Slower. We needed to go slower. "You don't have to," I said, stroking my thumb along the plump pout of her lip.

"You don't want me to?"

I laughed. I actually laughed, and the sudden movement made

my dick jerk, making it ache even more. "Of course I want you to." I kept my voice low and even. I didn't want to scare her off. If she knew how badly I wanted this, how much I ached for her, she might shut down again and push me away.

She sucked my thumb into her warm, wet mouth. Oh, God. I wanted my cock in her mouth so badly, I was practically vibrating with need. Every vein, every ridge, every inch of my swollen flesh wanted to feel that wet heat, but I held back. It took every ounce of restraint in my body not to pop my thumb out of her mouth and replace it with my cock, to plunge past those lush lips and surge straight to the back of her throat. I held back, groaning with the effort.

She slipped my thumb out of her mouth. "I haven't done this in a really long time. What if..."

She was worried I wouldn't like it. I hoped she wasn't thinking about what she'd seen in my office. I regretted that incident more than ever.

Feeling guilty, I pulled back. She gripped my hips, holding me in place.

"What if I don't remember how?" she asked.

Desire shuddered through me. I wasn't proud of my caveman feelings, but I was glad it had been a while for Gabriella. I liked that she hadn't given her mouth to another man in long enough to forget. I needed to be inside her mouth like I needed air to breathe, but I kept it light, grinning down at her. "It's like riding a bicycle," I said.

She laughed and then sucked me into her mouth. It felt so good, I almost came in two seconds. Her mouth was hot silk and molten lava. I somehow managed not to lose it like a goddamn teenager in the backseat of his parents' car.

My hips jerked, and I thrust hard. Her eyes flashed up to mine, watering with the effort of taking all of me into her mouth. Shit. I was evil because seeing her like that with half my cock already choking her made me want to shove hard and bury myself in the back of her throat. I pulled back instead, exercising monk-like restraint as she protested with a squeak.

With lightning speed, I tore open a condom, rolled it on, and took her in one long thrust. She cried out and locked her arms around my neck, holding me close as her walls pulsed and throbbed around me. When she rolled her hips against mine, grinding in an attempt to get even closer, I pulled back and stroked into her again. I hit the spot that made her crazy, and she squirmed, either trying to get more or trying to get away from the assault of my hard cock. I didn't know for sure until she started moving her hips.

I forgot the English language. Words spilled out in my native tongue. Words she couldn't understand. Words that may not have even been Spanish. I was talking nonsense. *Hablar papaya. Que chiva. Dicha. Tuanis. Te quiero. Amor.*

She spoke back in her own broken language, words my brain couldn't translate when all I had room for in my brain was the last coherent thought of making her climax before I gave in to the intense pleasure that threatened to end me. The gallant angel who sat on my shoulder won out over the devil prince who wanted to rip her apart, and I found a tempo that gave her what she needed.

Her orgasm rolled through her without warning and she spasmed around me, making it impossible for me to hold out one second longer. I thrust one last time as she broke underneath me. I found her mouth with mine and latched on, kissing her hard as I pumped into her, taking my own pleasure and losing my heart.

Chapter 26

GABI

When we were both so spent we could hardly move, Joey stayed on top of me, inside me, while we caught our breath. I traced his spine with a fingertip. He quivered under my touch, and another fluttery orgasm rippled through me like an aftershock.

His body pinned me to the bed, and I thought maybe, just maybe, I could stay this way forever, or at least another three days.

Guilt pricked the bubble of my happiness at the thought of returning home.

Home had everything I loved—my family, my job, my friends, and my house that I'd worked so hard to make my own—but there was no place I'd rather be than trapped under the cage of Joey's body.

The man was seriously talented in the bedroom. Although I'd just discovered orgasms, I thought I might be addicted to them. And to Joey.

I wasn't prepared for all the feelings that came up with mind-blowing sex. Joey must have been under a spell, too. He'd dropped the L-word in the heat of the moment, but it had been in Spanish, so it didn't count. Confessions of love during sex definitely didn't count.

"I'm crushing you," he said, shifting to roll onto his back.

I missed him already. He seemed to feel the same because his hand sought mine and latched on. He brought my fingers to his lips and kissed each knuckle. His beard was soft against my skin. He pressed a kiss to my palm, making me tingle with pleasure.

"You must be starving," he said, rolling to face me.

My stomach chimed in, rumbling loudly.

Joey rolled off the bed. "Get dressed," he said, pulling on his shorts. "I have a place to show you that will blow your mind."

I couldn't move. My legs felt heavy, and my eyelids drifted shut. I wanted to bask in the heat of Costa Rica and Joey's attention for a little longer.

Joey snagged my ankle and tugged me to the edge of the bed. "As much as I enjoy looking at you like that, clothing is not optional where we are going."

I raised up on my elbow and watched him get dressed. With little effort, he looked camera ready. His tousled hair and casual shirt were perfect for the relaxed atmosphere of Costa Rica. He looked good enough to eat.

Me? I was a hot, humid mess.

"I might need a shower," I said.

Joey scooped me up and set me on my feet. "Later," he promised, nibbling my jaw. "We will take a very long shower after the sun goes down."

I wrinkled my nose. "I smell like sex."

"Hm." He nuzzled my neck. "You smell delicious."

I trembled, looping my arms around his neck. My appetite had nothing on my newly awakened sex drive. "I'm not that hungry," I said. "Couldn't we just order in?"

"Nope," he said. "They only do breakfast here. We have to go out for dinner. You'll be glad we did." He kissed me. "I promise, you're going to love it."

There was that L-word again. It had been popping up like crazy.

My exhausted, sex-addled brain kept getting hung up on it. I reminded myself this was sex and nothing more.

"Are you sure I shouldn't tidy up a little?"

Joey swatted my butt. "Get dressed, baby."

We took a tuk-tuk, a yellow golf cart taxi, to the next beach town over. Even though Mossy Oak was hardly a bustling metropolis, it was like NYC compared to the sleepy beach town of Nosara. As darkness settled over the tangle of dirt roads winding through lush jungle, I wondered how the town survived. Howler monkeys and tropical birds were more plentiful than people. As we bumped along the road, the driver conversed with Joey in a friendly tone of Spanish dialect I had no hopes of translating.

Joey laughed and stretched his arm over my shoulders along the back seat. "He thinks we are newlyweds," he said, fiddling with the strap of my dress.

My heart pounded fast. The thought of being married to anyone, especially a known playboy like Joey, shouldn't get my pulse racing as if I'd been running a sprint, but it did.

Joey shifted to face me and put his hand on my knee. "If you were my new wife, I wouldn't let you out of our room for at least a week." His touch was feather-light, inching up my thigh. "I would keep you so satisfied you wouldn't want to move from the bed." The hot pads of his fingers scorched a path under the hem of my dress, and his mouth moved closer to my ear. "I would feast on your body." He parted my thighs, tracing the lace edge of my panties. "I would start right here, and I wouldn't stop until you begged." His thumb flicked my clit through my panties, and a moan escaped my clenched jaw. "'Screw me brainless, Joey,'" he teased, nibbling my ear.

I felt the smile on his lips as he trailed kisses along the sensitive shell of my ear. "I'm never going to live that down," I said, too far gone with what his hand was doing under my skirt to be annoyed.

His low laugh sounded in my ear. "I love it when you beg me," he said.

The tuk-tuk slowed to a crawl, and a group of pedestrians

crossed the street in front of us. We'd reached what must be the center of town. A small concentration of shops and restaurants lined both sides of the street.

My panties were soaked. I shifted my hips up and wiggled out of them as discreetly as possible.

"You ruined my panties."

"Next time don't wear any." He grabbed my panties and pushed them into his pocket.

The taxi turned down a narrow street and stopped in what looked like the middle of nowhere. Joey paid the driver, who said something in Spanish that made Joey chuckle heartily.

"What did he say?" I asked as the taxi pulled away.

Joey took my hand and led me along a stone path lit by tiki torches. "He told me the secret to keeping a woman happy."

My heart thundered in my chest, and my mind tripped down a forbidden path of what it might be like to share a life with this beautiful man. Waking up to the feel of his scruffy beard on my cheek, falling asleep in his arms, laughing at his jokes, and shattering to pieces under his talented tongue... The tightness in my chest made me ache for a something I hadn't wanted in a very long time.

"Are you going to share it?" I asked, keeping my voice light as if this were a game and not my heart on the line.

"Maybe," Joey said with a wink. He stopped and pulled me into his arms. "Have I told you how beautiful you look tonight?"

My head was spinning so fast, I couldn't think straight. This man was hitting all my buttons, making me long for things I couldn't want, making me crave a life that wasn't for me. "No." The word ripped from my throat, too raw to be the answer to his simple question.

"You are always so beautiful."

I knew he was a world class charmer, but God help me, when he said things like that and looked at me with those melted-chocolate eyes, I felt like the most loved woman in history.

There was that word again! The one that started with L and

ended with heartbreak. I blinked up at him, snapping a lid on the fantasy in my mind before it took root and blossomed.

"Thank you," I said when I found the courage to push words past the lump in my throat.

He kissed me. Soft and sweet. The touch of his lips on mine erased everything but him. It was way too easy to get lost in this man. Lost in his taste, his smell, and his touch, I became the purest version of myself. A woman only. Not a mother, sister, friend, daughter, or leader.

My needs boiled down to one thing: him. Joey was everything.

His tongue swept into my mouth. I swear, no one needed to tell Joey the secret to keeping a woman happy. He'd been born knowing it.

He rubbed his thumb across my lips, and a wave of desire pulsed between us, so palpable it hummed in the humid air. No wonder the tuk-tuk driver had thought we were newlyweds. We were acting like a couple in love. I suddenly wanted to be that couple in love, to live in a fantasy world, to feel what it was like to be half of another person's whole, even if it was for just three days.

A strange lightness radiated through me, bouncing around inside my chest and bursting through all my carefully constructed walls. I might have a whopping happiness hangover when I got back to Mossy Oak, but it seemed like a small price to pay.

"You are the most beautiful man I've ever seen." I swallowed roughly. "I hope you don't mind being called beautiful." I back-tracked, feeling as if my insides were showing, bleeding out. "You're really handsome." I was fumbling, not nearly as charming as Joey. "From the first time I saw you, I couldn't take my eyes off you."

Joey laughed, and I exhaled quickly, letting my tension go. Hearing his laugh filled me with satisfaction.

"Hot for teacher?"

"A little."

He bent to kiss me again and ended it way too soon to wrap his arm around my waist and lead me along the stone path to an open-air, beach-front restaurant with lights strung through the trees.

My jaw dropped as I swept my gaze around the tables nestled under a grove of trees. The sounds of laughter and soft jazz music filled the air. "It's magical," I said, unable to come up with a better word.

"Wait until you taste the food."

The food was fresh from the sea. The menu was delivered from the server's mouth in a rolling lilt of Spanish I didn't have a prayer of understanding, but thankfully, Joey ordered for both of us.

The food came out on small plates, one dish at a time, and we devoured everything. The food was excellent and the ambiance divine, but the conversation stole the show. It was the kind of soul-searching adult conversation I craved. We talked about everything from childhood memories to favorite colors to our most embarrassing moments.

For dessert, we ordered passion fruit gelato and talked about love. It may have been the starry sky overhead, or the bottle of wine we shared, or the cool press of Joey's lips on mine after a bite of ice cream, but my tongue loosened, and I confessed things I never thought I would.

"I love how love makes you feel invincible," I said.

Joey spooned a bite of gelato into his mouth and cocked his head at me. "I love how it makes you feel vulnerable." His eyes softened, peering at something in the distance. "That raw feeling in your gut... like you're being ripped apart."

My belly twisted. I knew the feeling all too well. "Like you're getting ready to jump off a cliff," I said, shivering a little when a salty breeze blew in from the ocean.

Joey slipped his arm around my shoulder. "And trusting someone will be there to catch your fall."

Our eyes met and held. Tension sizzled between us. My heart squeezed, feeling too big for my chest. I couldn't look away from him, but if I didn't, I might fall right off that cliff. I'd had plenty of love in my life, but romantic love was different. I hadn't felt it in years. The rush of love I felt for Joey couldn't be real. I'd thought I'd had my shot at true love and I wouldn't get another, but maybe I'd been wrong.

Joey cupped my shoulder, his fingers like hot little pads branding my bare skin. "Tell me about him," he said.

I didn't pretend to not know he was talking about Montel. "We fell hard," I said. "I was so young that I didn't think any of the bad stuff could happen to me."

"You don't mean Shane."

I stiffened. "Of course not. We were surprised, but so in love that it seemed like everything would be okay. I wanted to marry him with my whole heart, not just because I was pregnant." Remembering those early days with Montel was bittersweet, as always. We'd had so little time together. "Montel was amazing. Funny, and smart, and good at every sport—even bowling. Other guys tried to hate him, but it was impossible."

"Sounds like Shane took after his dad," Joey said.

I nodded, emotion clogging my throat.

"He's an amazing kid," Joey said. "I'm so impressed you raised him all by yourself."

"I didn't," I said. "My parents were there for me every step of the way. And Thatcher is like an uncle to him."

Joey arched an eyebrow. "I really need to meet this Thatcher guy you keep talking about."

My heart hammered in my chest. Was Joey jealous? I wanted to laugh. After all his shenanigans, he was jealous of Thatcher. "He's a good friend." I locked eyes with him. "That's all."

Joey captured my hand and lifted it to his mouth. "I'm sorry you lost the man you loved." He brushed his lips against my knuckles, his eyes never leaving mine. "But you know you can love like that again."

I dropped my gaze to the white tablecloth, feeling overwhelmed.

Joey tipped up my chin with two fingers. "You have too much love to give," he said.

I blinked back tears. The conversation had taken a detour I wasn't ready to explore. Joey sensed my discomfort and didn't push me. Instead, he signaled the server and asked for the check and a taxi.

"Are you ready for that swim?" he asked, steering the conversation into more comfortable territory. "The pool will be so much better at night."

Chapter 27

JOEY

The next morning, I woke Gabriella early. There was no time to sleep in when we only had two more days together. Part of me wanted to keep her in the room for the next forty-eight hours, but the other—more clear-headed—part won, and so we ventured out to my favorite beach for surfing.

We didn't have surfboards, but it was fun just to watch everyone else ride the waves. People came from all over the world to surf at the remote beaches of the Nicoya Peninsula.

Gabriella wore a leopard-print swimsuit, which was conservative from the front and scandalous from the back. The swimsuit made me think I'd made the wrong choice. I should have kept her in the room where I didn't have to keep my hands off her.

After a few hours of watching the surfers and lying around on the beach, we rented quads. We zoomed along the meandering dirt roads of the town, getting lost, and then ended up right back where we started without a care in the world.

We went to lunch at an outdoor spot on the beach and ate a

traditional meal of rice and beans with chips and fresh avocado slices.

Dozens of patrons sat at tables under the thin cover of a grove of trees, sipping Imperials to ward off the heat of midday. The air was hot and heavy with barely a breeze rolling in from the Pacific Ocean, and there wasn't a cloud in the sky.

"It's going to rain." I signaled for the check. "We should get out of here."

Gabriella tilted her head back to the sky. "Why do you say that? The sky is clear as glass."

This time of year, rain wasn't as frequent as it was during the summer and fall, but it could still pour at a moment's notice. Locals knew to wear clothes they didn't mind getting wet, and I knew in my bones when it was going to rain.

I pretended to study the sky as if I were preparing a lecture, then I shrugged and said, "It's Costa Rica. It rains."

Gabriella laughed and leaned back in her chair with a contented smile. Her skin glowed with a tan after only a day on the beach, and she looked like a local in her breezy sundress thrown over her swim-suit. "It's much too beautiful to rain." Her bottom lip pushed out in a stubborn pout. "I won't allow it."

I stretched my arm along the back of her chair. Even if we started our meal sitting across from each other, we ended up like this, sitting side by side, like honeymooners, sneaking kisses and caresses in between bites.

She looked like a different woman here on the beach. There was no belt at her waist, no buttons up her neck, and no pins in her hair.

"I like seeing you like this." I toyed with a lock of her hair, twirling it and watching it slide through my fingers.

Doubt flashed in her eyes. "I'm a mess. My hair is salty, and I have sand in places that definitely shouldn't have sand."

A grin curled my lip. "I like those places."

She smacked me on the chest, her hand lingering a little as she felt me up. She did that a lot—let her hand linger a moment too long whenever she touched me.

"Let's get out of here before it rains." My voice was gruff as I pushed back from the table.

"It's not going to rain," she insisted.

I bent and whispered in her ear, "Maybe I just want to be alone with you."

She hopped up from the table, grabbing her bag. "You should have just said so."

We headed down the beach toward our hotel. The day was half over, and I tried not to dwell on how little time we had left together in our bubble of paradise.

My free hand drifted to my chest, where I rubbed absently at my heart. The ink on my skin was there to remind me that love wasn't all fun and games. Usually the tattoo did its job, but it wasn't working. Maybe it was already too late. Maybe I'd stepped over the *falling* line straight into *madly*. Straight off the cliff. I stopped walking and tugged her hand until she stopped.

"What is it?" she asked.

I steeled myself and leaped. "I don't know how to say this..."

"What?"

"I really like seeing you." I plummeted, free-falling through the air with no net in sight.

"I like seeing you, too." Her words sounded raw, ripped from her throat.

I dipped my chin. "I like seeing you walk down the halls like you run the place."

She frowned. "I *do* run the place."

"Right." I grinned, thinking of Gabriella striding down the halls of PES. She was so hot when she was doing her job. "My point is I look forward to seeing you, whether it's hiding in the bushes at the park or struggling in a yoga class or waking up with crazy bed-head."

She touched a hand to her hair, which hung halfway down her back in a silky dark curtain. The heavy humidity had given it extra body, and it looked perfect.

I reached up and grabbed her hand from her hair so that I held both her hands prisoner. They felt tiny in mine. Such small hands, but so capable. It felt wonderful to touch her like this, out in the open. Or in a restaurant full of people. I wanted to do this at home. I wanted her to want the same.

I pinned her eyes with mine. "Do you understand what I'm saying?"

Her brow furrowed again, and I realized I wasn't making myself clear. Or maybe Gabriella was being thick-skulled on purpose.

I loved her, for fuck's sake. Did I have to spell it out?

I grabbed her face and planted my lips on hers. Her lips were stiff at first, still trying to figure out what the hell I was trying to say, but then they relented. We combusted like a match rubbed against a coarse surface. My hands shifted to cup her face as I poured every aching emotion into the kiss.

She kissed me back, grabbing my shoulders as her tongue met mine stroke for stroke.

Her mouth tasted like heaven, hot and salty and so sweet. I wanted to stay in this moment forever, kissing and touching as if we were the only two people in the world.

Without warning, the rain started. It fell in fat drops, dousing everyone on the beach as they scrambled for cover.

Rain soaked our hair and clothes and dripped down our faces, but we didn't stop kissing. We couldn't stop. We kissed until we couldn't breathe, until we were gasping and soaked through.

And still, I couldn't convey enough of what I wanted to say in one desperate kiss. I couldn't show her how much I wanted *more*. More than the accidental run-ins in the hall. More than the stolen kisses in an office. More than waking up next to her every once in a while.

The rain plastered us together, dripping into our mouths as we kissed desperately. I could never get enough of her. I didn't care if I couldn't breathe. Being kissed to death by Gabriella Salinger in the rain would be a good way to go.

We finally broke apart on a gasp and made a run for a nearby grove of trees. Ducking under the low branches of an almond tree, we cowered for cover.

"We could make a run for it back to the hotel," I said. It was a bit of a safe harbor under the trees, but not entirely dry. "Or we could just wait it out here."

"You were right." She laughed, peering through the branches at the heavy downpour that obscured the beach.

"I'm right about a lot of things." I smoothed her hair away from her face where it was stuck.

She reached up and caught my hand. A current sizzled between us.

"I think we should wait out the rain right here," she said, curling her hand around my neck.

She pulled my face down to hers and kissed me so hard I stumbled back into the tree. Her arms locked around my neck, and she ground against me.

I choked back a half laugh, half groan as our wet bodies slid together. "I guess I don't have to ask what you have in mind to kill time."

I scooped her up and knelt under the trees. We stretched out on the sand, my body covering hers. The rain pounded around us, providing only a thin veil of privacy, but we were both too far gone to care. Gabriella pushed my shoulder, rolling me onto my back. She yanked her dress up to her waist and straddled me. Her hair hung in a wet curtain around us as she reached down and fumbled with my shorts.

"Wait." I shook my head with regret. "I don't have a condom."

She freed my hard cock from my shorts. "I don't care."

I shifted under her, still hesitant. It wasn't like Gabriella to throw caution to the wind.

Her mouth came back to mine. "It's okay, Joey." She met my eyes, and what I saw in her gaze took my breath away. "Trust me?"

I hadn't trusted anyone in years, not since I'd had my heart broken. But I didn't hesitate with Gabriella. "Yes."

In one swift move, she shoved aside her swimsuit and sank onto me, taking what she wanted.

A hiss escaped my mouth as she rolled her hips, grinding against me. My hands went to her hips, and my fingers dug into her soft flesh so hard they left marks. A spark of lust in my chest exploded, consuming me.

I groaned when she picked up the pace, riding me fast and hard. She leaned down and took my mouth in a frenzied kiss. Our mouths battled like greedy flames licking up the air.

She sprawled over me, clutching my shoulders as she changed the angle. If she kept it up, I wouldn't last long, which was fine, considering we were in a bit of a crunch for time. As long as the rain held, we were hidden, but the weather could shift faster than a champion runner shooting off the blocks. And, when it did, the beach would come alive again.

We didn't have time for slow and sensual. Quick and desperate would have to be good enough.

Her eyes snapped to mine, and she must have seen how difficult it was for me to keep from coming while she rode me fast and hard, all the while making those soft moans and purrs of pleasure.

Her lips curved in a sensual smile. "Don't hold back."

She was slick with rain, her hands sliding across my wet shirt as she held me down. I wanted to touch her bare skin, but her clothes in the way made everything a little hotter. Her dress was bunched up to her waist, and the straps hung off her shoulders.

I wrapped my arms around her and felt her tremble as she rocked against me. Her lush mouth thinned into a determined line, and her eyes squeezed shut in concentration.

The hard points of her nipples pushed against her wet dress. I took one of those rain-slicked buds into my mouth, sucking right through her clothes.

She moaned and pushed me onto to the sand, her eyes wild with desire. She looked gorgeous as she used my cock to get herself off. This amazingly smart, completely-in-charge, most-put-together woman in the world was coming apart on top of me, grinding against me like a porn star on a public beach.

She made a noise of ultimate surrender, and it tipped me over the edge. "Are you sure it's okay?"

"I want to feel you," she said. "Can you give me that?"

I bent my knees and pushed into my heels, lifting her up as I thrust. I could give her that. I could give her everything she asked for. Hooking my arm around her shoulders, I yanked her mouth to mine and kissed her. Her tongue stroked mine, and I stiffened all over as a powerful orgasm crashed through me.

She moaned into my mouth, clenching down on me as I erupted inside her. Her pussy contracted around my cock as I shot off, and the clenching tightness tore a groan from my throat.

Wave after wave of pleasure crashed over me. It was too much. I was on fire. Exploding. Incinerating. Smiling like an idiot.

She rolled off me, adjusting her dress as I pulled up my shorts. We were fully covered in an instant. At first glance, we looked like two drunk Ticos taking a nap under the glossy leaves of an almond tree. Upon closer inspection, it was clear we were two spent lovers panting for breath. I reached across the sand for Gabriella's hand and linked our fingers.

The rain slowed to a drizzle, and I heard voices in the distance. It was time to move. I squeezed Gabriella's fingers. It seemed to be the only movement I could muster.

"I never..." She stopped, choking on a laugh.

"You never had sex in public before?" Not that I was an expert, but after that scorching session, I would have to put public sex on my favorite-things-to-do list.

"No," she said, and something in her voice, in that single word, told me we were talking about more than a romp on the sand. "I never had an orgasm before..." She cleared her throat. "Before you."

My mind went blank and then my heart pounded so hard, I thought my head might explode. I swallowed roughly, remembering our first time against the door in my apartment, how she'd looked at me like I'd turned her world upside down.

Shit. Maybe I had.

But she'd done the same to me.

Chapter 28

GABI

I didn't want to move. I'd never been so relaxed in my life. I watched the leaf-shaped blades of the ceiling fan stir the humid air without a single thought in my head. When was the last time I didn't have a mile-long list of urgent activities waiting for my attention?

My to-do lists were a thousand miles away, and they'd wait until I got back home. Until then, I was more carefree than I'd been in fifteen years.

Ever since I got married at twenty and became a mother a few months later, I'd been rushing from one place to the next. Having a baby, finishing school, becoming a widow and a single mother... It had been one thing after another for as long as I could remember. I hadn't lain still in a bed like this since I was a teenager composing a love letter to Freddie Prinze Jr.

Joey was asleep beside me, lying on his back with his feet hanging off the edge of the mattress. His soft, steady breath sounded over the mechanical whir of the ceiling fan. I grabbed my book from the nightstand and flipped to the page where I'd left off. I'd barely had the time or energy to read more than a few pages since

I'd been in Costa Rica, but I was more interested in the man lying beside me than the cowboy hero in the book.

I laid the book back down in favor of looking at Joey. There was nothing better than Joey Morales lying shirtless against the white linens with his hands clasped loosely over his ribs in peaceful slumber. His wavy hair fell over his forehead, obscuring the dark slashes of his brows. His full mouth smiled even while he slept.

I knew I shouldn't be staring at him while he was asleep, but he was so beautiful. The more time I spent with Joey, the more I liked him. It was going to be harder than I thought to go back to normal when we returned to Mossy Oak. The thought of only seeing him at work and at sporting events depressed me.

Maybe I could start doing more yoga; then I would see him on Thursday nights. And if I changed my running schedule, I would run into him more at the park. When Shane went to a friend's house for the night, we'd arrange an occasional sleepover at Joey's place. My skin flushed at the idea of Joey stretched out on his bed, waiting for me.

I realized I was planning a future with Joey, and I shut my eyes tightly. I pinched the bridge of my nose, trying to push away my ridiculous thoughts. I couldn't be in a relationship, not with Joey or anyone. I had too many moving parts in my life to accommodate a man.

And what would Shane think? His mother dating his track coach? It would never work.

Besides, this was Joey. He could have a different woman in his bed every night of the week. He wouldn't want me there on a permanent basis.

His chest rose and fell steadily with each breath. I watched the light play across his tanned skin, creating a display of shadow art across the dips and ridges of his chest. He mumbled something in his sleep and rubbed the scripted tattoo over his heart.

Maria.

Who was she? I had plenty of guesses. Mother? Sister? Favorite teacher? The most likely answer was the one that made my heart hurt the worst. She was someone Joey had loved enough to etch her name over his heart forever.

I lifted my hand and traced the letters spelling her name. Joey stirred and opened his eyes.

My palm flattened on his chest. "You're awake."

His hand covered mine, and he blinked up at me. "Were you watching me sleep?"

Heat crept up my neck, and I tried to think of a good reason I was propped up on one elbow, staring at him. "I was reading." I held up my book for proof.

"More porno books?"

I laughed. The book I was reading was a reverse harem with lots and lots of naughty interludes. "Guilty."

"Who would have thought that Principal Salinger read dirty novels?" he asked. "Is there a naked man on the cover of that one, too?"

"Not exactly."

"Half-naked?"

My cheeks heated. There were several half-naked men on the cover. I changed the subject instead of answering, sweeping his hair back from his face. "You smile in your sleep."

He laughed. "You were watching me."

"A little."

"You get this cute little line between your eyebrows when you sleep."

I slapped his hand away when he traced a line between my eyebrows. "That's called a wrinkle," I said. "You wouldn't know about them yet."

"Neither would you."

I grimaced. "I'm a lot closer than you are."

He stroked my cheek. "Do you know you snore?"

"I do not." Did I?

"It's more of a whistle, really." He made a soft noise with his teeth and tongue. "It's so cute."

I rolled my eyes, and he made a grab for me and pulled me on top of him. My T-shirt rose up, and his hand found my bare thigh.

"This is cute too." His voice was husky as he cupped my ass. Hunger blazed in his eyes as he pulled my face down to his and kissed me. "I like running behind you in those tiny shorts you wear."

"You're only running behind me because you can't keep up."

A laugh burst from his mouth. "We should race again," he said, toying with the hem of my T-shirt.

The ringing of a phone pierced the air. My heart jerked even though it wasn't my phone.

Unless there was an emergency at the retreat, Shane wouldn't be contacting me. And my mother was his emergency contact until I got back to the States.

"That's yours," I said.

"Let it ring." He pushed my hem higher up to my hips. When I stiffened, he stopped and relented. "Check if you must," he said, releasing me. "Then come right back."

I leaned over and looked at the screen of his phone. My throat tightened, and I forced the words past my lips. "It's someone named Angela."

Joey muttered something under his breath in Spanish and held out his hand, palm up, for his phone. I gave it to him.

"*Hola.*" He rolled off the bed and walked out onto the balcony.

Jealousy flared in my chest, and black spots swam in my vision. I sat up and tucked the sheet around my waist, watching Joey pad around the terrace. How could I have thought I could be with a man like him?

Angela, Maria, Caroline—the names were piling up. In a way, it made it easier to keep myself from getting too attached. When we got back home, I would recite those names whenever I missed him.

I made up my mind. There would be no more accidental meetings in the break room. No more stolen kisses. No more sleepovers. No more orgasms.

Ugh. I was definitely addicted to those orgasms. I'd become a fiend for them. Even as Joey was talking to another woman on the phone, I imagined his fingers trailing along my heated skin. How was I going to go back to a life without orgasms? And no Joey to give them to me?

The muscles in his shoulders rippled as he leaned on the banister. Despite the fact that he was talking to another woman on the phone, my body reacted to everything that was Joey. *God bless Costa Rica.* He was sexy from his messy hair to his bare feet. He sauntered back into the room, talking animatedly in heavily accented Spanish that *Spanish for Dummies* hadn't prepared me for. He sat down on the bed next to me and made an exaggerated gesture of impatience at the phone.

"*Sí. Te queiro. Adiós.*" He swiped his finger across the screen and hung up, then tossed his phone onto the nightstand. "Sorry about that," he said.

"It's fine." *It wasn't fine.* My heart was tearing in two. I knew enough Spanish to recognize endearments of love. *Te queiro. I love you.* Joey was quick to toss the sentiment around. He'd said it to me more than once in the heat of the moment.

"I have a big favor to ask." His eyes were luminous in the waning afternoon light.

My instinct was to give him anything. I paused and took a breath. "What is it?"

"That was my mother. She still wants us to come for dinner tonight."

"Your mother? You call your mother Angela?"

Joey grinned. "Everyone calls her Angela." His smile faded. "What did you think?"

My fingers clutched the sheet. "Never mind."

He pried my hands open. "You thought I would take a call from a woman while you were lying next to me?"

My cheeks burned, and I bit my lip. "It was silly. I'm sorry."

His laugh sounded, but it wasn't his usually deep rumble. Bitterness laced the low sound. "I can't blame you. My reputation isn't so good."

Both of us were thinking about that scene I'd witnessed at school, but neither one of us wanted to bring it up.

Joey traced a diamond pattern on the sheet over my leg, his eyes avoiding mine. The only sound in the room was the quiet hum of the ceiling fan and our steady breathing.

Finally, Joey cleared his throat. "If it's too much, I understand, but I would like you to meet my family."

My heart seized, and I felt terribly guilty. "I'm sorry for taking you away from them."

"No worries," he said. "Angela will get over it. She has three other children who live near her. She can handle one wayward son. Plus, I'll be back in June." His hand settled near the top of my thigh, and he set those dark eyes of his on me. "Will you come to dinner tonight?"

I tried to think things through, but my mind was as thick as mud. It was hard to deny Joey anything, and at the very least, I owed his mother an apology.

* * *

We borrowed Santiago's truck and drove to the next town over for dinner, which was a bustling metropolis compared to our sleepy surf town. The sidewalks were crowded with tourists, and the streets were clogged with tuk-tuks, scooters, and rental cars.

I gaped out the window at the sights and sounds. Everyone was having a good time. People of all ages strolled the sidewalks. Young families perched on benches licking ice cream cones, and couples holding hands peered into shop windows. Laughter, music, and eager shouts filled the air.

As we inched through the congested traffic, my nerves mounted.

"You're coming back here in June?" I asked, fidgeting with the hem of my dress.

Joey stopped in the middle of the street to let a pedestrian cross.

"I'm teaching a summer program for children who've fallen behind during the school year."

The tension in my shoulders eased while I studied Joey's handsome face in profile. Those who didn't know him well may only see his carefree smile and crinkling eyes and think he took nothing seriously. I knew better.

"You can't stop being a teacher, can you?"

He tossed me a genuine smile that made my heart swell. "I love the way kids come out of their shell when they are learning, you know? That gleam they get when they understand?" His eyes sparkled in the dark cab of the truck. "From the brightest kids to the ones who struggle, they all love learning."

My heart filled. Thankfully, I hadn't told the superintendent about Joey's after-school indiscretion. Losing him as a teacher would have been devastating to the kids at PES.

"Education is very different in Costa Rica," Joey said. "Not every kid has a chance to finish high school, so the early years are very important."

"Did you always want to teach?"

He shook his head. "I just wanted to sample the world and see what fit." He turned onto a side street and parked the truck between two golf carts. Shifting to face me, he lowered his voice conspiratorially. "I should warn you," he said. "My family is..." He paused, searching for the right words. "They are... nosy."

I laughed. "You've met my parents."

"Yes. They are wonderful. They never miss a meet or a game."

"They never miss anything." I rolled my eyes. "Don't get me wrong, I'm grateful to them. But sometimes..." I let my words die off, feeling guilty for my thoughts. My parents were my support system, my safety net, my soft landing. But they were also nosy and occasionally overbearing. I laced my fingers in my lap and blinked up at Joey. "Sometimes I wish it was just me and Shane." My cheeks flushed, and I sank my teeth into my lower lip. Had I said that aloud? It was something I had never even admitted to myself.

Joey untangled my fingers and gripped my hands in his. "Why

do you think I moved to America?" he asked. "I wanted my own life. I love my family, but I need to breathe."

The air between us pulsed with emotion. I let out a shaky breath. I'd never told anyone how I felt. Although I wished with all my heart that my husband hadn't died, sometimes I was thankful I'd never had to compromise with anyone when it came to raising Shane. I'd seen marriages rip apart because the couple couldn't figure out how to parent together. Montel and I never had to test our relationship over a disagreement on curfews or punishments. We never had to argue or take a stand.

My throat tightened with emotion. "I'm a horrible person, Joey. The thoughts I have about Montel..." I sucked in a breath, disgusted with myself.

Joey slid across the bench seat so that our knees bumped, and he wrapped his arm around my shoulders.

I leaned into his touch. "When he died..." I shook my head, forcing myself to form the words. "When he died, I was heartbroken." My gaze dropped to my lap. I couldn't look at Joey as I admitted my deepest secret. "But part of me was glad that we'd never had to struggle. It was easier to remember my marriage as perfect."

Joey gripped my chin and raised my face until I met his eyes. "Nothing can compare to your perfect marriage, so why try to love again?"

I blinked back tears. "It's easier this way."

He cradled my cheek. "It's easier not to love." His voice cracked. "To be alone or to fill your nights with meaningless flings. It's the same thing, you know?" He swept his thumb across my cheek, smearing the tear that had leaked from the corner of my eye. "Even good people have bad thoughts. It's how we act that matters; you see? How we treat people." He moved closer, his eyes searching mine. "You are not perfect." He cocked his head to the side and his eyes twinkled. "You snore, for one. And you're not so great at yoga."

I smacked him on the chest and shifted closer to him, craving the feel of his smiling mouth against mine. Desire rose, and the cab of the truck sizzled with electricity. Joey's eyes blazed, and his hand shifted to cup the back of my neck.

Then we were kissing, and all my dark thoughts were filled with light. His tongue touched mine. His taste filled my mouth. The jagged edges of my splintered heart softened.

When we broke apart, Joey pressed a kiss to my forehead. "You don't have to be perfect," he said.

My heart nearly exploded. For the past month, I'd been telling myself it was just sex between us. Lots and lots of exceptionally good sex. But now I wasn't so sure.

Chapter 29

Gabi

"You ready to eat the best food of your life?" Joey tucked my hand in his as we joined the steady flow of foot traffic on the crowded sidewalk. We walked by restaurants, bars, and brightly lit shops, and it dawned on me that there weren't any residential buildings in sight.

"Wait." I slowed my steps as we passed by the long line at the restaurant I'd noticed earlier. "I thought we were going to your family's for dinner."

"We are." He stopped and pointed up at the sign above the restaurant door. *Angela's.*

My jaw dropped. "Your family has a restaurant?"

He nodded and opened the door for me, gesturing me inside. The people in line gave us dirty looks as we stepped past them while they waited. We went inside the restaurant, and it was like being enfolded into a warm embrace. The smell of freshly baked bread and spices wafted into the candle-lit lobby.

"Did I forget to tell you we have a restaurant?" Joey asked, feigning innocence with his lifted brow.

"You know you did." I put my hand on his shoulder and gave him a little shove. "Why didn't you say?"

"I was trying to impress you." He led me through the crowded lobby to the hostess stand. "Did it work?"

I glanced past the hostess into the main dining room, where uniformed servers weaved between tables draped in elegant, white cloths. From what I could see and smell, it was obvious *Angela's* was a step above the restaurants we'd eaten at so far during my visit to Costa Rica.

This was a destination, not a meal. It probably took hours to get a table. Joey waved at the hostess, and she stopped what she was doing and escorted us to a corner booth where we slid into same side of the bench.

"*Gracias*," Joey said when she handed us two menus.

He didn't have to try to impress me, but it was working.

His leg nudged mine under the table, and chills raced down my spine.

"Is this why you are such a fabulous cook?" I asked, leaning into him.

He laughed and dipped his head to brush his lips across my cheek. "I've never made you anything but breakfast." His mouth trailed to my ear. "You haven't seen nothing yet."

The warm puff of his breath against my neck made me shiver. I remembered that delicious French toast he'd made and what he'd done with the syrup.

A loud throat-clearing noise sounded from close by. I leaned forward and saw a young woman in the black server's uniform with her hands on her hips, staring at us. She looked so much like Joey, she may as well have been wearing a nametag that read "Joey's sister."

She raised her chin and pursed her lips, flicking her glare between us.

Joey started to speak, but she cut him off with a rapid-fire Spanish that didn't sound like approval.

Joey responded in an easygoing tone, his musical laugh punctuating his words.

She glared at him harder and then turned her attention to me.

"I hope you're half as smart as you are pretty and you don't fall in love with my stupid little brother. He's a heartbreaker who never visits home."

Her advice hit every nerve in my body. I tensed, and Joey rubbed my leg in soothing strokes.

"I'll be home all summer," he said. "You'll be sick of me."

"I'm already sick of you." She tossed her head. "No manners," she said. "Introduce us, Fernando."

Joey slid his arm across the top of the booth.

"Gabriella, this is my older sister, Rosa."

Rosa's hand lashed out, and she slapped Joey on the back of the head. "I'm not that old."

He laughed and rubbed his head. "And you wonder why I don't come home," he mumbled with a sly grin.

"*Qué jeta!*" She narrowed her eyes at Joey, then turned to go. "I'm going to get Angela."

I tried to translate what Rosa had said. "That mug?" I asked when she was gone.

Joey chuckled. "She basically called me a jerk." He shrugged. "She always calls me a jerk. But I'm her favorite. I'm everyone's favorite."

I could see why. It was impossible not to fall for Joey's charm.

"Would you like wine?" he asked.

I thought of meeting the older version of Rosa in a few minutes and nodded. "Please."

Guilt pierced the bubble of my happiness. I thought of how I would feel if Shane came to visit me and was distracted by a woman. I needed some liquid courage to face Joey's mother.

A waiter approached the table, smiling broadly. "Fernando! *Cómo estás, mae?*" His gaze darted from me to Joey with open curiosity.

They exchanged a warm greeting, and Joey introduced him as Mateo, a cousin.

"A bottle of the best red you have," Joey said.

"Big spender." Mateo teased. "My rich American cousin."

"There's a big tip in it for you if you bring the wine before Angela comes out of the kitchen."

Mateo grinned and hurried off.

When he was gone, Joey turned the full wattage of his smile on me again. His attention was like a star, burning bright in the night sky, and I wanted to bask in the glow even if it burned. "You like Italian food?"

"If I said no, would we go somewhere else?"

Joey's smile didn't falter. "Of course. Would you rather have Chinese?"

My gaze slid back toward the kitchen. "Maybe."

Joey laughed and pulled me closer to his side. The warmth of his body comforted me and eased some of my anxiety about meeting his mother.

"Don't worry," he said. "My mom is much nicer than my sister. Rosa loves to give me a hard time."

I had a big enough family to understand.

"How many brothers and sisters do you have?"

"There are four of us."

"And everyone lives here except you?" I glanced around the cozy restaurant. "Do they all work here, or just Rosa?"

"Most of my family works here in some way or another," he said. "My father does the books, and my other siblings fill in when needed. My younger sister has her hands full with her own family, so she only comes in during the busy season."

I glanced around the packed restaurant. A line of people waited for tables, and every table was full. There was a cozy feeling in the restaurant, as if everyone knew each other.

"This isn't the busy season?" I asked.

Joey shook his head. "You should see it in January. The wait for a table is hours."

He leaned closer to me, sharing a secret. "I know where the back door is, though. I can always get a table."

Mateo was back with the bottle of expensive wine and some crusty bread with sweet cream butter. He poured a taste for Joey and winked at me. "He doesn't know shit about wine," he said in a conspiratorial whisper.

Joey made a show of swirling and sniffing the wine before shrugging and offering the glass to me for a taste. It was delicious. Full-bodied with hints of cinnamon and tart blackberry. "Perfect."

Mateo filled two glasses. "Are you sticking around for a while, Fernando?"

"No. Just a quick visit."

"Have you seen Victor? Or Alejandro?"

"No," Joey said, sipping his wine. "I'll see plenty of them this summer."

All this talk of summer plans made me think of how much I would miss Joey while he was in Costa Rica.

Mateo darted a glance in the direction of the kitchen and said something in Spanish with a grin before hurrying off. Joey slipped his arm around me and brushed a kiss against my temple just as a woman approached the table. One glance at her and I knew she was Joey's mother.

She was one of the most beautiful women I'd ever seen. My stomach clenched as she scrutinized me.

Joey slid out of the booth and kissed his mother on both cheeks. "This is Gabriella," he said.

She extended a slim hand to me. "I'm Angela."

I shook her hand as Joey sat beside me again. "Joey has wonderful things to say about your cooking," I said.

She arched a brow. "*Fernando* isn't so bad at cooking himself. It runs in the family." She glanced around the restaurant proudly. "My grandparents opened this restaurant when they came over from Italy. My grandmother was also Angela."

I followed her gaze around the bustling restaurant. It had the homey feeling of a third-generation family business.

"I can't wait to try the food," I said.

"You won't be disappointed. We make the best lasagna outside of Italy." She turned to grin at Joey. "Your father is on the line tonight," she said.

"Oh no, I was going to order the snapper."

"He's gotten much better." Angela's smile reminded me very much of her son's. "Fernando's father is an accountant," she said. "He only fills in with the cooking when we are short-staffed." She turned toward Joey. "You should go say hi to him. It might bolster his mood. He is biting everyone's heads off."

Joey raised an eyebrow at her. "Does he have on his apron?"

"Go find out." She nodded her chin at the kitchen, her dark eyes dancing in the low light.

"I'll be right back," Joey said as he slipped out of the booth.

Angela waited until Joey disappeared into the kitchen before leaning her hands on the table. "Can I sit for a minute? Rest my tired bones?"

I nodded, although there was nothing tired looking about Angela. She had energy zinging off her in waves. From her warm smile to her curling hair, she exuded vibrancy—another thing she had in common with her son. It was obvious where Joey had gotten his charm and effervescence.

"I'm glad I have a minute with you," I said. "I want to apologize for taking time away from your visit with your son."

She narrowed her eyes at me, then smiled. "Thank you for that. I do wish he would come home more," she said, leaning her elbows on the table. "We barely see him anymore."

As a mother, I certainly understood. The prospect of Shane going away to college in a few short years was already weighing heavily on my mind. What if he moved to a foreign country and only came back for brief visits? What if his brief visit was monopolized by some hussy eight years older than him, someone who would have sex on a public beach? I shuddered at the thought.

"You must be looking forward to him being home all summer," I said.

Her face lit up. "Yes! We are all so excited to have him back."

"Your son is a wonderful teacher," I said. "The children adore him." They weren't the only ones. Everyone at PES loved Joey.

Angela scrutinized me but smiled again. She and Joey had that in common. They seemed to smile naturally and radiate happiness. "Maybe you will make him happy," she said. "Do you like children, Gabriella?"

I raised my glass and sipped while I stalled for time. What a loaded question. And not at all random. The sly fox had to have sent Joey to the kitchen on purpose so she could quiz me.

"I work at an elementary school," I said, setting down my glass. "I love children."

"Do you want children of your own?"

I leveled her with an intense stare of my own. "I have a son," I said.

"You are a mother!" she exclaimed. "That is wonderful. So you understand how much I love my son, and how much I want him to be happy." Her gaze darted toward the kitchen, and she leaned across the table to whisper, "You are the first woman he's ever brought here. He must be serious about you."

My eyes went wide, and I stuffed a piece of bread into my mouth. I swallowed without chewing and choked.

Angela was on her feet instantly, patting me on the back. "Goodness," she said. "You have to chew."

I gulped down a sip of water as Joey came back to the table and slid into the booth beside me. "He had on his apron," he said, showing me the picture he'd taken on his phone.

Joey's father was a thinner version of him, with dark hair graying at the temples. He wore an apron with sunglass-wearing lobsters, and a huge smile stretched his mouth.

"I better get back to the kitchen," Angela said. "But I will stop by with dessert."

Joey said something to his mother in Spanish, and they both laughed. They looked so much alike that it made my chest ache. "It was wonderful to meet you," Angela said to me. "Remember to chew."

When she was gone, Joey leaned back against the booth and stretched his arm across my shoulders.

"What happened?" he asked. "You were tense when I came back from the kitchen. I shouldn't have left you alone with my mother."

"Your mother's English is very good," I said, leaning against his side. He felt so solid and warm. I wanted to melt into him.

"What did she say?" He lifted his wineglass and drank.

"Let's just say I get the feeling that she wants you to settle down and give her grandchildren."

His eyes met mine, and he set his glass down with a thump. "Doesn't she have enough of those already?"

"Apparently not."

Joey took my hand. "I'm sorry. My mother is too nosy for her own good."

"It's fine," I said. "Don't be upset with her."

He blew out a frustrated breath and gathered me against his side. "I can't stay mad at Angela," he said with a low laugh that vibrated against my chest. "Her lasagna is too good. You'll see."

Chapter 30

JOEY

We lay on our sides, facing each other, lazily touching and saying everything that entered our minds.

"What happened with Montel's family?" I asked.

She shook her head. "They aren't around."

I wanted more, but I let it go. "They're missing out."

Her drowsy eyes lifted to mine. "I know, right?" She smoothed my hair away from my face. "They never liked me much. They thought Montel was stupid to marry me and burden himself with a family." She shrugged. "We were young. Too young."

"Shane doesn't want more from them?" I asked.

"He doesn't complain. My family is a lot to handle. They fill any void before it arrives. Maybe someday when he's older..." She trailed off, sounding sleepy.

She closed her eyes. But I fought to stay awake, determined to savor every moment we had together. I thought about the entire year we'd spent together at school. The accidental run-ins that were completely planned. The staff meetings when we couldn't take our eyes off each other. Bumping into each other in the break room after I'd dropped off a batch of forbidden muffins.

I'd lied when I said she snored. She was a quiet sleeper, barely moving throughout the night, while I was a bed hog. I slept like a starfish with my feet hanging over the mattress.

I lay awake for a long time, listening to the steady sounds of Gabriella's breathing and the tide crashing against the shore. Our time in paradise was coming to an end, and I didn't want to miss anything because of sleep. Eventually, I couldn't hold out anymore, and as I drifted off, I wondered what it would be like when we returned home. Would I be able to pass Gabriella in the halls without thinking of our time here together? Would she ignore me?

The next morning when I woke, Gabriella was already on the terrace. She sat watching the surfers in the distance. A tiny smile lifted the corners of her mouth, and she'd never been more beautiful.

My heart pinched just thinking about saying goodbye and picking up where we'd left off in Mossy Oak: hiding in supply closets and sneaking kisses at yoga practice.

I padded out to the balcony and greeted her with a kiss on the cheek.

"Hey," she said. "I thought you were going to sleep forever."

"You look beautiful."

She laughed and shoved a hand through the thick curtain of her hair. "You're lying. I look like a mess. My hair has gone crazy in this humidity."

"Your hair is perfect."

I stood and rested my hand on her shoulder. We watched the ocean in silence for a long beat. It was early, and the night chill still hung in the air. A few surfers glided over the turquoise waves as if they were floating.

"Can you teach me to do that?" Gabriella asked.

"Of course I can." I hauled her up from the chair.

She laughed. "Now?"

I tugged her into the room. "Now is the best time." The early waves were perfect for beginners.

"Can we get coffee first?" She dragged her feet, holding her ground. "I need coffee."

My heart skipped a beat. I couldn't believe it was her last day in Costa Rica. I was staying until the end of the weekend, so we wouldn't see each other until Monday morning at school.

Could we go back to pretending? Or would we avoid each other at school for the rest of the year? I didn't want this vacation to end.

I pulled her into my arms and nuzzled her neck. Her skin was warm, and her soft hair tickled my cheek. I kissed a path across her collarbone, pushing her shirt aside to get to more skin.

When we went back to work, could I walk by her in the hall and not picture her wearing nothing but my T-shirt?

She put her palm on my chest, electrifying me with her touch. "Joey."

Her smoky voice stirred my blood. It took all my willpower to resist dragging her back to bed for the rest of the day.

"We can surf later." She slipped her fingers under the elastic band of my shorts.

My fingers circled her wrist, stopping her exploration. "We'll miss the best waves."

She wrapped her arms around my back and settled her cheek against my chest. "What have you done to me?"

I stroked her hair and dropped a kiss on top of her head. She was in my blood. I was in hers. "We did this to each other," I said.

We stood holding each other for a while, soaking up our last morning before the rush of life began again. It was easy to see this was more than a fling, more than sex.

"Come on." I crossed the room and rummaged in my bag for my swimsuit. "We will grab coffee in the lobby and get some boards from Santiago. I'll teach you how to ride the waves." *And you will fall madly in love with me.*

She worried her bottom lip between her teeth. "What if I'm not any good?"

I found her swimsuit and tossed it to her. "With me as your teacher, you're going to be great."

* * *

Gabriella was better than great. She was amazing. She learned to surf quicker than anyone I'd ever seen. She'd claimed that Shane had gotten his athleticism from his father, but she was selling herself short. Gabriella had more talent in her little finger than most people had in their entire body.

My plan to make her fall in love with me by way of surfing totally backfired. Watching Gabriella soar over the waves with her arms spread wide and a smile lighting up her face made my heart swell to the point of bursting. I was officially gone for her... head over heels in love.

After our successful surfing experience, we were starving. We threw on some clothes, got a tuk-tuk into town, and ate fancy sandwiches at a vegan café.

When we finished eating, we joined the tourists and locals for some window shopping. Gabriella slid her arm around my waist and snuggled close to me, something she'd never do if we were back in Mossy Oak.

I steered her toward the ice cream shop. "We need some of that."

"Mmm. What's your favorite flavor? No, don't tell me. Let me guess." We stepped aside to allow three kids to run by on the sidewalk. "Mint chocolate chip?"

"No."

"Butter pecan?"

I grimaced. "Not even close."

"Chocolate cherry?"

"Yuck." We stopped in front of the ice cream shop. "You're just naming every flavor that comes to mind."

"That's how guessing works," she said with a laugh. "What am I supposed to do?"

I reached for the door. "Think about me. Think about what I might like."

A woman struggling with a baby, an ice cream cone, and a wayward toddler nearly plowed me over. I grabbed the woman's elbow to steady her as the little boy came barreling through the door. When she looked up at me, I froze.

"Maria," I said.

"Fernando!" she cried. "What are you doing here?" She asked in Spanish.

A montage of memories played out in my mind. Our first kiss behind the bleachers. Our first drive to Liberia, which we'd thought of as the big city. Our first time getting drunk off cheap wine and passing out on the beach.

I'd never forgotten Maria. She was my first love. My most painful memory. The reason for the ink on my chest.

The little boy wailed. He'd dropped his cone, and the chocolate ice cream splattered on the sidewalk in front of the door.

"Oh, Diego," Maria said in the voice of every frustrated mother.

"Papá!" Lucia leaned toward me and grabbed a fistful of my hair. She had a tight grip for such a little thing and refused to let go.

I laughed and scooped her out of Maria's arms. "Lucia, you little chunk. Come here!" I snuggled the little girl, blowing a raspberry into her the chubby folds of her neck. She'd gotten so big since I'd seen her last summer. She was a beautiful girl, like her mother, with enchanting dark eyes and round cheeks. She smelled like sunshine and baby shampoo.

"She's grown so much," I said.

"She's hardly a baby anymore." Maria smiled and wiped the tears and chocolate from Diego's rounded cheeks. "What are you doing here?"

"It's spring break," I said, switching to English to include Gabriella. "We are on vacation. Gabriella, this is Maria."

There was an awkward pause as Maria and Gabriella stared at each other for a long moment. The former love of my life and the current love of my life didn't seem eager to become friends.

"Nice to meet you," Gabriella said finally. "Can I get him another ice cream?"

"That's kind of you." Maria's English was rusty and stilted. "We will share this one, please."

Lucia yanked my hair so hard I saw stars. "Hey," I said, untangling her fingers.

Gabriella cleared her throat. "I'll go get in line before it gets any longer." The worry line was back between her brows. "What flavor did you want, Joey?"

"Is it still vanilla?" Maria asked.

"Yes," I admitted.

"He is so boring." Maria's laugh tinkled like a bell.

"I'm not boring. I'm classic. What's yours?" I asked Gabriella.

Her eyes darted from me to Maria. "Chocolate," she said.

"Another classic."

Gabriella reached for the door. "I'll be inside."

When Gabriella was gone, Maria switched back to Spanish. "Have you seen Victor or anyone else?"

I shook my head. "Not enough time."

Maria reached for Lucia, who didn't want to give up her hold on my hair. "Thanks for taking her. She's such a little flirt. And everyone is Papá."

"She's beautiful."

Maria beamed up at me. "Isn't she?" Lucia giggled as her mother tickled her chin. "Maybe I will see you this summer," she said.

"Maybe." My throat went dry. I wasn't as excited to return to the surf and sand of Costa Rica as I usually was. I glanced into the ice cream shop where Gabriella stood in line. Three months away from her seemed like an eternity.

Maria laughed and grabbed me for a quick hug. "Wipe the stars from your eyes, Fernando. You will scare that woman away looking at her like that."

Sadness settled on my chest. I'd scared Maria straight into the arms of my best friend. She'd broken my heart and ruined me for relationships for a long time, but that had been a long time ago. I was grateful that Maria had dumped me before we'd made it down the aisle. If not, everything would have been different. I would have come back home after I finished college in Texas. I would have never become an American citizen or a Spanish teacher. And I wouldn't have met Gabriella.

Chapter 31

GABI

Joey came up behind me in line and slipped an arm around my waist, pulling me back against his chest. I pulled away, putting space between us. Tears threatened, but I bit them back.

"What's wrong?" Joey took my shoulder and turned me to face him.

I chewed my lip. "That was her," I said, pointing at his chest.

The color drained from his face. "Yes."

My cheeks flushed. At least I had a face to the name now. I cringed, realizing Maria was even lovelier than I'd imagined. She was drop-dead gorgeous, and so were those children. We inched forward in the line, but I no longer wanted ice cream.

"You never mentioned..." I swallowed thickly, remembering the way the little girl had reached for him. "You never talked about the children."

He blinked as if pulling himself back to the present. His smile flickered, but there was something serious in his face that was very not Joey. The intensity of his eyes sent a shiver down my spine. "What?"

I'd felt the connection between the four of them like an earthquake under my feet. They'd been so natural together. She'd embraced him, and I'd torn my eyes away, unable to watch it if she kissed him.

"The baby. Is she yours? And the boy too?"

The color drained from his face. "You thought those kids were mine? Don't you think I would have mentioned being a father?"

My heart ached. "She called you Papa."

Joey scoffed. "Maria said she calls everyone that." He took my elbow and drew me out of the line, then outside to the sidewalk. "Is that what you think of me?" His voice rose to a fevered pitch. Gone was the confident, teasing tone that made me shiver with anticipation. "That I would have children with a woman and leave her for another country, never knowing my own kids?"

My stomach clenched. Had I been wrong? "I thought..."

His eyes turned dark and stormy. "No. You didn't think." He stepped closer to the street and waved down a tuk-tuk. "Let's get out of here."

Joey didn't say a word on the ride back to the bungalow. Confusion and anger battled inside me. I'd been so jealous of Maria, I'd jumped to conclusions. I should have known that Joey would have mentioned children.

I'd never seen him go quiet for this long. He was usually so easygoing, but I could feel the anger radiating off him in waves.

When we got back to the bungalow, he went out to the terrace and stood staring at the setting sun.

"I guess this is it." I came up beside him and braced my hands on the railing. "Our last sunset."

Joey tilted his chin at me. "Why?"

I frowned, staring out at the magnificent view. "Because I'm going home in the morning."

A bitter laugh escaped his mouth. "There are beautiful sunsets in Mossy Oak. I've seen them."

"I know. But we can't watch them together. You know that."

He turned his back to the display of vibrant colors in the sky. "Why not?"

My jaw clenched, and I shook my head. "You know all the reasons."

His eyes narrowed, boring into me. "None of them are good enough."

"We work together."

He shrugged. "I'll quit."

A thin red line blurred my vision. "You can't quit."

"We can't work together, Gabriella. Don't you see?"

"It isn't ideal, but we don't have a choice."

"I can't be in the same room with you and act like I'm not in love with you."

My heart seized. He'd casually tossed out the L-word, as if it weren't the most important feeling in the world.

"But the students..." I couldn't digest this information. It was too much. Joey would upend his life for us to be together? "They love you."

"And I love them," he said, finally reaching for me. His hand closed around my wrist, and he tugged me to his chest. "But I love you more."

I stiffened and pulled away from him. "What about my son? How does he fit in?"

"Shane already knows about us."

My heart leaped into my throat, pulsing so fast it blocked my breath. "What?"

"Shane told me to go for you a month ago. Trust me, he doesn't mind. He likes me."

The line of red expanded in my vision, blurring the view of the sunset, my thoughts... everything. "No."

"Yes." Joey smiled. It was his easy, confident smile, although a little more dim than usual. "Shane wants the best for you. He wants you to be happy." His expression tensed. "What you saw that night at school with Caroline..." He shook his head, frowning at me. "I know you think I have a lot of women. That I'm a gamer."

I squinted up at him. "A player," I said.

His eyes found mine, and all traces of his smile disappeared. "I'm not like that, Gabriella. Caroline and I weren't in a relationship. She just wanted to be with someone when she came to town for work. It was easy between us. No strings. No demands. I hope you understand."

The tight coil of jealousy in my belly loosened. I'd judged Joey harshly without hearing his explanation. I'd jumped to conclusions more than once. Caroline, Kaitlyn, Angela, and Maria. Jealousy had clouded my vision.

"It's not like that with you," he said. "I care about you."

Panic seized my heart. "Joey—"

"Don't say you don't care about me, Gabriella. I know you do, or you wouldn't have come here. You wouldn't have been jealous of Maria or suspicious of Lucia and Diego."

The pain in my chest spread until my entire body felt like it was being squeezed in a vise. I didn't want to talk about my feelings, and there was one surefire way to steer the conversation back to solid ground.

I hooked my fingers in his belt loop and tugged him closer to me. "Maybe I came here because I wanted more sex with you."

His eyes flashed at the bluntness of my words. The storm raging inside him darkened his features. I'd never seen him so angry.

"More sex?" His voice pulled tight enough to crack. "Is that what you want?"

I read the unspoken question in his eyes. *Is that all you want?*

In answer, I slid my hand to his fly. As soon as I touched him, his body responded. *Yes.* This was my way out of this tense conversation. We would go back to Orgasmland where everything was hunky-dory. Beneath the thin fabric of his shorts, I felt him respond.

He wanted sex, too. It was impossible to deny when my hand was on the evidence.

He grabbed my wrist and pushed my hand away. "Stand up," he growled.

I pushed up from the chair, my feet scrambling to find purchase on the slick tile floor. My chest rose and fell with the short pants of my breath. A shiver rushed down my spine, at odds with the heat spreading through me.

"Take off your dress."

The lush gardens outside our bungalow provided some privacy, but we weren't completely hidden from view. Someone strolling along the beach could see onto our terrace if they happened to glance past the thick buffer of jungle.

"Do it, Gabriella."

With a final glance at the deserted beach beyond the trees, I reached around to undo my zipper. My breasts jutted forward, and my nipples rubbed against the lace of my bra. The shiver running down my spine exploded, sending pulses of desire through me.

The zipper gave way under my clumsy fingers, and the straps of my dress fell off my shoulders. I shimmied, pushing the dress over my hips.

His hand drifted to his shirt as he watched me step out of my dress. His strong fingers flicked the top button open and then the next. I saw the scripted M of Maria's name, and jealousy flared again.

"Keep going." His voice was a deep rumble that caressed my bare skin.

I slid the straps of my bra off my shoulders and unhooked the clasp. My lace bra fell to the floor, and the humid air kissed my naked breasts. Goose bumps spread along my skin despite the late afternoon heat.

He shrugged out of his shirt. "Panties too."

My eyes strayed to his tattoo, and an angry spark had me yanking down my panties. I wanted to make him forget Maria completely. Part of me wished I'd never seen her, so I didn't picture her face every time I looked at the tattoo. She had pretty eyes, a sprinkling of freckles across her cute button nose, and rosebud lips. I was more jealous of her than ever after I'd met her.

Joey unzipped his shorts and shoved down his boxers. His heavy erection sprang free. Desire thundered through my veins as he stroked himself idly, watching my every move.

The sun was perched on the horizon between sea and sky, and a golden glow spread across the terrace. Joey's skin gleamed bronze, his muscles rippling as he stalked toward me. His hands snaked around my waist, and I lost my balance, falling against the hard wall of his chest.

"What do you want from me, Gabriella?" His voice was sandpaper against silk. His teeth nipped my jaw, and his scruff scraped my cheek. He gathered my hair in one hand and tugged my head back, exposing more of my neck to kiss and bite. "Do you want this?" He spun around and walked me backward until my back hit the wooden railing on the terrace. His hard length nudged my thigh, and I squirmed, desperate to get closer. "Words, Gabriella." He tugged my hair again, hard enough to make my eyes water. "I need to hear your words." His voice was a guttural groan that sent a rush of hot liquid pooling between my thighs.

"Yes." The word tore from my throat. "Yes, I want you."

He gripped my hip, his fingers scorching hot against my flesh. "You want sex."

"Yes." My voice was all breath, barely audible.

His fingers dug into my hip and tangled in my hair. "Hot sex?" He yanked. "Dirty?" His knee pushed my legs apart.

"Yes," I cried, arching against the wooden railing, on fire for him.

"You want orgasms from my mouth and my cock." His eyes burned into mine. "My fingers."

I nodded.

"Say it." His growl made my belly flip and my knees weak.

"I want—" I couldn't speak when his hands shifted to cup my sex. One long finger dragged across the seam of my wet folds. "That," I said, taking the easy way out.

I heard the low rumble of his laugh. "Then I will give it to you," he said, plunging a finger inside me. "I would give you the world if you wanted it, baby." He pushed another finger inside, and I bucked against him. "But you just want sex, so I'll give you that."

Every nerve ending came in my body alive when he stroked me, his confident fingers finding the secret spot that only he'd ever found. I almost lost it and came right then, but he pulled his hand free.

"Not yet," he said with a wicked grin. Then, his mouth was on mine, and he was kissing me with rough abandon, his mouth taking everything I had to give.

I kissed him back, desperate for more. I opened my mouth to the sweep of his tongue and slid my fingers through his hair. He kissed me as if this were the last time our mouths would meet, and I met every thrust of his tongue with a demand of my own. There was nothing gentle about the meeting of our mouths. We were devouring each other, kissing with a passion I hadn't known existed.

He'd said he'd give it to me rough and dirty. It was what I needed to convince myself that sex was all there was between us. I didn't want room for that four-letter word he'd dropped in my lap like a present I couldn't accept.

When he ripped his mouth from mine, I chased his kiss, yanking his hair and grinding against him. I'd never seen anything so sexy as the devilish gleam in his eyes when he broke free and spun me around so my back was to him. He pushed me against the wooden railing and suddenly I was bent over and exposed to him. His hands gripped my hips, and I felt him drop to his knees.

I tried to close my legs, feeling vulnerable in this position, bent over the railing with my legs spread wide and him behind me, but his hands were firm, preventing me from moving. His palm moved to the small of my back and held me firm to the railing, pinned and spread for his pleasure. He dragged a finger along my slick folds, tracing me from top to bottom. The velvet warmth of his tongue followed.

I writhed against the railing, gripping it with white-knuckled fingers. An un-ladylike sound tore from my throat. Real cuss words, not the cutesy ones, tumbled out of my mouth. "OhmyGod," I groaned.

He paused, and I felt the rumble of his laugh against my inner thigh. "That's it, baby," he said, coaxing me with his sexy accent. "Come for me."

It didn't take long before I obeyed his command. I had never had it like this before from behind, trapped and unable to escape the onslaught of licking and sucking. He devoured me, pressing his nose into me and flicking his tongue against my clit until I was a mass of nerves, trembling against the wooden railing.

He wiped his mouth against my thigh and crawled up my body, placing wet kisses everywhere. Over the curves of my cheeks, along my spine, between my shoulder blades... His mouth was all over me, kissing, biting, and sucking until flames licked through my core, threatening to consume me.

Joey leaned over me, and I felt the iron length of him nudging my entrance. He was so hard, and I was so wet that he almost slipped right in. I rocked against him, desperate to soothe the ache inside me. My body was one giant, pulsing throb that needed him.

"I'm going to fuck you hard," he said in a hoarse whisper near my ear. "I'm not going to be gentle."

He seemed to be waiting for me to answer, as he wasn't fulfilling his promise yet. I nodded, and he lined himself up where I needed him most.

"I won't hurt you, baby," he said. "Tell me to stop, and I will." He pushed into my tight entrance, only an inch, and stopped. "Words, Gabriella. Say you understand. I'm going to use you so hard you'll have trouble walking tomorrow, and the whole flight home you're going to be squirming in your seat, trying to get comfortable, thinking about my dick inside you."

I trembled, clutching the railing with bloodless fingers. I didn't like that he was talking about my flight home, away from this paradise, but I found my voice and managed a shaky, "okay." I'd never had rough sex before. I'd read about it, of course, and there was usually a safe word. "Don't we need a safe word?"

"No," he said. "Just say stop. That's the only word you need." He placed a kiss at the top of my shoulder and then I felt the smart smack of his hand against my ass.

I barely had time to register the intense pleasure/pain combination before he thrust into me, slamming all the way home.

Chapter 32

JOEY

I wanted to punish her. Her words had killed something inside me, and I wanted her to feel the same pain I did.

If she thought I was the kind of man who would father children and abandon them, then she didn't know me at all.

I pounded into her, grabbing her hips and holding her against the railing, fucking her so hard her feet left the ground. She cried out, saying words that made no sense. I listened for her to stay stop, but she was saying the opposite: *more* and *please* and *Joey.*

She gripped the railing and hoisted herself higher, offering me everything, except the one thing I really craved—her love.

I gave her pain and pleasure. I branded her with my handprint. I fucked her with a view of the setting sun, oblivious to the beauty of nature's show because my heart was ripping in two. Sparing her no mercy, I slammed into her over and over until her perfect pussy clenched in orgasm.

"Fuck," she said in an awed voice.

I almost laughed, because Gabriella was creative with her cursing. I'd never heard her say anything vulgar. Her version of cursing was suitable for a kindergartner or grandmother. But all she could think of was one word. One very appropriate word.

"I'm not done yet," I told her.

My dick was iron hard and scorching hot, seeking relief, but I ignored my own needs. I flipped Gabriella to face me and carried her to the bed.

Our lips locked as we tumbled onto the mattress. It creaked and groaned under the weight of our sweat-soaked bodies. I shoved my tongue into her mouth, wanting to taste every inch of her. I took her again, filling her with one hard thrust. She was tight from her orgasm, her pussy so snug around my cock, it was hard to fit. I sucked in a sharp breath, adjusting to the surrounding tightness. Her muscles clamped down around me. I couldn't move.

And then I had to move.

I pulled back and plunged into her, giving it to her so hard, so rough, she cried out and clutched my shoulders and scraped my back with her fingernails. I kissed her greedily, taking, taking, taking... until I lost myself in her. The animal inside me took over as I fucked her for what I thought might be the last time. Because even though I loved her, I wanted all of her, not just the parts she was willing to give me. I would rather starve than live off the measly scraps Gabriella was willing to offer. I wouldn't be half alive, always hoping for more. I wanted all of her or nothing.

Words popped into my head. Dirty, filthy words of lust and pleasure. I spoke in Spanish because I was too far gone to translate. The words flowed off my tongue, punctuating the air around us with my dirty demands.

God, I was going to miss her. Miss the spirited flash in her dark eyes and the reluctant curve of her smile. Miss catching a glimpse of her in the halls and stealing glances in the break room. Miss her smoky voice and the rosy scent of her perfume. Miss every moment she wouldn't give me.

I was angry. At her for not wanting more than sex. At myself for not being able to accept that. Gabriella was breaking me apart, flaying my heart open and bleeding me dry.

I gave it to her in punishing strokes, pinning her to the bed and thrusting into her over and over until the bungalow filled with her moans of pleasure. She went wild beneath me, making noises that spurred me on, faster and harder. I held her down, pumping into her as she tightened and trembled, her muscles strangling my cock.

Her body clamped down on me so tightly, I thought I would explode. I forced myself to wait. I didn't want it to end, for us to be finished.

When I couldn't hold back any longer, I came with a shudder. Burying my face in her neck, I allowed myself to linger in the bitter-sweet moment.

My tattoo had failed me. I hadn't paid attention to my own warning, and I'd fallen in love with a woman who didn't want anything to do with me outside the bedroom.

I held on tightly for a moment and then forced space between us. My anger burned out, leaving me with only disappointment. I rolled onto my back and stared up at the ceiling fan spinning in lazy circles. The fullness in my chest disappeared, leaving me feeling hollow.

I took a moment to get my breathing under control and then went to start a bath. When the water was just right, I went back into the bedroom. Gabriella barely opened her eyes when I gathered her in my arms and carried her onto the terrace. I lowered her into the warm water and gently soaped her body until she was clean. She leaned her head back as I massaged shampoo and then conditioner into her long hair.

I had used her hard, so I pampered her, lifting her from the tub and drying her with a towel. She snuggled against my chest when I carried her back to the bed. I tucked her under the sheet and filled a glass of water from the sink for her to drink. Then I got in behind her and cradled her back to my front until she fell asleep.

When her breathing was shallow and steady, I disengaged and rolled onto my back. Staring at the dark ceiling, I felt my disappointment grow with every beat of my heart. I'd never thought the married life with kids was for me, but I was craving it like a missing ingredient. The one woman I pictured a future with only wanted me for my body. I would have laughed at the irony if it wasn't so damn sad.

Gabriella muttered something and snuggled against me. For a woman who didn't want a relationship, she was clingy in her sleep. I pulled her closer to my chest, knowing I should give her up before I was completely fucked. But I also knew I'd been fucked the moment I kissed her.

Book Review of "The Round Up" by Janet Freeman

BY VALENTINA BLUERIDGEBOOKCLUB.COM

1 star
5 hot peppers
1 book boyfriend hearts

DEAR READERS,

If I had anything else do to with my time, I wouldn't have finished this book. That just goes to show you how horrible it was. I was on a long flight with nothing else to do, so I finished this ghastly piece of fiction, although it is a gift to call it anything other than pure smut. I don't know if I can do this job anymore. I'm so disgusted with the crap that is out there. Don't we have any good erotica authors anymore? It used to be I would get a story with the sexy times... not anymore.

Plot Overview:

Something about cowboys and ranches and a jaguar?? I don't know how the jaguar got to Montana, but it is causing chaos all over the ranches and even made national news. Enter Bridgette Connelly to save the day. She's a city girl from NYC who wants to save the world one jaguar at a time. Somehow, she gets entangled with four lonesome cowboys, and that's where things start to get murky and the plot disappears faster than five-alarm chili at a cook-off.

Pros:

• Trope: Reverse harem, cowboys

• Why choose when you can have four handsome cowboys wrangling for your attention?

Cons:

• Multiple men to please. I mean, really? I can imagine accommodating more than one man in bed, but these men were draining. They never left her alone for one second. She couldn't even go to the bathroom by herself. Worse than toddlers.

• Worst meet-cute ever: Bridgette is lost on the back roads, so she decides to get out and walk. Who does this? I almost threw my book, but since I was on a plane at the time, it seemed like a bad idea. What if I hit someone in the head?

• Screwball ending: Bridgette saved the jaguar, and they made him into a pet. WTF did I just read?

To sum it up, skip this one, readers. And if you have any suggestions for me to read, please email me @ Valentina@ BRBC.com. I'm getting desperate, and if things don't change, this may be my final review.

Chapter 33

GABI

"You got taller," I said, reaching up to hug Shane.

He hugged me back, stooping a little. "You always say that when we are away from each other for a few days."

"Because it's true." I didn't want him to stop growing up; I wanted him to slow down a little.

He tossed his duffel bag in the back seat and narrowed his eyes at me as I got behind the wheel. "Why do you look like that?" he asked.

I patted my hair, which was in its usual sleek ponytail. "Like what?"

"All tan and happy." He pulled out his phone, which he'd just gotten back after a week of no technology at camp. "Did you go somewhere?"

My neck itched, and my cheeks felt hot. "I took a quick trip with a friend from school."

He smiled at his phone, thumbs flying. "Me, Emma, and Jake want to come back to Camp Rock Bridge this summer as counselors."

"Emma C. or Emma W.?"

"Both." Shane scrolled without glancing up from his phone. "You think I can?"

"What about basketball camp?"

"That's in July. And football doesn't start until the second week in August."

I frowned, already counting the weeks Shane would be away this summer. "You have the entire summer planned."

He stopped scrolling and waited. "Is that cool?"

Even though I would miss him, I wouldn't stop him from living his life. "Sure."

"We still have the family weekend in Edisto the first weekend in August," he said. "Maybe Coach Joey can come."

My fingers tightened on the wheel, and spots swam in front of my eyes. I blinked rapidly, trying to focus on the road. "What?"

"Maybe Coach Joey will come with us for the weekend to Edisto."

"Why would he do that?"

"Come on, Mom. I know you're dating him."

I pulled off the highway into my parents' neighborhood, my heart racing. "I'm not dating Joey."

"That's who you took a trip with, though, right?"

"Why do you think that?"

"Because you're being so secretive, and you look weird."

My heart jumped to my throat. "I don't look weird."

"Who did you go with then?"

"Uh..."

Shane laughed. "Everyone knows the tea on you and Coach Joey," he said. "You're always huddled up together at track meets. And I saw you kissing at yoga."

I snorted. "We weren't kissing." Not until we were locked in Kennedy's office, we weren't.

"Well, I thought you were going to, and I didn't want to see it, so I left."

I parked in front of my parents' house and cut the engine. "Joey and I are just friends. We run together sometimes."

"And take trips to the beach." He smirked. "I don't know why you're hiding it. We talked about you a long time ago, and I told him I was cool with it. I guess. I mean, Coach Joey is dope."

"You talked about me?"

Shane nodded. "I'm not a little kid anymore," he said. "We can talk about your relationships and stuff. You don't have to hide."

I hoped my cheeks weren't as red as they felt. I needed out of this conversation. "What about you and Erin?" I asked, turning the tables.

Shane shrugged. "What about her?"

"Is she your girlfriend?"

"No. She was never into me. She likes Jaden. I guess I'm not her type."

I studied my son. "Smart, handsome, and athletic isn't her type?"

He rolled his eyes. "You're my mom. Of course you have to say that stuff."

I patted his hair, which was in desperate need of a cut. The springy curls had enough weight to hang over his forehead into his eyes. "Your dad would be..." I stopped, too choked up to finish.

"Really proud of me," he said for me. "I know." He ducked away from my hand before I had a chance to smooth his hair. "He would be proud of you, too. And he would want you to be happy. He wouldn't want you to be alone."

Emotion clogged my throat. "I'm not alone." I swallowed thickly. "I have you."

"I meant a boyfriend or husband or something."

My stomach tightened. "I'm not ever going to have another husband. Your father was the only man who will ever have that title."

"Mom?" Shane asked, leaning closer to me across the console.

I looked into his big brown eyes. Shane was almost all his dad, except his eyes were all me. "Yeah?"

His eyes were wide with concern. Little flecks of gold and amber burst out from his irises. "Can I get real with you for a minute?"

"Of course."

"Forget about what Dad would want. What do you think *I* want for you?"

I'd never given it consideration. Our relationship went the other way around. I took care of Shane. I wanted things for him. I never expected he might want things for me, too. I blinked rapidly as tears threatened. "I don't know."

"I want to know someone is there for you when I'm not around anymore."

I gulped. I didn't like to think too hard about the inevitable day Shane would leave.

"I worry about you," he said. "It would be nice to know you had someone like Coach Joey to take care of you when I'm gone."

I'd never wanted to cry more than I did right then, but I held myself together. We were getting ready to have supper with my family, and I didn't want to break down right before we walked in. One of my mother's talents was sensing tears and drama a mile away.

I cleared my throat and pulled Shane into a hug. His soft curls tickled my cheek. He no longer had that little boy smell of feet and maple syrup, but he was still my baby—except he was wiser than me. A whole lot.

* * *

When we got home, Shane went straight to his room to connect with his buddies on his online game. I could hear him yelling and laughing, and the sound pricked my heart.

I missed Joey's laugh.

He would tease me, saying I missed more than that, but it was true. I missed his laugh the most. His laugh filled me up inside, as if I'd just eaten Thanksgiving dinner.

I puttered around in the kitchen, made lists of everything I needed to accomplish in the upcoming week, and finished all Shane's laundry he'd brought back from a week at camp, but still I hadn't heard from Joey.

My phone buzzed, and I lunged so fast I almost pulled a hamstring. I'd hoped it was Joey, but it was Kennedy, on the book club text thread.

Kennedy [5:58 p.m.] : I'm so pissed I could scream.

It was so out of character for Kennedy to be mad, I had to double check the sender.

Sloane [5:59 p.m.] : omg what happened?

Mia [5:59 p.m.] : Do I need to have someone arrested?

Kennedy [5:59 p.m.] : Can you meet at Hawthorne's?

Thatcher [6:00 p.m.] : I'm closing up the shop now. I can be there in five.

Lacey [6:01 p.m.]: I'm meeting Beckett for dinner, but I can reschedule.

Kennedy [6:01 p.m.] : Don't ruin your night on my account, L.

Lacey [6:02 p.m.] : Sorry

Mia [6:03 p.m.] : I'm at the office, but I could use a lunch break.

Gabi [6:04 p.m.] It's dinner time, M!

Kennedy [6:05 p.m.] Gabi's back!! I want to hear all about CR.

I wanted to hear all about why Kennedy, who was as serene as Mother Theresa, was mad. Normally, I wouldn't leave this late at night when Shane would be home alone, but he'd proven he wasn't a little kid anymore with his wise advice.

I popped into his room and told him I was going to meet my friends from the book club and I'd be back before bedtime.

He shoved his headset to the side long enough to tell me to have fun, then went back to his game.

By the time I drove into town and joined my friends, they were already tearing into a large pepperoni.

My heart overflowed at the sight of them. Maybe I was emotional after spending so much time having Joey pluck at my heartstrings, but I almost teared up when I sat down with them.

"Look at you!" Sloane hopped up from her chair to hug me. "You look so tan and..." Her voice faded. "What's wrong?"

I shook my head and took the seat next to Kennedy. "Nothing."

"Not nothing," Kennedy said. "What did he do?"

I swiped at my tears.

Mia narrowed her eyes at me from across the table. "If you need him roughed up, I know a guy."

Kennedy put her arm around me. The soft sweep of her hair tickled my cheek as she pulled me in for a hug. "What happened, honey?"

I sniffed loudly. "He told me he loved me."

"Jesus." Thatcher slammed his beer on the table. "Have him arrested, Ms. James."

Mia scowled. "Shut your man hole."

"Can't you see she's hurting?" Sloane filled a glass of beer from the pitcher on the table and pushed it toward me.

"Do you love him back, or what?" Thatcher asked.

I buried my face in my hands. Joey was everything I'd ever dared to want in a man. "It's complicated."

"Boy, is it." Sloane came to sit on the other side of me and patted my shoulder. "You don't have to make any decisions right now. He isn't going anywhere."

"A man tells a woman he loves her, it's a big deal," Thatcher said. "What did you say back?"

"I don't remember. It was quite a moment."

"Please tell me you didn't say thank you?" Thatcher curled his lip. "That's the worst."

Had I thanked Joey? Everything was a blur. I was more confused the more I thought about it, and I missed him like crazy. And maybe I did love him a little. What was I going to do at work tomorrow? I wouldn't possibly be able look at him without blushing. Would I have to avoid him again? For how long? *Forever.*

I needed to steer the conversation in a different direction. "What's going on with you, Kennedy?"

Her cheeks turned pink. "You know that yoga retreat I booked at Camp Rockbrook for this summer?"

I grabbed a slice of pizza and stuffed a bite into my mouth, nodding enthusiastically instead of answering. For the last few months, Joey had consumed my thoughts. I'd been a horrible friend.

"They double-booked the dates with a triathlon club." Kennedy's shoulders slumped. "This was going to be the first retreat in North Carolina, and I was dying to show everyone what we have to offer. Now it's ruined. Stupid triathletes."

"Maybe you can work something out," I said. "Maybe you can split the time or share the facilities."

"I'm not sharing my time with a bunch of uptight triathletes."

"I'm surprised at you," I said. "You're the one telling me not to put people in boxes."

"Yeah," said Sloane. "Maybe these triathletes are super chill. Lacey's friend Xan is nice."

"The one who put the roofie in her drink?" Mia asked. "I still want to nail that guy to a wall."

"What?" Kennedy looked horrified.

"That's not what happened," I said, wishing Lacey were here to set everything straight. "Xan is a good guy."

Kennedy gulped her beer. "If he's a triathlete, I doubt it."

I laid my hand on her shoulder. "You should contact him and see if he knows the people who booked the Camp Rockbrook. Maybe he can help. Lacey will give you his number."

"Gabi, I don't expect you to fix my problems. I just wanted to drown my sorrows with some friends."

"Cheers," said Sloane, raising her glass of wine.

We all tapped glasses. I wished figuring out what to do about my feelings for Joey was as easy as sharing space with uptight triathletes.

* * *

The next morning, I still hadn't heard from Joey. He hadn't even texted to tell me he was back in the country. I'd hardly slept the night before, wondering and worrying about him.

I'd gotten used to seeing him, and I'd missed him so much over the last few days.

Guilt pricked my conscience as I strode down the silent halls of PES. I hadn't missed a man since Montel. My heart squeezed at the betrayal. I'd held on to Montel with clenched fingers for so long. It felt like losing him all over again to admit I wanted the love of another man.

"Ask Mr. Morales to come to my office first thing after announcements," I told Mr. Collins, who'd beaten me to the office even though I was forty-five minutes early.

"Oh!" he said, jumping to his feet with a guilty expression. "Haven't you read your emails?"

I hung my coat on the rack and glared at Mr. Collins over my shoulder. "Of course I've read my emails."

Well, maybe that was a white lie. I hadn't read *all* my emails. I'd skimmed the important ones and was waiting until I was officially back on the job to give them a thorough reading.

Mr. Collins cleared his throat. "Maybe you should read your emails," he said.

I went into my office and sat behind my desk. I fired up my computer and logged into my email account. I skimmed my inbox, noting a correspondence from Chelsea Taylor that made me roll my eyes as well as an email from the superintendent regarding end-of-grade testing results.

My shoulders inched up to my ears when I saw the email from Morales, Fernando, with the subject line: Resignation.

With trembling fingers, I clicked on the email.

It has been my pleasure. Blah, blah, blah. *Sorry to leave this wonderful school. Another opportunity has come along.*

He's quitting? I checked the date on the email. Two days ago. Correction—he'd quit. Right after we'd finished our conversation. He'd sent this from Costa Rica.

My vision doubled as I read the email again and again, until my eyes strained, and then I leaned across my desk and pressed the intercom for Mr. Collins.

"Yes?" he answered.

Was it my imagination, or was there a touch of snarkiness in his one-word question?

"Can you get Mr. Morales on the phone for me?" I asked.

"I can try," he said.

I didn't imagine the note of exasperation in his voice. "Find out where he went," I said, disengaging before Mr. Collins had a chance to answer.

The next few minutes ticked by slowly. I tried texting Joey again, but he didn't reply. I read his resignation email again and again, searching for clues but finding nothing.

After my fifth time reading Joey's email, a vein pulsed in my forehead, and my vision blurred. I leaned my elbows on my desk and hung my head in my hands.

I jabbed the intercom button again. "Did you find him?"

Mr. Collins's reply came over the intercom immediately. "I can't get him on the phone," he said. His voice lowered in a conspiratorial whisper. "I heard he went to Sapphire Valley Academy."

My blood boiled. Sapphire Valley stole all the best teachers. We hated Sapphire Valley. How could he do this?

I grabbed my purse and flew out of my office.

"Where are you going?" Mr. Collins asked, his eyes as huge as dinner plates.

"Can you handle announcements? I'll be back as soon as I can."

Chapter 34

Sapphire Valley Academy had been trying to recruit me as the head of their language department for months, so it had been a breeze to get a job there. One phone call and everything was set. I was going to be over the foreign language department, which included French, Latin, Spanish, and Japanese.

Even though I was getting a promotion and an increase in salary, leaving PES had been hard. I'd agonized over the letter I sent to each one of my students' families, promising to stay in touch and to see them at the Fun Festival in two weeks. I'd arranged for Mrs. Costello to sub my classes until a permanent replacement could be found. The kids liked Mrs. Costello almost as much as they liked me. She was a kindly, grandmother type who sat on the floor with the kids and read them stories in Spanish.

I was going to miss my students, even Sally Ann, but I was going to miss Gabriella more. By now, she probably knew I'd quit. I wondered how she felt. Was she as angry at me as I was at her? Or did she understand why I'd done it? Did she know I'd left because there was no way I could work with her? Not when I was in love with her and she only wanted one thing from me.

I parked in the teachers' lot and took a moment to collect myself. I had to forget about Gabriella. She didn't want me, so why should I waste time on her? I wasn't the type of man who chased women. There were plenty of fish in the sea—even if none of them were as beautiful, smart, or sweet as Gabriella.

After another minute, I snapped out of my sadness and reached into the back seat for the muffins I'd made. Two dozen chocolate chip.

A muffin went a long way to making friends with the most important people at the school: the assistants, the cafeteria workers, and the custodians.

Having already met the headmaster informally a few times, I was pretty sure the school would be a good fit, but it never hurt to bring bribes.

I went straight to the headmaster's office. My new boss, Mrs. Ackerman, was nothing like Gabriella. She was a free spirit with silver braids that hung to the middle of her back. She was closer to my grandmother's age than mine, and she ruled the school with an angelic energy.

I stopped at her assistant's desk first.

"How're you doin'?" I asked, offering the muffins.

She sniffed appreciatively. "Oh Em Gee! Chocolate chip!" She clasped her hands together. "I shouldn't. I'm watching my weight.
"

"One won't hurt. Take it for later."

She blushed and reached into the container. "You really know how to get in good with the staff."

If she only knew how good I was in at PES. "People love my muffins." I smiled, and the poor girl blushed from the roots of her hair to her neck. *Here we go again.* The curse of my Costa Rican accent was that women loved it too much. They claimed everything I said sounded sexy. I cleared my throat and closed the container. "Is Mrs. Ackerman here yet?"

"Everyone calls her Angie," she said. "And I'm Beth." She took a bite of the muffin and grinned as she chewed. "Fernando, right?"

"It's Joey."

"Well, Joey, your muffins are scrumptious. I can see why everyone loves them. Can I have the recipe? My book club would love them."

I leaned onto the counter and grabbed a pen and paper. "It's no secret." I scribbled down my favorite recipe website and slid the paper across her desk. "Every week they post a new flavor."

Angie's office door opened, and my heart stopped beating for a few seconds when I heard Gabriella's voice. She was using that authoritative tone, which was a few octaves lower than her normal voice. I was going to miss hearing her voice during staff meetings.

My heart finally kicked into gear again, and I straightened up from Beth's desk. Seeing Gabriella was like a punch to the gut. She was gorgeous with her hair pulled back from her face, emphasizing the symmetrical beauty of her face. Her brown eyes locked on mine, and color rose on her cheeks.

My stupid heart ached with the need to touch her.

She wore that blue top with the bow at the throat, which I'd imagined undoing so many times it was practically a memory.

Tension filled the air as we stared at each other. Gabriella's eyes fired daggers at me. I fired back.

I cocked my chin at her. "Hello."

A storm flashed in her eyes. "Hello."

The strain between us pulsed like a heartbeat. Her gaze drifted over my crisply ironed shirt and tie and froze on the container in my hand. Her jaw dropped.

"You're the muffin man?"

"Everyone knew it was me."

Her eyes went wide. "I didn't!"

My blood pounded in my head so loud, I couldn't hear myself think. "What are you doing here? Shouldn't you be at school?"

Angie's eyes darted from me to Gabriella and back. She cleared her throat. "Gabi's here because she's mad that I finally stole you away. I've been trying to get Gabi over here for years, but she won't budge. She insists public school is where she's needed."

"It's true, and you know it." Gabriella shifted her glare from my muffins to Angie. "Public schools are in need of great teachers and leaders."

She was feisty when she was passionate about something. I loved watching her temper flare.

Angie smiled sympathetically. "We are doing everything we can to ease the stress of public education. Fernando is going to volunteer at several schools as part of his position as language director."

Gabriella's dark gaze swept back to me. "Language director?"

I nodded. The job came with lots of perks: better pay, flexible schedule, and no Gabriella to haunt the halls. I nodded at my new boss. "I'm eager to be part of the team."

Gabriella scoffed. "I thought education was your number one priority."

A vein pulsed in my forehead as I locked eyes with Gabriella. She knew exactly what buttons to push to anger me.

Angie stepped between Gabriella and me, breaking our staring contest. "I can assure you, the quality of education at Sapphire Valley Academy is superb." She stepped aside. "Fernando, why don't I show you your new office?" She led the way down the hall. "Come see, Gabi. Maybe when you come over to the dark side of academy learning, you can get one like it."

"Never," Gabriella murmured.

We went down the hall, following Angie through a maze of offices. She pointed out the break room, and I stashed the muffins on the counter for everyone to enjoy. Then she stopped in front of an empty office.

"This is yours," she said, flipping on the lights.

The office was bigger than Gabriella's, with a standard desk and chair, filing cabinets, and a window that faced a rolling green field.

"Make yourself at home and let me know if you need anything." She stepped into the hall and leveled her gaze at Gabriella, then at me. "I'll leave you two to get straight."

As soon as Angie left, I strode to my desk, putting as much space as possible between me and Gabriella. I couldn't be near her without wanting to touch her, and I hated myself for that. I'd left PES because I couldn't bear to be around her, and here she was.

I put my laptop bag on my desk and leaned my hip on the corner, trying my best to look casual as I faced the woman I loved who, unfortunately, didn't return the sentiment. "What are you doing here, Gabriella?" My voice sounded as weary as if I'd just crossed the finish line of a marathon.

She pushed the door closed and marched across the room, then launched herself into my arms. Her hands wound around my neck, and her mouth locked on mine. She parted my lips with her tongue and licked inside.

Her mouth was like a drug. I was so addicted. Our tongues stroked together, and my anger faded.

"How dare you leave me?" she muttered between kisses.

I held her away from me. "I told you I was going to do it."

"You didn't text or call last night. I was worried."

I wanted to keep my distance, but my hands had a mind of their own and slipped around her waist. Her words made my heart ache. "You were worried?"

She nodded and kissed my jaw, her mouth cool and her breath warm on my freshly shaved skin. "When I saw your email this morning, I thought I was going to explode. I hate that you left. How could you?"

Anger flared in my chest. "I quit because you wouldn't let me love you, and..."

"And what?"

I scraped a hand through my hair, working up the courage to say the words. She'd already rejected me. What did I have to lose? "And maybe if we don't work together, you would give us a chance."

Her eyes glazed over, and she stared at something beyond my shoulder. "What about Maria?"

My throat clogged, and I swallowed roughly. "What the hell does Maria have to do with anything?"

She lifted a hand to my chest. Her fingers trailed over my heart. "She was the love of your life."

I covered her hand with my own and trapped her palm against my heart. "Maria broke my heart. Her name is there to remind me not to fall in love again." But it hadn't worked. I'd fallen for Gabriella, fallen hard without a net.

She blinked up at me. "Do you think it's possible to have more than one true love in your life?" Her voice was a raspy whisper.

I nodded tightly. "Of course I do."

She smiled. "Montel was it for me. My soulmate."

I stiffened at the sound of his name. I knew it was ridiculous to be jealous of a dead man who'd never gotten to know his own son, but my chest burned with envy. I wanted to tell her all the things I could give her that Montel couldn't, but it was a cruel reminder of the devastation she'd endured.

"And then I met you." She shifted her hand to curl around my neck. "I came here because I realized I was going to miss seeing you every day, and I don't want that to end. And I don't want to have to sneak around or go all the way to Hog Bottom for dinner."

"Hog Bottom isn't so bad."

She narrowed her eyes at me. "You know what I mean."

My chest swelled so full of hope, I thought it might burst. Was she saying she loved me? I needed to know for sure. "Say the words, Gabriella."

She straightened my tie. "I want you. I love you."

I tried to keep my cool, but it was impossible. I felt like I'd been waiting my whole life to hear those words from her lips. My hand stole around her waist, and my mouth descended to claim hers.

She locked her arms around my neck and kissed me until we were both breathless. We broke apart and gasped for air.

The pink of her lipstick was smeared, and her sleek ponytail was skewed to the side. My sweet Gabriella looked like a mess, but I was in worse shape. My breath came in shallow pants, and sweat pricked the back of my neck. My dick was so hard, it was painful. And I had to meet my new coworkers in a few minutes at the staff meeting. "You're going to make me lose my job on my first day," I said.

Her tongue tentatively slid along her lower lip, as if she was savoring the taste of me. "Aren't you going to say it back?"

I grinned. "I love you too."

We kissed again, and I pulled back with reluctance, adjusting myself in my pants. "I need to go to a meeting."

She stepped back and skimmed a hand along her ponytail. "Your place, tonight at six o'clock? Shane has tutoring until seven."

I rolled my eyes, already frustrated with the short amount of time we'd have together. I would take it though, because she loved me.

When I nodded, she smiled and walked to the door. Her hand went to the knob, and I missed her already. She stepped into the hallway and shot me a sexy grin. "Have a horrible first day," she said.

Chapter 35

Joey was waiting for me at the main door to his house.

He opened it wide and ushered me up the stairs to his apartment. The smell of tomato sauce, thick with fresh herbs, wafted down the hall from the kitchen.

"It smells so good in here. What is that?"

His hands cupped my cheeks, and he bent to kiss me. "I knew we didn't have much time, so I put something in the oven."

Joey's version of putting something in the oven smelled very different from mine. A beeping noise sounded, and he hurried into the kitchen.

"Do you need any help?" I asked.

"I got it," he called.

The beeping stopped, and I heard the creak of the oven door and the slide of pans over metal racks. A moment later, Joey came back into the living room.

"Dinner's cooling on the counter," he said, wiping his hands on a dish towel. "There's enough for you to take home for Shane."

God bless America! This man was everything: sexy, sweet, smart, and thoughtful. I threw my arms around him with enough force to make him stumble backwards.

He caught me around the waist before we could both fall.

"Shane knows about us," I said.

"Smart kid."

"He called me out on it, and I admitted it."

"You did, huh?"

"He approves, by the way. He said you were... dope."

Joey laughed. "Yeah? That was nice of him."

I stretched up on my toes and ran my nose along the faint shadow on his jaw. "I like your shave," I said, reaching up to thread my fingers through his hair. "But you need another haircut."

"Or what?" He squeezed my waist, lifting me higher onto my toes. "You can't fire me anymore."

"How was your first day?" I asked as he walked me backward.

"Not as horrible as you wanted it to be."

My legs hit the sofa, and he set me on my feet.

"I'm very sorry to hear that."

I reached down to grab the hem of his shirt and dragged it up to his chest. He let go of me long enough to lift his arms and toss the shirt aside, then wrapped his arms around my waist again.

My greedy hands stole between us to spread across his chest. He felt the same—smooth skin, hard flesh, and a soft smattering of hair—but everything had changed.

He was mine. I could touch him. I could kiss him. I could share a pizza with him at Hawthorne's.

A buzz of excitement raced through me at everything we could do together. I pressed a kiss to his chest, inhaling the musky scent of him. His hands dipped under my shirt and spread over my back.

Pressing kisses to his chest, I paused and traced his tattoo with my tongue. I'd always wanted to kiss his ink, but I'd never felt like I had the right. Now every inch of Joey was mine, even his heartbreak.

My hands dipped lower. Touching him was a familiar pleasure. I knew the way to make him moan and stutter incoherently in at least one language. His low growl filled my ears when I stroked him over his pants.

"I'm sorry I left you like this earlier today." I popped open the button on his pants.

He gasped. "How sorry?"

I slipped my hand under the waistband of his boxers. "Very sorry."

The doorbell rang, and we both froze. Our eyes locked.

"It's probably just a neighbor. I'll get rid of them." He eased back and bent to grab his shirt. "You can wait in the bedroom if you want."

"You mean hide there?" I asked.

His big brown eyes searched mine, but he didn't answer.

The doorbell rang again as we stared at each other.

"Gabriella?"

A month ago, I would have already been hiding in the bedroom, but my feet were rooted to the spot.

I crossed my arms over my chest. "Get the door," I said. "I'll stay right here."

His brows rose. "Really?"

"Really." I cocked my head at him. "Or do you want me to get it?"

Joey grinned. "Go ahead." He reached around and gave my ponytail a yank. "I dare you."

"Oh no, you didn't."

His laugh rumbled, and he swatted me on the butt. "Get the door, baby."

"You quit your job for me. The least I can do is answer your door."

I strode to the door, and Joey followed, tugging on his T-shirt. I opened the door and saw Chelsea Taylor in the hall, holding a white box.

Her eyes widened when she saw me, but the rest of her face didn't move. Botox made it almost impossible to look surprised.

"Ms. Taylor," I said, adopting my professional voice even

though the last time she'd seen me, my butt was hanging out of my dress. My cheeks were flushed, and my ponytail was lopsided, thanks to Joey.

"Ms. Taylor," Joey said in a voice he reserved for misbehaving students and Frodo. "I asked you not to come to my home."

Ms. Taylor's eyes bounced from me to Joey, as if she couldn't decide where to look. She finally focused on Joey. "Don't worry, Kaylee isn't with me. And you aren't her teacher anymore."

"That doesn't mean you can disturb my privacy."

Her smile dimmed. "I brought you a cake." She offered Joey the box. "We hate to lose you at PES."

Joey took the box. "Thank you."

"It's chocolate," she said.

He slid his arm around my shoulder. "Gabriella's favorite."

Ms. Taylor darted a glance at me. She probably wished she'd gone with a different flavor.

"We were just sitting down to dinner," I said, reaching for the door. "Thanks for the dessert."

Ms. Taylor peeked around my shoulder into the living room, as if she couldn't believe what she was seeing. "It smells delicious."

I slid my arm around Joey's waist and gazed up at him adoringly. "Joey is the most amazing cook."

He beamed and dropped a kiss on my forehead. "Thanks, baby."

Ms. Taylor's forehead twitched, and a faint line appeared between her brows. I was pretty sure we broke her Botox.

The baffled expression was still on her face when I closed the door.

Joey strode into the kitchen and tossed the cake box on the counter. "Everyone in town is going to know about us now," he said.

I came up behind him and wrapped my arms around his waist. "Good."

His hands came up to rest on mine. "I wish I wasn't leaving for the summer," he said. "It seems like we never have enough time."

I thought ahead to the summer. Shane would be gone, and I would be mostly on my own. I would have my job to keep myself busy, but summers were completely different from the school year. The students wouldn't be around to keep things interesting. My work would be preparing for the upcoming year, scheduling building maintenance, and hiring teachers. Duties that I could perform without difficulty.

I leaned against Joey's back, hugging him tighter. "I have some vacation time I haven't used," I said. "Maybe I could visit for a week."

"I'd like that." He turned around to face me, and we kissed.

My phone sounded. It was Shane's ringtone, so I answered.

"Hey, Mom," Shane said. "We got done early."

"Okay," I said. "I'm coming." I hung up and stuck my phone back in my pocket. "What were you saying? Something about not having enough time?"

Joey laughed. "Good thing there's always tomorrow."

Epilogue

GABI

Santiago was waiting for me at the Nosara airstrip instead of Joey. My disappointment must have shown on my face because Santiago laughed good-naturedly when he lifted my suitcase and stuffed it in the back of his truck between two surfboards and an assortment of fishing gear.

"Sorry I'm not Fernando." He reached into a cooler and plucked out a frosty bottle of Imperial. "Although most people think I'm much better looking. And I have beer."

He popped the top and handed me the ice-cold bottle. One sip later, and some of the stress from traveling all day melted away.

Santiago watched me drink with a knowing smile. "You hungry?" He shoved aside a bucket and reached into another cooler. "I have fruit."

He laid out a feast of papaya, pineapple, and banana on his tailgate and handed me a plate. Even though food was the last thing on my mind, I didn't want to be rude. I selected a few of each and thanked Santiago.

"You can eat on the way," he said, closing the tailgate.

Grateful that Santiago sensed my urgency to be away from the airstrip, I settled into the cab of the truck with my refreshments.

The food and drink took the edge off my travel weariness but didn't erase my need to see Joey as soon as possible. We hadn't seen each other in six weeks since I had visited him in June for a long weekend.

"Where is he?" I asked.

"At Angela's." Santiago pulled out of the airstrip and onto the main road. "He told me to tell you he's sorry he couldn't pick you up."

I clutched my plate in my lap as we bumped over the dusty, pothole-filled roads. I'd been looking forward to many things about Costa Rica, but the roads weren't one of them. At one point, we had to stop because there was a skinny cow standing in the middle of the road.

"That's the sorriest-looking cow I've ever seen."

Santiago laughed and tapped lightly on his horn to shoo the animal. "That's a horse," he said.

The creature ambled out of the way, and I stared after it. Santiago was right. It *was* a horse. "That's the sorriest-looking horse I've ever seen."

"That it is," Santiago said. "How is your Spanish coming?" he asked in his native tongue.

"Muy bien."

"Would you like to speak in Spanish or English?" he asked politely.

Everyone in Costa Rica was so nice. They went out of their way to make visitors feel welcome.

Most people knew English and were happy to have someone to practice with. Costa Ricans were happy in general. And who wouldn't be happy surrounded by the sea, the mountains, and all the fresh air?

The last time I'd visited Joey, I'd gotten to know Santiago a little better, and I was glad to have some unexpected alone time with Joey's oldest friend.

"English, please." If I was going to pump Santiago for information, it was better to do it in a language I could easily understand. "How long have you known Joey?"

"Since we were kids."

I sipped my beer, hoping he would elaborate, and he eventually, he did.

"Fernando was a brat. He used to beat me up and take my lunch."

I choked on my beer. "What?"

"Just kidding. Fernando was too skinny. He couldn't beat anyone. But he could run fast." His eyes crinkled in the corners. "He never let anyone win in a race."

"I beat him all the time." Okay, so I cheated and took any advantage I could get, but I still won. Sometimes.

"That's just because he's watching your ass."

I rolled my eyes. "That's what he says."

Santiago shrugged. "What else do you want to know?" he asked. "Maybe something about Maria?"

"That's okay. I'm good with Maria." She was in the past. I had no room for worrying about the past.

"That's good." He was quiet for a moment and then exhaled. "Maria dumped Fernando and took off with one of our best friends. He tell you that?"

"Not exactly." We hadn't gone into details, but I was fine with that. I really didn't want to know more now, but Santiago seemed determined to tell me.

"She crushed him. They were going to move to America together when he finished college, but she had already moved on before then, you know?" Santiago glared out the window. "It ruined him for a while. He got that tattoo with her name because he said it would remind him never to be so stupid to fall in love with a woman again."

The cab of the truck became thick with tension, and Santiago fell silent. As we bumped along the road, I got the feeling he was purposefully staying quiet until I gave him some sort of reassurance.

"I can't promise not to hurt him," I said. "But I love him."

Santiago glanced away from the road and appraised me. "He's my brother," he said.

I nodded. "Is it weird I call him Joey?" This was what I was dying to know. Joey had insisted it didn't matter that I called him his American name while everyone else he loved used his given name, but I didn't completely believe him.

Santiago shrugged. "Not if it isn't weird to him."

Frustrated, I set my plate on the floor by my feet and faced Santiago. "He says it isn't."

Santiago didn't get it. "What's the problem, then? It's just a name. My friends call me all sorts of things. *Mae. Carepicha. Dolor de huevos.*"

I knew *mae* was a term of endearment, something used between friends. And *picha* was dick, but the last one stumped me. Costa Rican slang didn't always make sense.

"Pain in the eggs?" I asked, flipping through my Spanish dictionary.

Santiago chuckled. "Something like that. My point is, you can call him Fernando or Joey or dickface. He's still the same man."

This made me think of Romeo and Juliet. *A rose by any other name...* It made me feel better that Shakespeare had come to the same conclusion. Good enough for Shakespeare was good enough for me.

We stuck to the lighter topic of Joey's youth for the rest of the ride. Santiago told me about how he'd been forced to rescue Joey the first time they'd gone surfing, and how they'd started a business together selling snacks to tourists stuck in construction traffic.

When we pulled up to the back entrance of Angela's, Santiago wrapped me in a bone-crushing hug. "You're all right with me, Gabriella," he said.

He walked me to the back door, and we stepped into the lively kitchen in the middle of dinner service. Cooks bantered in Spanish, servers loaded their arms with trays, and busboys hurried by with dishrags. The smell of garlic, freshly baked bread, and fragrant herbs hung in the air.

"This way." Santiago led me through the busy kitchen to the main dining room.

The restaurant was packed. Conversation and laughter drowned out the soft jazz playing over the speakers, and a buzz of energy filled the homey space. Excellent food and fabulous service made it hard to be unhappy at Angela's.

I searched the floor for Joey's family. During a busy dinner hour, I expected to see his mother flying through the dining room like a live wire, one of his sisters carrying a tray, or his cousin Mateo pouring wine. It was odd that I didn't spot any of them.

I tugged Santiago's arm, suddenly worried. "Where is everyone?"

Santiago's eyes twinkled. "You'll see." He grabbed my hand and led me through the maze of tables. "Do you have a big family at your home?"

"Pretty big."

He tucked my hand in his elbow and smiled at me. There was no doubt that he was handsome with his bronze tan, wheat-blond hair, and devilishly dark eyes, but I didn't see how anyone could say he was better looking than Joey.

Finally, we arrived at a private dining area set apart from the main floor by a folding screen. I stepped around the side of the screen and came to a halt when I saw Joey's entire family seated at a long table.

My mouth dropped open as I scanned their faces. Joey's parents, his sisters and brother, his cousin Mateo, and a few others I didn't recognize were gathered at the table, drinking wine and passing baskets of bread. Joey rose from his chair and grabbed a bouquet of flowers.

A hush fell over the table, and everyone turned toward me. His long strides didn't bring him to me fast enough. I hurried to meet him halfway and threw my arms around his neck, nearly tackling him.

Everyone at the table erupted in a loud cheer.

Joey crushed me to his chest, lifting me off my feet. I buried my face in his neck, smelling his familiar scent of spice and sunshine.

"Watch the flowers," someone cried, but Joey didn't listen.

His arms tightened around my back, and he took my mouth in a possessive kiss. The table cheered again, and Santiago boomed his familiar line: "Get a room!"

Finally, Joey let go of me and presented me with the bouquet, which was no worse for the wear.

"You miss me?" he asked, grinning.

"A little." I kissed his cheek, rubbing my face against that familiar scruff. "What's all this?" It was unusual that all the members of his family would be sitting down in the middle of a busy dinner hour.

"I thought that since you were missing supper with your family right now, we would have it with mine."

I glanced from Joey to the table, where everyone who mattered in his life was seated. Tears filled my eyes, but I choked them back. These people mattered to me now, too. They were Joey's, so they were mine.

He put his arm around my waist and guided me to my seat next to Santiago. I sat and clasped my hands in my lap, trying not to cry.

A server came up and filled our wineglasses. Another delivered bread and appetizers. Joey's father raised his glass and toasted happiness.

"I have something for you," Joey said in a low voice that made chills dance along my spine. "Come with me."

He pulled me from my seat and led me through the kitchen. A door stood open to a supply closet, and he pulled me inside. Grinning, he shut the door behind us. "I have a thing for closets," he said. "It was in that closet at school when I first fell in love with you."

He led me to the center of the small space and pulled a small box from his pocket. My heart plummeted to my stomach as if it was on a roller coaster ride.

"I'll never try to replace the husband you lost," Joey said. "But I love you so much, Gabriella. I want you to be mine."

Heat filled my chest and spread to my cheeks. "I love you too."

He lifted the lid on the box, revealing a platinum ring made of two gracefully twisting rows of diamonds entwined in an eternity band.

My pulse raced, and my throat went dry. "Are you asking me to marry you?"

A wistful smile curved his lips, but he shook his head. "No. I respect you too much for that. I know you don't want another husband right now. But maybe someday..." His words trailed off, and he cleared his throat. "Maybe someday, you'll change your mind, and you can ask *me* to marry *you*." His brows pinched together. "This ring is because I want you in my life. I want you and Shane to—"

I shut him up with a desperate kiss, showing him how much I'd missed him, loved him, and wanted him. The noise of the restaurant faded into the background, and it was just the two of us in the closet, stealing a kiss like old times.

Tears filled my eyes as I pulled back and took the box from Joey. My hand shook as I plucked the ring from the velvet lining. The diamonds shimmered in the light, entwining into infinity.

Lightness filled my chest as I stared at the ring. I started to slide it onto my finger, but stopped after the first knuckle. Something wasn't right.

Montel would always be a part of my story. Every time I looked at Shane, I would think of the love we'd shared and the life we'd created. But it was time to have a life of my own again. Time to have a future. With Joey.

My breath hitched when I pushed Joey's ring into his palm.

His hand closed over mine, and his eyebrows rose. "It doesn't fit?"

"It's not that." I slid the gold band Montel had given me so long ago off my left hand and switched it to my right hand. Tears filled my eyes as I lifted my left hand. "I think it would fit better on this hand."

As soon as the words left my mouth, Joey snatched me off my feet and claimed my mouth in an intoxicating kiss. For a moment, I worried that he would drop the ring as his hands roamed over my back. His tongue slid against mine, and I stopped thinking about anything besides getting closer to him.

We panted for breath when we parted, our chests heaving and eyes glistening. Joey set me back on my feet and reached for my hand. He'd miraculously managed to hold on to the ring, and he slid it onto my finger with a smile that rivaled the brightest ray of sunshine on a summer day.

I stared at the twinkling symbol of everlasting love on my finger with a sense of wonder. I'd never thought I would find a love like the one I'd had with my husband, but I'd been wrong. I'd never been so happy to be wrong in my life.

"*Te amo*, Fernando," I said, stretching up on my toes to press a kiss to Joey's smiling mouth.

His grin grew, and he kissed me back. Before I knew it, he had me backed up against a wall lined with boxes. Our lips locked together, and it seemed like nothing could tear us apart.

Except a knock on the door. We parted reluctantly as the door creaked open, and Santiago's head and shoulders filled the crack.

"I didn't mean *this* room," he said, laughing. "Food is on the table. You want us to start eating without you?"

We adjusted our clothes, fixed our hair, and emerged from the closet with matching goofy grins. When Joey held his hand out to me, palm up, I laced my fingers with his and we joined his family.

Next time, we'd join mine.

. . .

THE END

DO YOU WANT MORE FROM JOEY AND GABI?

Grab this BONUS Epilogue from Joey's point of view when you sign up for Jill's Newsletter

Acknowledgments

If you're reading this that probably means you got to the end of Joey and Gabi's love story. Thank you so much for giving this book a chance. I hope you enjoyed it.

As a parent of teenagers, I really poured a lot of my feelings for my kids into this book. Part of me wants to keep them under my wing as long as possible, but the other part knows that the whole point of them is to let them go. It's bittersweet watching them grow up. While writing Gabi, I reveled in my feelings for my nearly-grown children. My main job has always been a mother, and I tell my kids that I have to earn my mom dollars. That can mean anything from making them a snack to listening to their problems. I hope they know that I will always be there for them, even while I let them go.

This book was so fun to write. I always strive to give my readers the best book boyfriends. I hope Joey Morales lived up to your expectations and inspired a few trips to Costa Rica.

Here's the part where I thank everyone under the sun for helping me get this book baby into the world. Feel free to skip a few paragraphs and join back at the end.

Thanks to Angie, Connie, Cyndi and my Beta BFFs—Jennifer L, Desiree, Jennifer H., Ashley, Martha, and Amy. Couldn't have done it without you!

Thanks a ton to the yoga community at Y2 Yoga in Charlotte, NC. It is the best community of yogis and teachers anyone could ever ask for. I tried to recreate it as best I could in Namaste, but nothing can replicate Y2!

Thanks to my family. To Grace for listening to my story ideas, to

Michael for reminding me not to sit in the same chair too long, to Drew for telling me repeatedly "No man would ever do that," and for stopping me from adding secret babies to the story, to my mom for being my number-one cheerleader and fan.

This book was inspired by a trip to Costa Rica in 2019. I hope I did the country justice and made you long for a visit. Start planning your trip today! You won't regret it!

Even though I love to travel, there is no beating my home state of North Carolina. We have the best beaches (please forgive me Florida), incredible mountains (still love you the most Colorado), and the most gorgeous leaves for your peeping pleasure.

I hope you loved Mossy Oak and want to visit again soon. Thanks for reading!

About the Author

Jill Brashear is a hopeless romantic and author of swoon-worthy contemporary romances that will leave you breathless. With a pen in her hand and a heart full of love, Jill weaves tales of passion, longing, and happily-ever-afters that will make your heart skip a beat.

Also by Jill Brashear

ALOHA SERIES

Try Easy

Try Me

Try Right

Try Over

BLUE RIDGE BOOK CLUB

Love, Lacey Donovan

Blue Collar Crush

Sincerely, Thatcher Hayes

STANDALONES

Win, Lose, or Love